STRANGELY FUNNY

2 1/2

EDITED BY SARAH E. GLENN

MYSTERY AND HORROR, LLC
TARPON SPRINGS, FL

STRANGELY FUNNY 2 1/2
EDITED BY SARAH E. GLENN
COVER ART BY MONSTERMATT PATTERSON
DESIGN AND LAYOUT BY GWEN MAYO

Copyright © 2015 by Mystery and Horror, LLC
Published by Mystery and Horror, LLC

All stories in this anthology have been printed with the permission of the authors.

This is a work of fiction. Any resemblance to any actual person living or dead, or to any known location is the coincidental invention of the author's creative mind. This includes historical events and persons who may have been recreated in a fictional work.

ISBN-13: 978-0-9915825-9-4
(Mystery and Horror, LLC)

Library of Congress Control Number: 2015936776

Printed in USA by Mystery and Horror, LLC
(www.mysteryandhorrorllc.com)

TABLE OF CONTENTS

1
Knewscast
By Kevin Quirt

13
The New Kid
By Tim McDaniel

23
The Pillow
By Fred McGavran

33
Inheritance
By Kristina R. Mosley

49
The Snout
By Matthew Pegg

67
Alien Dust
By Chelsea Nolen

77
Outsourcing
By Gary Piserchio & Frank Tagader

93
The Demon of City Hall
By Rosalind Barden

105
Sadie's Selkie
By C.A. Rowland

113
Getting A Head
By Joette Rozanski

123
Folkesmuir
By John Grey

135
Hell's Working Girl
By Dan Foley

145
Unimpressed
By David Neilsen

159
Stephen, the Well-Adjusted Vampire
By Katrina Nicholson

173
Beehives of the Dead
By Elizabeth Allen

183
The Other Half
By A. Steven Clark

191
Dead to Write
By Chantal Boudreau

DEDICATION

This book is dedicated to our co-conspirators,
the authors of
Strangely Funny 2 ½

Thank you all for keeping news of this special anthology quiet
until we were ready to share it with the public.

KNEWSCAST

By Kevin Quirt

Paul glances at his new co-anchor and recalls the last bit of advice his mentor ever gave him: If you're a knewscaster and you don't predict your replacement coming, it's time to go. The advice came just before Paul stole the anchor job from him. He flinches at the memory, but the audience won't find any cracks in his granite resolve. His eyes pierce the camera lens as he reads the teaser for the next dire news prediction.

"Tomorrow, a popular local restaurant will serve E. coli-tainted beef as part of its lunch menu. Eleven people will become seriously ill. Find out which restaurant your family should avoid, after the break."

The new co-anchor, Kelly, adds an unnecessarily perky comment on personal responsibility in ensuring meat is properly cooked. Paul feigns interest until they cut to commercial. He tries to maintain eye contact but Kelly starts to review her notes for the post-break interview. His eyes drop, allowing him to imagine the buttons of her blouse popping open, giving him a peek at her ample breasts. That's why she's here. Kelly's the eye-candy, a cheap ratings grabber, but she's out of her league if she thinks her fluff news predictions justify a share of the CKWS (Know the News Before It Happens with Ottawa's #1 Knewscast!) anchor desk.

Gerry, the news director, had to be trying to get into more than just her good looks by fast-tracking her career. Kelly had moved from weather prediction to fluff news predictor to predicting co-anchor in less than two years. The audience liked that she got out into the community, was approachable and professional. It had taken Paul a decade to get this near the pinnacle of his profession and he'd done it with guts and talent: predicting the news before anyone else did.

As a news preporter, Kelly's predictive talent was knowing when someone was going to fall into some luck. She had a knack for catching video of a person watching their jackpot numbers come up or the look on a child's face when a lost puppy finds its way home. Gerry constantly raved about how her segments were a hit with male and female demographics--for different reasons, he winks, holding the latest list of stalkers. Gerry had "suggested" that she'd make a great co-anchor.

Paul should have seen this coming. His talent involved predicting crime and human tragedy. He was the best at picking when and where a piano would fall on a schmuck getting robbed. The station's ratings took off after he claimed the anchor desk and people stopped going to any area where Paul predicted danger. He was a local legend, holding CKWS's anchor chair for over twelve years.

Maybe Gerry knows Paul's overdue for a talent burnout? Predictions are like incoming snowballs: they only travel so far and they can only hit one person. When the prediction hits, there might be some residual spray for someone else with talent to pick up. Only one person gets hit and only if their talent aligns with the prediction, like Kelly's does with luck. If you lose your sensitivity, as everyone does with age, then the predictions start flying right past you.

Paul hasn't made a real prediction in over a year. A lesser knewscaster would have quit, but losing his talent to see the future hasn't hurt the ratings at all. Paul's second talent is making up a great story. With no predicted facts to hinder him, he's free to pick any headline grabbing body count. To fill the rest of the broadcast, he's fed stories from the staff preporters.

It helps that viewers avoid the locations he mentions. No one around means no death. Paul's credibility remains intact. According to his fans he's still number one, saving lives every night. Let Gerry push him out for Kelly Cleavage? Not a chance. She can have this local dump when he's ready, which could be soon. Paul King has a shot at a network gig.

The din of the studio dies off as the stagehand counts down. Kelly's on. Paul doesn't have to read another piece for a bit, so he pulls a mirror from his jacket to check his makeup. Kelly banters with the political news correspondent about a predicted sales tax

—

2

hike. Her preparation is paying off.

Paul chews the inside of his cheek and sneaks another imaginary peek into Kelly's blouse as she blathers on. Anything to distract from her voice. Out of the one in 100,000 lucky enough to be a precog (Thank-you, cell phone radiation!), why her?

Paul's camera light turns on. He prepares to read his own "prediction" concerning an elderly man living on Meadowlands Drive who will have a heart attack shoveling snow tomorrow morning. It's Paul's route to work and with tonight's predicted snowfall, he doesn't want the old farts pushing snow in front of his Silverado again.

Before he can scare the septuagenarians into hibernation, Kelly places her fingers to her forehead and shouts that she has some breaking news. Paul's camera light blinks off.

Kelly inhales. "It's about an intruder. Here! At the station! Tomorrow! I see a body on the floor!"

Gerry yells through Paul's earpiece, "Why didn't you pick this up? Is this real?"

Paul's lips move but he doesn't make a sound. He stares into one of the inactive cameras and gives the director a let's go to commercial look. The earpiece crackles again. "Unless you know she's talking out of her ass, let her carry the ball."

Is Gerry throwing him under the bus? He'll be finished if people realize she caught a crime prediction instead of him. Sweat threatens to crack his makeup.

Paul inflates his posture to demonstrate his dominance of the anchor table. He gives the control room the nod and his camera turns on. "Thank-you, Kelly, for that introduction. You must have picked up some residual after the prediction hit me. Don't worry about speaking out of turn. With practice you'll be able to tell the difference between actual predictions and what you just experienced."

Paul looks towards Kelly and gives her a nod and a smile so the camera can capture this tender mentoring moment. Kelly looks back, eyes wide, mouth agape. He was expecting to see annoyance or petulance, but agape? Is he missing something here?

"Go on!" Gerry yells through the earpiece.

"There will be a murder at the station tomorrow," he says, glancing back at the camera. That works. She did mention a body, right?

There's silence in the studio. Paul hears a quiet "Awesome" through his earpiece.

The dark eye of the camera stares like a dilated pupil, expecting more. An idea forms. "And the victim will be a...knewscaster." He looks back at Kelly, her mouth still open.

Gerry barks into Paul's earpiece. "That's great! Now, commercial! Tweet the headline so everyone has a chance to tune in!"

The last camera light blinks off, indicating that they are off the air. Gerry sticks his head outside the booth and yells at Paul. "Stick with the code! You can't say who! We're back on in 90! Drop the other stories and talk about this one. But no damn details!"

Paul smirks. He knew the code would buy him time. The broadcast code is beautiful in that it requires knewscasters not to cause undue stress to an individual or family by providing the name of a future criminal or victim. The story given to the public is that the code protects the viewers from mediocre precogs who can barely predict the difference between a fart and shitting their pants. In fact, it protects the station from the liability of having the wrong person named. More important, it's a huge ratings booster. Not naming names forces people to watch. Otherwise they would set their browsers to scan news items for any mention of their name and could skip the news entirely. That Paul King would break news on where and when a death would occur, keeps people coming back night after night. After all, it could be them.

Kelly sorts her notes and murmurs that she doesn't have any more information to talk about.

Gerry shrugs his shoulders. "I don't need more information, sweetheart. Just look concerned for the viewers." Gerry yells so everyone hears. "This is what live news is all about! Remember: D-L-D: Details Limit Discussions and we still have thirty minutes to fill. We need speculation, people!"

"What about?" Kelly says, not looking up.

"Talk around it. No names of course, because of the code and all that. Oh God... I need experts, stat!" Gerry hollers to Frankie to take over in the booth. Gerry runs out of the studio, as Frankie peers up from behind the booth with a blank stare and uses the wrong end of his Bic pen to push up his spectacles.

Paul and Kelly wince as Frankie blasts feedback through their earpieces. He yells, "Um, guys. Forty seconds until we're on air, well more like 35 now...shit, probably 30 seconds by the time I'm done talkinnnng...now."

Paul spins towards Kelly. "How much do you know?"

"I don't know," she says, then looks him in the eye. "You should know."

Paul stops. Of course he would have picked up something like this if he still had his talent. "You know the code forbids me to say anything,"

The silence between them grows awkward.

"Kelly?" Frankie says over the earpiece. "Gerry just called about moving you and Paul to the interview chairs so viewers could see your Iraqi side. Does this make any sense to you?"

The crimson that flushes into Kelly's face tells Paul that his co-anchor understands perfectly that Frankie had misheard the phrase "rack from the side."

Frankie follows up with, "Ooooh shit. You guys have been on for like 10 seconds now."

Paul sits in his office, staring out into in the empty bullpen. It took longer than usual for the place to clear out. Preporters were trying to get the inside scoop on who was the victim. Paul chastised them for not sticking to the code. As far as he knew, Kelly hadn't said anything to anyone either. He grabs one of his Knewsie award plaques and runs his fingers over the relief of Nostradamus in front of a microphone. The remainder of the knewscast had been a perfect balance of tension-heightening, last-second scrambling, plus enough discourse to let the audience think they were being informed. Gerry had been able to scrounge up some talking heads before the end of the broadcast: a criminologist who was asked how insane someone would have to be to attack a precognitive news station; a retired social worker who discussed how the station staff would deal with the traumatic aftermath of tomorrow's tragedy; and an expert on media ethics who stormed off the set after she heard the first two talk.

It was thirty minutes of fantastic speculation. Paul had been in the interviewer zone. His nods were timed perfectly with Gerry's cutaways to him. A convincing performance to make the audience forget that predicted events are avoidable. They tune in every night to see if they need to avoid their fate, but an audience is willing to suspend that belief to relish the drama around a prediction of the "inevitable."

But there are still two problems: First, how can he even trust Kelly's prediction? She can't even evade her stalkers. The woman has no talent for predicting crime. It wouldn't be the first time a precog had misinterpreted a prediction. The second problem is that at the end of the broadcast, Gerry told the crew it was business as usual tomorrow. He expected everyone at work to cover the story.

For once, people will be around when Paul's prediction is supposed to be fulfilled. If a murder doesn't happen at the station tomorrow, then people will know that Paul is full of it. Now he's stuck hoping for a murder.

But murder's a bit over the top for Paul's taste. How about an attempted murder? Yeah, that will do just fine. Now we have a story: an unjust fate for a damsel in distress, Ottawa's favourite female co-anchor, thwarted by Canada's infallible Precognitive Knewscaster of the Year! That works. Kelly practically begs to be the damsel.

If the network gets wind of this, their bigwigs will eat this up and beg him to ditch this local gig. He'll set his own terms. Gerry will kiss his ass. This'll be fantastic! Their current anchor, Sam Bentley, has more salt than pepper on top and Paul's contact says the network bigwigs are worried he's losing his edge. JBS Nightly News has been sniffing around since Paul won his fourth Knewsie award but they've yet to pull the trigger and pick him. JBS has to be the one to make the offer. If he approaches them, they might want a demonstration that he still has it. On the other hand, if they know Paul's prediction saved his co-anchor's life, on live television no less, they won't ask for any more proof. And since national anchors focus on national and international news, they're rarely close enough to future news to be hit with any predictions; he could coast for years in the new job.

Paul yanks the strips of teeth whitener out of his mouth and calls his contact at JBS to let him know the prediction. He sounds very interested and promises to call his bosses. Now all Paul needs is someone who looks like they could commit murder.

He brings his Knewsie plaque down the hall and into Kelly's office, placing it on her keyboard. It's been a weekly tradition to help inspire and remind her which one of them is The Man. She always brings it back the next day without comment. He looks around and finds her stalker list pinned to the cork board. At the top of the list is Tommy Vincent. Tommy Ten, security calls him. His

—

M.O. is to arrive at ten every morning and ask for Kelly. Every day he brings in new computer-generated composite images of what their children will look like. He's just crazy enough for people to assume he can make the jump to violence. Paul repositions his plaque, propping it up in front of Kelly's monitor and gives it a pat, promising that he'll see it again soon. He looks up Tommy Ten's number, grabs his jacket, and leaves to buy a burner phone.

The voice on the other end of the line sounds agitated, disjointed; like someone woken up with a staple to the forehead. "Who…whoever this is, get lost! I need to keep this line free!"

Paul plugs his nose to disguise his famous baritone. "We have a mutual friend who's in great danger. Do you know who I am talking about?"

"Kelly!" Tommy replies, his voice now crisp. "I saw the broadcast. How do you know her?"

"Don't worry about that. She's scared and she needs you."

"Really?"

"Yes, really."

"Well, the guards and the restraining order-"

"All the station's idea. Not hers. They need her to appear unattached so the male audience thinks they have a chance with her. It's all about the ratings."

"Bastards!"

"Yes, bastards," Paul replies. "She asked me to call you and help you get in. I need you to be behind the station, by the fire exit at ten o'clock tomorrow morning. I'll leave the door open. You come in. Don't let anyone see you or she'll be in trouble with her bosses. Follow the hall to the right until you get-"

"I know where her office is."

"Uh, good."

"And she and I will be alone, right?"

"Right."

"Nobody touches Kelly but me!"

"Ten o'clock, then," Paul says, as he hangs up the phone. *Get ready, network news. Paul King's coming.*

No one's around when Paul props open the back door. Gerry has already shooed away the police, citing freedom of the press. Gerry isn't going to tolerate the police thwarting any crime he can catch on camera. Thank goodness for the presumption of innocence.

Even if there was a pre-cog cop on the force, cops can only stop crimes in progress.

Paul hears every decibel the news director can muster when Gerry learns how many studio hands are taking the day off, citing a hazardous workplace. In Gerry's mind, there's no reason for them to take the time off since only a knewscaster's at risk, but Paul might have called the station union rep last night, suggesting collateral damage was possible. Fewer people at work means it will be easier for Tommy to move through the building unseen. Assuming the yelling means that the morning bullpen session has started, Paul walks in. The place is empty except for Gerry and some prereporters.

Gerry raises his hands to call attention and tells them that they will be broadcasting live all day and that the networks are going to follow the story in real-time. "Does everyone have their hand-held camera? The networks don't want to miss any results." Everyone except Kelly holds up their camera.

"Results?" Kelly asks, shaking her head. "You mean if someone is killed or not."

Gerry slides beside Kelly and puts his hand on her knee. Paul watches her leg twitch but Kelly holds her composure. He speaks in a reassuring tone, "Kelly, this is what reporters dream about. Being in the centre of a story that has captured the nation's imagination. I can understand you being afraid, but we'll all look out for each other. Right, everyone?" There's a few mumbles and a couple grunts through the room. "So, grab your camera and keep it with you or you're fired."

Kelly plucks Gerry's hand off her knee like she's removing a snotty Kleenex. "Gee, thanks, guys, but I'll take care of myself." She stands and strides down the hall to her office. Gerry and Paul tilt their heads slightly and gaze as her hips bop out of the bullpen.

Paul's amazed that Kelly even came in today. She'd made the prediction, so she had to know she was the intended victim. It shows some bravery. Or stupidity. Her prediction might not have been clear. Crime's not her thing. Maybe she believes Paul's assertion that she only got prediction residual and she doesn't really know what's going to happen. Gerry has told everyone to stick to their normal routine. Kelly's schedule has her in her office, working on her blog from 9:30 to 10:15.

All that's left to do is hope that Tommy arrives on schedule and then "predict" his attack in the nick of time, catching the would-be killer just as Tommy finds Kelly (with security right behind Paul, out of camera sight.) Everyone will assume the worst. No one will believe Tommy's story, even if they bother to check the phone records. No harm will come to Kelly, except maybe a scare. A crazed stalker goes to jail and Paul King is hailed as a hero for saving the hot damsel. That's award-winning journalism!

Paul hums and visualizes accepting an award for bravery when Gerry bursts into his office. "I just got word that the network wants to do a live interview with you right now. Sounds like they're looking to introduce you to their audience." Gerry gives Paul a punch in the shoulder. "You'll remember to bring along your favourite news director, right?"

"Yeah, you bet, maybe," Paul says, thankful he took the time to apply his own makeup this morning. Only a few touch-ups are needed, so he turns to the mirror.

"Get yourself gussied up quick, big guy. You got five minutes. They need your mug in front of a camera by 9:50."

"I'll be there," Paul says, practicing his 'you can trust me to predict the news important to you' smile.

"One last question, Paul, and it's the big one," Sam Bentley says, already lifting his eyebrow in anticipation of an intriguing answer. "Will your premonitory prowess allow you to prevent this potential murder?"

Paul leans forward and stares into the camera. "Thank you for asking the tough question, Sam." He lifts his own eyebrow to prep the audience for his bombshell response. "I've played this scenario close to the vest. I even let my co-anchor break the story because I didn't want to give away too much information."

"Tell us why."

"One simple reason, Sam, and it's the reason I went into this business: to strike fear into the hearts of those who would harm the innocent. I want criminals to know that I know what they're planning, and that as a knewscaster, I will expose their crime before it happens." Paul's voice rises. "I want the murderer to come in today. I want him to try to get away with a crime on my watch. I want to make an example of this man, and send a message across North America that Paul King protects the innocent!"

"So you know it's a man, then."

"I know more than that, Sam. I know who his intended

victim is and that he plans to strike at ten this morning," Paul says, nodding his head and crossing his arms.

Paul sees Sam check his watch while a wide-eyed Gerry leans out from behind his camera.

"It's already three minutes past ten," Sam states, his eyebrow yanked up to his hairline.

A word erupts from Paul that gets the network a hefty fine and he bolts from his chair, grabbing his camera as he runs from the studio. If Tommy didn't like Kelly's reaction to his arrival, she's probably dead already. If Kelly's still alive, he'll turn the camera on and hit Tommy with it. If she's dead, well, best to leave it off until someone covers the body. Damn, damn, *damndamndamn!* If she's dead he can kiss the JBS job good-bye.

Paul runs down the hall with Gerry in tow. He bursts into Kelly's office with a gasping, "I'll save you!" but freezes when he sees Tommy lying unconscious at Kelly's feet. She has her camera pointed at the broken Knewsie plaque beside Tommy's head. A welt in the centre of his forehead forms before their eyes into the reverse relief of Nostradamus at the mic.

"Oh, that's going to make a great visual," Gerry says, peeking over Paul's shoulder. "Make sure you get a close-up on that." Kelly's shaking but grinning at the same time.

"Why don't you let me handle it from here, dear?" Paul says, reaching for her camera. Kelly snaps out of her trance and yanks her camera out of reach.

"Oh, no thanks, Paul. I still need to watch the video from when I had the camera hidden by the back door. I had a vision that's how he would come in." Kelly gives Paul a knowing smile. "But I almost didn't believe it because the door should have been locked, right?"

"Maybe, uh…" Paul searches for a story but nothing comes. It takes him a second to figure it all out. She wants him to know that she has video of him unlocking the door, looking like an accessory to attempted murder. He plops down on her couch. Why isn't she ratting him out?

"Well, maybe I can forget the whole door thing," she muses. "It's not like video of how the door became unlocked would make or break the story, right?" Kelly smiles, sitting down beside Paul and placing her hand on his knee. "Hey, maybe you could interview me and make me look good for the big networks out there. I hear JBS might be looking for a new anchor. Maybe they'd be interested in me. Wouldn't that be cool? Me, a big-time network anchor?"

Paul drops his head into his hands and groans. "Sounds like a great idea," he says. "Would you mind if my first question was: How would someone with no talent for crime pick up on all of this?"

Kelly pats his knee again. "That's probably not a good question for the interview, but I'll let you in on a secret." She leans in to whisper in his ear. "I did see an intruder and a body on the floor, but I didn't see a crime. I just saw my career hitting the jackpot."

Based in Ottawa, Canada, Kevin Quirt writes speculative fiction in between the learning experiences provided by his three children. A psychology major with an interest in asking what could be amazing about the here and now, Kevin's fascination with the human experience is explored using fantastic circumstances. His work has appeared in the Spirit Legends: Of Ghosts and Gods *anthology and he was identified as a rising talent by* Penumbra e-magazine.

THE NEW KID

By Tim McDaniel

It started in the seventh grade. That was when the new kid came to our school, the Antichrist I mean, and he sat right behind me in English class. Most of the girls thought he was so cute, so dark and mysterious with his black leather jacket and slouch. And the guys liked him, because they'd heard he'd been kicked out of the Catholic school. But I immediately hated him.

He'd whisper things, really disgusting things, stuff you don't even hear on cable. And then he'd look so innocent when I turned around to glare at him. Then I would be the one to get in trouble with Ms. Soperson -- "Stop visiting with Harold, now, Joan, and continue with your reading." It made me so mad. It was unfair, and I sure didn't want people thinking that I liked him.

And, of course, because of who he was, he had these powers. One time when I was at my locker I saw him standing in the hallway, looking at me with a kind of secret grin. I glared at him and slammed my locker shut, and then it was like the floor turned to ice, and my feet went out and I fell right on my behind. I looked like an idiot. Steff and Taffy laughed at me, and even Kyle saw.

And one time he walked by my table at lunchtime, when I was sitting alone because Steff was in the bathroom, and he put something on the table and walked away. When I looked I saw it was a huge black and yellow spider, like a tarantula only bigger, like with a glandular problem. I knocked the tray onto the floor, and everyone looked, but of course by then he had already made the spider disappear. I could've killed him. I'm sure I saw Kyle laughing that time.

I tried talking to my parents, but they wouldn't listen.

"Oh, he's just showing you he likes you," Mom said. "That's how boys are." Mom was putting the Florida vacation pictures into the big scrapbook.

I was sitting on the floor at the coffee table, having a second piece of chocolate cake. "Oh, Mom. This is different. He doesn't like me. And I sure don't want him to like me. Why don't we have any ice cream?"

"It sounds to me like someone has a crush on a certain boy," Dad sang out from the kitchen, where he was drying the dishes.

"Does not!" I said. "He's the *Antichrist*, Dad! That means he hates everyone."

Mom closed the book and looked at me with her serious face, her lips tight. "Now, dear, we didn't bring you up to judge people. He can't help being the Antichrist. He was born that way."

I didn't appreciate this little lecture. I figured I was pretty liberal. Blue Lake had two black families, and so I had a black friend -- well, not a friend, but you know. I knew her. And I was OK with Catholics, and I even knew a gay guy who lived two doors down, and if there had been any Jews in Blue Lake I'm sure I would have got along with them fine too. But this new kid, Harold, was just...

"He's just mean."

Mom closed the scrapbook and put it on a shelf in the entertainment center. "And you have blonde hair. He was born that way, sweetie."

"Can't be easy, being the Antichrist," Dad said from the kitchen, among the clatter of the dishes. "Gotta be a lot of pressure on a young kid. Famous father, the weight of prophecy, and everything. Must have a hellish home life."

"Well, I don't care. I hate him."

"Give him a chance, dear," said Mom. "You'll see. It'll all work out. You know, I used to think your father had an annoying laugh, when we first met. Now it doesn't bother me. It's like that."

I stomped up to my room.

"Joanie." I tried to ignore him and work on my chapter questions, but he wouldn't stop. He leaned over his desk and poked me with a pencil. "Hey, Joanie. That's your name, right?"

Ms. Soperson was on the other side of the room, helping Corwin. I turned to Harold. His green eyes glittered like stones at the bottom of a pond, and his black hair hung into his eyes. I guess I could see why some girls liked him. I sure didn't. "It's Joan, not Joanie." I turned back, nose in the air, but he kept talking.

"Hey, Joanie. You like Kyle." I stiffened, but pretended not to hear. If Steff had said anything to him, I would kill her. Bite her head off. Just kill her.

"Well, take a look at your boyfriend now, Joanie. What's he doing over there, anyway?"

I had to glance over. Kyle was three desks away. His face was all screwed up, like he was in some kind of pain or concentration, and he was shifting around in his chair. Then he put his pencil way down his pants and scratched himself with it. He bit his lower lip. I guess he was still itchy, so he put his whole hand down his pants to itch. I couldn't believe what I was seeing.

"Kyle!" I whispered. I wanted to warn him that people could see.

He didn't hear me. "Kyle!" I said again, a bit louder. Maybe a little too loud.

"Kyle?" Ms. Soperson! "Do you have a problem?"

Kyle looked up, his face bright red, his eyes wet, his hand still down his pants scratching. I guess he didn't know what to say. And now some people were staring.

So I leapt to his defense. "It's all Harold's fault, Ms. Soperson! He made him do it!"

Well, that made just everybody look at me, and at Harold, and at Kyle.

"I've had enough of you blaming Harold for everything, Joan. But I'm talking to Kyle now. Kyle?"

Kyle at least had a little time to jerk his hand out of his pants, and think of something to say. "I don't feel too well, Ms. Soperson. Can I go home?"

"No, you may not. You can go see the school nurse, if you're feeling bad. And she'll decide if you can go home."

"But..."

"Well? What is it, Kyle?"

Kyle looked around, then got up and went over to Ms. Soperson and whispered in her ear. "Your crotch?" she said. Then the whole class whooped, and Ms. Soperson realized she had said it out loud.

"OK, everyone. I'll be right back." She took Kyle's arm and

hustled him out of the room, and now her face was red, too. Everyone was laughing. I looked at Harold. He wasn't laughing, but he had this satisfied smirk on his face.

"You jerk!" I spat at him.

"Sure am. But did you see the look on his face?"

"He never did anything to you!"

"You're right. But hey, I am the Antichrist. I don't have to be fair." He leaned back in his chair. "Anyway, I'm sure Kyle appreciated that you made everyone look at him!"

"That was you!" I don't know what happened to me then. Everything went red, and I don't even remember but they told me later that I jumped out of my desk and it tipped over and I grabbed him. But I remember having my knee on his chest, and using both hands to pound his head into the floor, my hands full of his hair, and he was just laughing. Then the other kids were grabbing at me.

They said I was hysterical, and sent me home. Later I had to see Mr. Capelle, the counselor.

"I guess you know why you're here, Joan."

Mr. Capelle was sitting on the edge of his desk, looking at me with a look of concern on his creased pink face. I was sure that he practiced that look in front of the mirror. But I had to answer him.

"Because I beat up Harold Damien."

"That's right. You know, he had to go to the Emergency Department."

"I'm glad!"

"I know that you don't mean that, Joan. His parents could have called the police. You're lucky that they chose not to."

"I don't care."

Mr. Capelle nodded, reaching up to scratch his mostly-bald head. "I understand you and Harold haven't been getting along too well."

"He's mean."

"Yes, well, you know he is the Antichrist, Joan. We shouldn't be surprised that he is also mean. That would naturally follow, wouldn't it?"

I hated to admit it, but that made some sense. "I guess so. But I hate him."

"I see." Mr. Capelle slid himself off the desk and walked around it, frowning like he was thinking really deeply. He sat in his chair and looked over at me. "You know, Joan, usually we only hate people that we don't know well enough."

"I know him well enough."

"I understand you think you do. But Harold's parents have made a suggestion, and I think it's a good idea." He clasped his hands together in front of his face, so I knew he was going to get all official on me.

"You know, Harold is new here in Blue Lake. He doesn't know many people, or have many friends. You've lived here all your life. What we're going to do, is make the two of you kind of partners. A team."

"Partners?"

"That's right. You'll be his guide and his friend, spending an hour and a half with him, every day after school. And you know something? I think the two of you will become fast friends."

"Please Mr. Capelle, don't make me do that."

"Oh, it won't be so bad. You'll see. Your parents have already agreed. And, Joan, to make sure there's no more fighting, I want you to come see me every Tuesday and Thursday, just for the two of us to talk." He smiled. I wanted to smack his fat pink face with a golf club or something.

"Hey." Harold was sitting on the steps, playing with a magnifying glass.

I remembered I had to play nice. "Whatcha you looking at?"

"Nothing."

I sat next to him, not too close. "Then what are you doing with the stupid magnifying glass?" Then I noticed. "Oh, you're burning ants? That's sick. I used to do that when I was a little kid."

Harold smiled. "Yeah. But I'm not killing them. See? I just burn off a couple of legs on each ant. I must have done fifteen of them by now."

"That's horrible!" But I couldn't stop watching him. "How can you aim it so it just burns off a leg?"

"You got to hold the ant down, but really soft, so you don't squeeze the guts out. Watch." Harold chose an ant of those walking along the concrete step, and gradually lowered a finger until it was just resting lightly on the ant's back. I couldn't believe how gentle the touch was. At first the ant just staggered a little, and then scrabbled, and then Harold increased the pressure just enough to make the ant lie on its stomach, legs spread out.

"And now I just focus the magnifying glass on one of the legs." He took the glass in his other hand, and shifted it around until a tiny spot of burning sun appeared on the step. It tracked towards the ant, and found a leg. The leg withered in the spot and curled up. Harold released the ant and it limped away. The burnt leg dropped off its body after a couple of steps.

Harold looked at me. "Sometimes I do the front pair, or the middle pair, or every other leg. Well? What do you think?"

"I can't believe you could do that."

"It's not hard."

"What are you talking about? You must have practiced like, for hours. But I guess you got nothing better to do with your time."

"You could do it, too."

"Why would I even want to?"

"Just try it."

"I could do it if I wanted to. I just don't want to." But I watched the ants crawl by. I wondered if I could make one stop and lay down, like Harold had.

"OK," I said. "Let me try. But don't burn it."

"OK."

"I mean it. Don't."

I really didn't want Harold to burn the ant's legs off. I wanted to do it myself. Just to see if I could, you know.

"Hi, Kyle." For once, Harold was sitting at the far side of the lunchroom.

He looked up from his fries and nodded, and I sat down right next to him. "What are you going to do for your science project?" I asked him, opening my milk. It was hard to speak, because my throat felt closed up.

"I don't know. Hey, Greg." Greg and Mandy -- she always laughs too loud -- sat down at our table.

"I have a great idea, but I need a partner," I told Kyle. "Mr. Lanyon said we could have partners if we want."

Kyle was looking down at his lunch, and a strand of his yellow hair was just touching the end of his nose. I wanted to stroke that hair. "Yeah," he said.

I picked up my sandwich and tried to sound real casual. "So, you want to be partners?"

"Yeah, I'll think about it."

Then Steff came up, and Kyle pushed Greg's sack lunch to one side so Steff would have room for her tray. Greg didn't mind, because now he was sitting closer to Mandy.

"Hey, Steff," Kyle said.

Steff put her tray down. I don't know why she smiles when she's got those ugly braces. "Hi, Kyle," she said, so sweetly. She couldn't be more obvious, sticking her chest out at him. "Do you have a partner for the science project? I really need help with my volcano thing."

"Sure!" said Kyle.

"But I thought you were going to be my partner?" I said.

"Sorry. I thought about it, like I said!" He looked away from me and smirked.

And Steff looked at me out of those big blue eyes of hers. "What's your project, Joan? Something about how to lose weight?" Everyone laughed.

"A conveyor belt spoon!" Greg said.

"It's glandular!" I said.

Steff said, "Or grandiose." She probably just learned that word.

"Hey, don't make fun of Miss Piggy," said Greg. Everyone laughed again, and I heard Kyle the loudest. It was so immature. No one's called me that since third grade. I just got up and left. And I was still hungry.

After school, I just wanted to run home, but I had to meet stupid Harold, or he would report me to the stupid counselor and I'd get in trouble.

"I saw you and your friends at lunch today," he said.

"Who didn't? And they're not my friends." We were out by the baseball diamond, and Harold was climbing around on the backstop. I thought he would laugh at me the way the other guys did, maybe call me Miss Piggy too. But he was quiet. I sat on the ground and threw some pebbles, but I kept stealing looks at Harold. He looked like he was just concentrating on climbing, his hair curled over almost into his eyes. And of course he was wearing his black leather jacket. Yeah, he was kind of cute. Too bad he was such a jerk. "Harold?"

"Yeah?" He looked down on me, from up there, smiling. His

teeth were really even.

He knew what I was going to say even before I said it. But I said it anyway. "How did you do that thing, with Kyle, the other day?"

Harold jumped down. "The crotch-rot?"

"Yeah. If that's what you call it." I picked up another pebble and looked at it.

"You don't mind that I did that to him?"

"Ha. I don't mind."

"Your boyfriend?"

I looked up at him. "He's not my boyfriend. I hate him." I felt myself smiling, then, in a way I never did before. A new kind of smile. "I want him to get that crotch-rot again, only worse."

"You serious? 'Cause it's not something you can just fool around with, and then walk away." He was looking right into my eyes.

I looked right back. My mouth was dry. "It's not fair, what he did to me," I said in a whisper. "I'm serious."

He looked at me doubtfully.

"I'm serious, OK?" I said, standing up.

"Partners, Joan?" I knew he wasn't talking about the science project. And I thought of Kyle, and Greg, and Steff. I thought of them fighting to sit next to me at lunch, because they were scared of what I might do if they offended me.

"Yeah, Harold. Partners."

Harold smiled the widest smile. He took his jacket off and swung it over his shoulder. "It's not hard to learn," he said. "And you know what, Joan? We're going to have so much fun!"

"So, Joan, things are going well with Harold?"

"Yeah, Mr. Capelle. Just fine."

He smiled. "Ah, that's good. See? I thought you two would become friends. From what you've told me, and from what Harold's parents have said, I don't think you need to come to see me like you have anymore. Unless you want to just chat."

I got up. "Thanks, Mr. Capelle." I got up to leave.

Mr. Capelle shuffled some papers on his desk. "Oh, Joan?"

"Yes, Mr. Capelle?"

"You live not far from Kyle Reardon, isn't that right?"

"Yes, Mr. Capelle."

"I don't suppose you have any idea of where he's been the last two days? His parents said he got on the bus as usual, but he's been absent from class."

I thought of Kyle, lying there behind the bushes behind the Math Annex, pinned to the ground, unable to speak, blood smearing his mouth, his smirk gone, his eyes full of terror. I'd have to visit him again soon.

"Sorry, Mr. Capelle. I don't know where he is." I turned towards the door, smiling.

And that's how it started, Harold and me. And you know, he was right -- we did have a lot of fun. By the end of the school year the whole school -- even the teachers and Mr. Capelle -- knew to give us respect.

Oh, don't think I don't know what Harold is, what kind of guy he is. I'm not stupid. I go along with him, sure, but it's for my own reasons. And one day dear Harold is going to be surprised.

I'm learning things about him, see. His secrets. Stuff he'd hate to get out. One day I was in his room, and I borrowed his diary. Photocopied the good parts later -- stuff about the wet beds, the teddy bear. The whining about his dad. Like he's got it bad; he was never the fat girl in the class. But when the time is right, I'll let him know what I got on him, and then we'll see.

And the whole world will see. They think Harold is bad? Just wait till they see what happens when I'm in charge.

Boys. They haven't got a clue. Ha!

Tim McDaniel teaches English as a Second Language at Green River Community College, not far from Seattle. He lives with his wife, a dog, a cat, and an impressive collection of plastic (and wood and cloth and glass and etc.) dinosaurs. His short stories have appeared in a number of magazines, including F & SF *and* Asimov's.

THE PILLOW

By Fred McGavran

Louise would never order anything that was not right for me, so I do not blame myself for anything that happened. When the box arrived, she was out on her regular Wednesday circuit to the grocery, the podiatrist, and lunch at the club with our younger daughter Carol. I carried the box in from the porch with some difficulty: it was about a yard long, two feet wide, and weighed more than the laundry baskets Louise made me carry up from the basement. When I shook it, nothing inside moved.

I set it on the kitchen table to open it, but the metal brads wouldn't budge. I was cutting them out with a paring knife when Louise and Carol returned, still flushed from the club's house chardonnay.

"What are you doing?" Louise cried. "You'll ruin it."

"I'll watch him, Mother, while you go to the bathroom," Carol said, taking the knife away.

It was no surprise to me that Carol had gone through two husbands with hardly any alimony or child support to show for the experience.

"Let me do that," Louise said upon her return.

She found a screwdriver in one of her secret drawers, pried out the brads, and opened the box. Inside, wrapped in plastic so thick that my knife had barely lacerated it, was a pillow.

"Here," she said. "Use it for your nap."

"Did he eat his lunch, Mother?" Carol asked.

On days when Louise is out, I open the can of beef barley soup she always leaves, smear some inside a bowl, and dump the rest down the disposal.

"Why is it so heavy?" I said to distract them.

"Magnets," Louise said. "They realign your spine as you

sleep."

"I didn't know that the spine was magnetic," I said.

"It's the latest medical breakthrough," Louise snapped.

They were looking at me with the expectant stare of prison guards just hoping the prisoner will resist. So I lugged the pillow upstairs, where Louise stuck it into a pillowcase.

"Ow," she said as she punched it to fluff it.

When I lay down, it felt like a log under my neck. I tried to turn it around so that the softer side was up, but she turned it back.

"The magnets have to be under your neck to work," she said.

So I closed my eyes, thinking that I would turn it around again as soon as she left. Instead I fell into a deep dreamless sleep like the afternoon naps I took decades ago after cutting the grass and drinking two beers with lunch. When I awakened, I felt so refreshed that I slipped downstairs and was boiling water for tea before Louise and Carol could change the subject of their conversation from me to the disagreeable men Carol was meeting on the internet.

"I don't know how much longer I can handle him by myself," Louise was saying. "And assisted living costs a fortune."

If the cup had not rattled in the saucer as I slipped into my den, they would not have known I was there.

"Don't spill, Walter," she called after me.

"Don't live" is what she meant.

I spend many hours in my den, resting my hands in the indentations on my blotter and trying to remember whether any of the people in the photographs on the wall are still alive. There is a dark stained area where I place my saucer. I was staring at a photograph of a man who could have been me receiving a plaque from another man who may have been important once.

As I tried to remember, something trembled at the edge of perception, like a water strider on a pond. I looked down at my desk. Nothing. Then to my right it moved again. Leaning forward, I saw the paperclips in the magnetic holder quiver. Suddenly one leapt out and stung my ear like an angry insect.

"Ow!" I cried.

"He's spilled something," Louise exclaimed and rushed to my aid.

"Look, Mother, he cut himself," Carol said, turning my head to the side.

She dabbed my ear with a tissue.

"He never cuts his fingernails," Louise said.

She hurried off for scissors and a nail file, leaving the rest of the afternoon to grow cold with the tea. In the evening, when it was time for me to go to bed, Louise placed my neck on the hard part of the pillow as firmly as an executioner positioning the neck of the condemned on the guillotine.

"I don't think it's working, Mother," Carol said.

"We have thirty days to return it," Louise said turning off the light.

Have you ever come home from war by sea, when the waves that were so black at your crossing were now turquoise and laced with foam? Our destroyer escort was as low in the water as a Venetian galley; blue water broke over her bow, and when the California hills rose on the horizon, the crew danced on the deck and cheered. For the first time since we had moved into the condo, I heard the magic singing of a bird through the window treatments. I got up very carefully so that Louise would not spoil it and went to the window to touch the warm place the sun had made on the shade.

I still remembered those huge breakfasts we had on bright Saturday mornings, and tiptoed downstairs to the kitchen. Photos of Zoë, Carol's teenage daughter, Denise and her children in Buffalo, and Lewis and Grace and their children in Los Angeles shuddered as I reached for the refrigerator door. Inside it was as empty as when I was a bachelor. No eggs, no sausages, no bacon, not even a loaf of bread with the crust flecked blue with mold.

"What are you doing in there?" Louise demanded.

Surprised, I let the door swing shut. The magnet holding Zoë smacked me in the cheek. As I peeled it off, the other magnets let go, hitting me in the forehead and cheeks, while the West Coast and Buffalo grandchildren fluttered down.

"Now look what you've done," she said.

"I was just looking for breakfast."

"Here," she said. "I'll do it."

She reached into a cupboard for Raisin Bran and then stepped over the pictures to the refrigerator for the almond milk.

"We don't even have any eggs," I said.

"Eggs don't have a long refrigerator life," she said, backing me to the kitchen table and setting Raisin Bran soaked in a tan fluid before me.

If I had not been starving, I would have let it go.

"Let's go to Denny's," I said, remembering a name we had heard on TV.

She looked at me as if I had suggested we go into the Amazon jungle and eat live insects. I walked around her to the sink and poured the cereal and almond milk into the disposal.

"I'm sure you'll enjoy it, dear," I said. "They're one of Oprah's sponsors."

Two hours later found us seated at a Formica table at Denny's, me admiring a huge plate of scrambled eggs, sausages, and pancakes, and Louise sniffing a glass of prune juice as if it might contain strychnine. Just as I cut into the sausage with my knife and fork, my spoon hit me in the glasses.

"What have you done now?" Louise cried.

Then her utensils unwrapped themselves from her napkin and flew at my head.

"Stop that," she said. "Everyone's looking at us."

The only one looking at us was a four year old in the booth behind her, who had struggled free of his mother.

"Don't stare," his mother said.

"You don't have to take that from her, Bud," I said to the boy and settled into the best breakfast I had had in years.

All the way home, Louise talked about the risks of speaking to other people's children. It was coming back to me that there had been a time I could ignore her. So I took the newspaper and went to my den, while she disappeared into the basement. When she emerged an hour later, she was carrying our son Lewis' old football helmet. Like many adult children, Lewis had left his "stuff" in our basement, including a complete set of college textbooks that had never been opened.

"If you keep on bumping into things," she said, "you have to wear this."

The penholder on my desk had turned and was pointing at me.

"Let me try it on," I said.

It was a pretty good fit and only made a little "thock" when the pen struck the side.

"Isn't that better?" Louise said in a distant voce.

"Let's go to the club tonight for dinner," I replied.

We made an unusual entrance: I in a houndstooth sport jacket, bow tie, and football helmet, Louise in her usual vintage smock, and Carol in something sequined that emphasized her paunch. Undulating so that light flashed from every jeweled piercing, Zoë manipulated her PDA to avoid eye contact with any of the startled diners.

"Would we like to check the football helmet, sir?" the maitre d' inquired.

"We would not," I replied.

As we made our progress through the dining room, several "thocks" on the helmet confirmed that I had made the right decision.

"Grandpa," exclaimed Zoë, "that woman threw a knife at you."

Turning, I saw Dorothy Cuttlesworth Ames, doyen of a constricting circle of the city's wealthiest widows, holding a fork in her right hand and staring at the empty fingers of her left.

"I didn't think you were a southpaw, Dorothy," I said to allay her embarrassment.

After we were seated, our waiter removed Mrs. Ames' steak knife from the back of my helmet.

You reach a time in life when your hearing is not good, and wearing a football helmet does not improve communication. Perhaps I was a little quick to order a drink, about the last clear memory I have of that evening. Louise and Carol followed my lead, however, and soon I was amusing Zoë by moving her silverware around by tilting my head.

Dinner itself was something of a trial. A straw, of course, solved the difficulty with the wine, but I did not yet understand the fine muscle skills necessary to insert food through a facemask. To the horror of my wife and daughter, several mouthfuls ended up in my napkin. Zoë, however, looked on with the same curious expression with which she watched *The Dog Whisperer*.

Departing, I received a standing ovation from the other diners. By the time valet parking had found Carol's van, Zoë had reabsorbed herself in text messaging, and Louise and Carol were mouthing to each other that they would talk as soon as I was in bed. In a heightened state of awareness after two glasses of wine and a cup of coffee through the straw, I decided to forestall their plans.

Have we spoken yet about triangulation? It is a pejorative term in psychology to describe one member of a family confiding something nasty to another about a third family member, the target, so that target is isolated and unaware that she is the victim until it is too late. Louise had practiced this art upon me with Carol for years. Thanks to the time difference, however, whenever Louise called Lewis in Los Angeles, he was into his second martini and too distracted to follow her argument. Although she lived in our time zone, our older daughter Denise had become unresponsive after we refused to pay her country club bills and renew the lease on the Lexus. At 11 o'clock that night, when I thought Lewis would be getting his second wind, I called him on his cell.

"It's your mother," I said. "I'm afraid she's starting to lose it."

"I'd like to help, Dad, but I just can't leave Grace and the kids alone out here without them going crazy in the malls. Can't Carol handle it?"

"She's in denial, Lewis," I said, pausing for dramatic effect. "Could you call Denise? I'd do it myself but she's been uncommunicative after I refused to pay for her last divorce."

So that is how Denise received a call from her California brother at 2 AM that her mother was about to die. Physicians tell me that there is no one more intransigent about a declining mother's care than an out-of-town daughter wracked with guilt for having deserted her mother years before. Denise was able to find a live-in for the kids, a kennel for the dogs, plus make a ten o'clock flight here the next morning. I can't tell you how exciting it was for me to witness her arrival in an airport limousine just as Louise and Carol returned from lunch at the club. Before Louise was out of the bathroom, Denise had reignited one of the nastiest sibling rivalries of the last century.

"Of course you don't see it," she said in a savage whisper to Carol just as the toilet flushed, announcing their mother's imminent appearance. "You're too close to her."

I was a little surprised that Denise had not commented on my football helmet, but I always stay out of the way when my wife and daughters scream at each other. Have I mentioned that after her third divorce, Denise let herself go and outweighed her mother and sister together by at least 150 pounds? Perhaps it was intimidation, or perhaps Denise reassuming her role as big sister and mother's protector after a lapse of forty years, but the battle ended in compromise. Louise and the girls got into the airport limousine for a tour of local assisted living facilities. They returned after dark with a gripping story of having toured all the best units, several boxes of Chinese food, and a plea for my credit card to pay the limousine driver.

"Royal Oakes is by far the nicest," Carol announced. "But they won't have a double unit open up until someone dies."

"I didn't know we were looking for a double unit, Carol," I said to distract Denise from staring at my helmet. "Someone has to be here for you and the kids."

"That's right, Carol," Denise said, dumping most of the cashew chicken over a huge pile of rice on her plate. "What do you have to drink with this, Dad?"

I found an ancient bottle of St. Emilion behind the mayonnaise, too good for the occasion, but I wanted to keep her on my side. The next morning after breakfast at Denny's, we checked Louise into a Royal Oakes single. I'll bet she appreciated that last full breakfast. We left her arguing with a big boned woman in hospital blues about the best time to start her on Depends.

And here the story might have ended. Carol would arrive around noon several days a week to take me to the club for lunch, or to drop Zoë off while she toured local spas and tanning salons, and we always had dinner together Friday at the club. Every Sunday we would visit Louise for lunch. She had developed quite a taste for cashew chicken, although I never did find the right wine.

One afternoon, however, when I returned from the barbershop and went upstairs for my nap, my pillow was missing. I hoped Carol had not tried to wash it.

"Carol," I called down. "What did you do with my pillow?"

"There's been a recall," she said. "I sent it back."

The next few days passed like one of those episodic dreams that distort your sleep, and you arise achy and sticky with sweat.

"There have been reports of serious injuries," Carol explained when I told her to get it back. "At least you won't have to wear that ridiculous helmet anymore."

What do you say when the fatal diagnosis is uttered, and all that is left is to call hospice and pull down the shades? At our last dinner together at the club, I spilled my water twice, could not taste the fritters Diablo, and nearly aspirated my straw. I lost it during our exit when I saw several diners waving metallic objects at me as if to reflect the evil eye.

"Chill, Gramps," Zoë said. "They're taking pictures with their cells."

In my weakened state, I did not realize Carol was driving us to Royal Oakes instead of back to the condo.

"We're so lucky to have found a double," she explained with a bright deceptive smile. "They moved Mother in today, and I have your pajamas and socks in the trunk."

So, wrapped tight in plastic, I spent the first of many nights at Royal Oakes. A slow decline is like entering detox with no hope of every escaping the addiction, where all the shakes and tremors lead to ever more painful bondage. Who, oh who will hear my cry and come to my succor? I am "le prince d'Aquitaine à la tour abolie."

Perhaps the worst part was reacquiring a certain intimacy with Louise, who slept in a bedroom as small as mine on the other side of our common bathroom. To pass the time, I pressed my call button whenever she pressed hers to see whose caretaker would arrive first. If my caretaker, Teddy, arrived first, Louise would have to give me one of her plastic cups of warm cranberry juice. If LaRhond, her caretaker, won the race, then I had to give Louise one of my Pop Tarts. The shortest response time was 20 minutes, the longest 2½ hours. When I commented favorably on Teddy's performance to the charge nurse, she reassigned LaRhond leaving Teddy our only caretaker. So much for rating employees by performance.

Unlike the condo in the old days, I could not evade the beef barley soup or boiled zucchini by pouring it down the disposal. Teddy always sat beside me and poked a spoon in my mouth whenever I came up for air.

"Gotta eat this shit, man," he said. "We catch all sorts of shit when somebody starves."

As you might expect, Louise offered no sympathy. Her presence was like the television, which was never turned off. We were just another ancient couple dozing through empty days, while at night the staff wheeled huge squeaky machines and gurneys through the halls to keep us from going to sleep. Like King Richard imprisoned in the tower, I waited for a minstrel to pass by who would recognize my song and not betray me to the guards. My only relief was an occasional visit from Zoë, who had learned to drive my old Mercedes and was teaching me to surf the web on her PDA to obtain my credit card number for gas.

"Let's do eBay today, Gramps," she said, moving in for the kill. "What would you like to bid on?"

"Pillows," I whispered, feeling that wild surge of hope that only someone at the edge of death can know when the doctor suggests an experimental therapy.

"What kind?" she said. "There are 19,738 listed."

"Use 'magnetic' as a modifier, dear," Louise suggested, her first coherent statement in months.

Zoë found them in a nanosecond.

"New or used, Gramps?"

"Try 'original,'" I said.

And that is how Zoë got my credit card number, and I started on my return to life.

The next few days seemed endless, punctuated only by calls from my credit card company asking if I had really ordered six pairs of cross training shoes or a video game about stealing cars. I was so weak that Teddy despaired of borrowing enough for child support to stay out of jail.

"You gottta take care of your friends, man," he would say, peeling me off the toilet in the morning. "Can't be here for you if you ain't here for me."

In the corridor outside our room, I heard the aides talking about hospice and how long it would be until they had to move Louise back to a single and clean the place up for the next couple. I had not bothered to put on my glasses the day that Zoë arrived with the pillow.

"This the right one, Gramps?" she asked dropping it on my chest.

It was as heavy and inflexible as the lead aprons dentists drape you with when they X-ray your teeth.

"Yes, dear, yes," I whispered. "Just place it under my head."

Instead, she tucked the pillow under her arm. I could not see her clearly, but her head seemed curiously enlarged. When she bent over to kiss me goodbye, the procedure was interrupted by the facemask on her helmet. Instead of leaving me the pillow so I could return to life, she took it for herself so she could audition for *American Idol*. Oh, yes, the minstrel had recognized my song and had sold me back to the evil prince.

"Teddy," I whispered when he came to bind me up for the

night. "You into eBay?"

"Whoa," he said. "What am I gonna eBay with, man?"

"Go to 'pillows, magnetic, original.' I'll give you my card number. Pay whatever they ask."

"You gotta wait 'til the last minute so they don't bid 'em up on you," he said, confirming my respect for his genius.

I let him order a second football helmet for himself to reinforce our bonding.

At last a faithful minstrel had heard my lament, and the door to my prison creaked open. The day of my release, Teddy appeared with a pillow, bent me forward, and placed the hard part under my neck.

"Yes," I cried, feeling the rich surge of life return. "One good night's sleep, and I'm free."

"You want your helmet, man?" he asked.

"Tomorrow, when I'm ready for the club."

"You gonna be quite the couple," he said.

"No, I don't think Louise will be up to it."

"She loves her pillow, man. When I give it to her, she says she ain't never felt better."

"You gave Louise a pillow?"

"An' I get her a helmet, too. 'Joe Namath No. 12' jes like you."

From Louise's room, I could hear the remote control for the television spinning slowly on her bedside table before dropping onto the floor. I had not thought that it was magnetic.

"Don't wait up for me tonight, Walter," she called. "Carol and I are going out."

Fred McGavran is a graduate of Kenyon College and Harvard Law School, and served as an officer in the Navy in Vietnam. In June 2010 he was ordained a deacon in The Diocese of Southern Ohio, where he serves as Assistant Chaplain at Episcopal Retirement Homes in Cincinnati. The Ohio Arts Council awarded him an Individual Achievement Award for The Reincarnation of Horlach Spenser, *a story that appeared the Harvard Review. Black Lawrence Press published* The Butterfly Collector, *his award winning collection of short stories. His action novel* The Arminius Codex: The Hunt for the Last Roman Eagle *are on Amazon Kindle. For links to stories and, see www.fredmcgavran.com .*

INHERITANCE

By Kristina R. Mosley

Milo and Cate stood in their living room, looking at the boxes and furniture she inherited from her grandmother. "Your grandma had a lot of crap, didn't she?" he asked.

Cate didn't respond. She looked down, brown hair covering her face.

"What's wrong?" she asked.

"Don't call my grandmother's things 'crap.'"

"I didn't mean anything by it."

She sighed. "I know you didn't. I'm sorry. I'm still a wreck."

"Of course you are," Milo said, embracing his wife. "It hasn't been long."

They held each other for a few moments, Cate's face buried in Milo's gray t-shirt. "We need to figure out what to do with this stuff," she said, her husband's chest muffling her words. They separated.

"What were you thinking?" he asked, running a hand through his shaggy blond hair.

She shrugged. "I'll probably just stick everything in the attic. I want to go through it first, though."

They looked at the boxes scattered around their living room. "Where do we start?" he asked.

Cate pointed to a box at her feet. "This works," she said. She opened the box and found old photos. Milo helped her sift through the albums, framed portraits, and loose snapshots. He picked up a photo of a baby girl with chocolate frosting smeared across her face. She grinned enthusiastically at the camera. He read the description on the back. "Catherine Marie Russell, age one."

She laughed. "First birthday, I guess. Just shows that I've always liked cake." She picked up an album and flipped through its pages, stopping on a black and white picture of a smiling woman. Her light hair was tightly curled, and she wore a light-colored one-piece bathing suit.

She seems so happy, Cate thought. She turned the album so her husband could see the picture. "Milo, look."

"Wow, is that Earline?"

"Yeah."

"How old was she?"

Cate looked at the date on the back of the photo and subtracted. "Eighteen or nineteen, I think."

"You look like her."

"You think so?"

"I mean, you're darker, but your facial structure is similar. You have the same smile. You're both pretty ladies," he added, smiling.

"But I'm prettier, right?"

"I don't know, Cate. Your grandma was pretty hot."

She laughed, and they continued to dig through the boxes of memories. Soon, only an old army trunk remained. Scuffmarks covered its dark green surface, and the latches and lock were tarnished and dull.

"I wonder what's in it," Milo mused. "Unlock it."

"There's no key anywhere," she replied.

"Guess I'll open it." He walked into the office and returned a few moments later, unbending two paperclips.

"You're going to pick the lock?" Cate asked.

"Yes."

"I didn't know you could do that."

He laughed. "I'm a very mysterious man. Now, step back."

She moved away. Milo stuck the paperclips in the lock, moving them around until he heard a faint click. He lifted the lid. Inside sat an old, dusty burlap sack. Cate reached down and opened it, revealing a dirty, yellowed skeleton wrapped in heavy chains. She gasped, jumped away, and looked at her wide-eyed husband.

"Why would your grandma have a skeleton in a trunk?" he asked.

"Maybe it's a Halloween decoration."

"It looks real, though."

"So, you think you know everything, Mr. Med Student?"

"I know bones. Do you think your grandma killed him?"

"What? Grandma would do no such thing."

"Don't worry. I was dead long before Earline met me," a deep male voice said.

Milo and Cate looked around their living room for another person. No one else was there. "Was that the skeleton?" the husband asked.

Cate nodded.

They screamed. Milo grabbed Cate's arm and pulled her across the living room. He stood between his wife and the trunk.

"Please don't be alarmed," the skeleton said. "I don't want to hurt you." He tried to free himself from the chains. "Also, I'm chained up, so it would be hard for me to hurt you even if I wanted."

"You stay right there," Milo said nervously.

The skeleton put his hands up in a surrendering gesture. "All right."

"How are you talking?" Cate asked.

"I'm fairly sure it's magic."

"But, there's no such thing," Milo argued.

"All right, Mr. Med Student," the skeleton began, "how do you explain me?"

"The skeleton's not really here." He ignored the bones and turned to his wife. "You know what's really going on?"

"What?" Cate wondered.

"Your grandmother's house was old, and the attic wasn't well-ventilated. There was mold or something in the boxes. We inhaled it, and now we're hallucinating."

"Doesn't that take some time?"

"Maybe it's been long enough. It could've been days. Who knows? We're hallucinating."

Cate shrugged. "Maybe Grandma had a skeleton in a trunk."

"Why are you being so nonchalant about this?" Milo asked.

"I believe the skeleton. He's not going to hurt us. I wonder if he has a name?" she said.

"Why would you wonder that?"

"I'm human. I have to name things." She walked over to the skeleton. "What's your name?"

"I don't think I have one, or at least I don't remember what my name was in life. I've been dead a long time," he responded.

"What did my grandma call you?"

"I don't think I can repeat that in polite company."

"Hmm." Cate narrowed her eyes. "I'll call you Paco," she said to the skeleton. "I knew a Paco once, a guy I went to school with."

"So?" Milo asked.

"The skeleton reminds me of the guy."

"Dude looked like a skeleton?"

"He was pretty skinny…"

The skeleton turned his empty eye sockets to her. "I think it is an excellent name."

"Thank you, Paco." She smiled.

"My God, you're friends now?" Milo exclaimed.

"You don't need to be rude," Cate said. "He's dead. He's been through enough."

Milo rolled his eyes.

She turned to the skeleton. "How did you end up in the trunk, Paco?"

"Earline called me. I supposed I was there to fight for her, but she didn't know what to do with me. She was scared, so she wrapped me in chains and threw me in this trunk."

"Why would you need to fight for her?"

"There was an evil man. She needed my help. I don't know much else."

Cate walked closer to the trunk. Milo put out an arm to block her. She glared at him but stopped.

"What evil man, Paco? What did he look like? What was his name?"

"I didn't know. I don't think Earline did, either. He wore a black suit. He was tall and thin, even by my standards. Darkness covered his face. He seemed very old."

"How so?"

"It's hard to describe. He seemed out of place, like he didn't belong in the time in which he lived. Also, he smelled musty."

"What did he do?"

"He caused a lot of trouble, that's what he did. Earline told him to leave, and I pushed him a bit. He left after that," Paco said.

"Weird," Milo muttered.

Cate's eyes widened. "Grandma's journals."

"What?"

"I got Grandma's journals, remember? There might be something in them."

Milo picked up an old composition book. Its corners were bent, and the white on its cover was almost brown with age. He handed it to Cate. "Here you go."

Cate opened the notebook. Her grandmother's neat cursive greeted her. She leafed through the yellowed pages, hoping to find a clue in Earline's past that would explain why her life was now topsy-turvy. She skimmed the pages.

"Share with the class," Milo said.

"I love stories," Paco added.

Cate looked up. "Okay, I found something." She cleared her throat and began reading. "*A man came up to us at the reception, claiming to be Ronnie's cousin Samuel. Later, Ronnie said that he didn't know him, but since his family was so large, he didn't know all of his relatives.*

"*There was something about Samuel that seemed...strange. First, he dressed all in black. Secondly, he was pale, as white as a sheet. He didn't seem to belong at our wedding. He would've fit in better at a funeral--in the coffin.*

"*Samuel congratulated us. His smile was too big. It wasn't a happy smile, either. He looked like a snarling animal. He asked if he could drop by our house some time. Ronnie quickly said yes. I didn't like it, but it was the right thing. I have to be welcoming to my new family after all.*

"*Samuel walked away, and we visited with other relatives. I looked over to where he was, but he had vanished. I didn't see him for the rest of the wedding reception.*"

"Creepy," Milo said.

She flipped through the pages. "*A robin flew into the kitchen window. I went outside. The poor thing's neck was broken, and it didn't move. I didn't want it to be dead. After a few moments, the bird moved. It soon found its feet and flew away.*"

"Oh my God, Scruffles!" Cate gasped.

"What?"

"When I was eight," she began quietly, "a car hit my dog Scruffles. Dad buried him in the backyard. I stood over his grave, wished for him to come back. The next day, he did, but he wasn't right. He was dirty. He limped. He didn't want to eat or play. Scruffles didn't obey anyone but me, and he didn't want to leave my side. Mom freaked out and ran into the house with my brother, but Dad stayed outside with Scruffles and me. He just said, 'Send him back, Cate.' Somehow, I knew what he meant. I thought hard, and Scruffles closed his eyes again. Dad sent me in the house with Mom and Kyle, and he reburied my dog. I understand what I did now, Milo. I brought him back from death."

"What?" he squawked. He moved his mouth like a fish gulping. "What?" he said again.

Paco's jaw was open, like he had his mouth wide in surprise.

"So, I'm pretty sure I can raise the dead, and Grandma probably could, too."

Milo was silent, still wide-eyed.

"Are you okay, honey?"

"Yeah," he said. "It's just a lot to take in."

"How do you think I feel?"

"Keep reading, Cate," Paco said. "We don't know about the man yet."

"Oh yeah." She flipped more pages. Several entries later, the words were scrawled quickly, hardly legible, like her grandmother wrote in haste.

"Ronnie and I were asleep," Cate began. *"I dreamed of a man in a black suit. I knew he was dangerous, and I tried to find help. A noise woke me, but Ronnie didn't seem to hear it. I put on my housecoat and went to see what it was. A figure stood in the backyard.*

"As I approached, I saw the figure was a skeleton wearing rotten clothes and grave dirt..."

"That would be me," Paco interjected.

"I screamed, but no sound came out," Cate continued. *"The skeleton told me not to worry, that he was there to protect me. He said that I called him. Neither the skeleton nor I knew how I did that."*

She turned the page of the worn notebook and continued. *"The back door creaked open behind me, and I heard a yelp. I knew it was Ronnie. I didn't know how to explain the skeleton, and I didn't really try. Bless him, he didn't get upset or anything. He just stood there with me, trying to figure out what to do with it. Then, the man in black showed up."*

"Oh, shit," Milo whispered.

"He knew my name. Something was familiar about him, but I

didn't know him. His face was black, as if covered by a mask of shadows. Ronnie stood between the man and me, intending to defend me. The man said something under his breath, and Ronnie crumpled to the ground. I rushed over to him. I didn't think he was breathing. It wasn't fair, I thought. Why was the only thing I had taken from me?"

"Okay, question," Milo said, raising his hand. "If your grandpa was dead, how the hell are you here?"

"I have no idea," Cate replied. She continued reading. *"I shouted at the man to leave. The skeleton got between the stranger and me, repeating what I said. He pushed the man, but the man shrugged him away. The man mumbled something about me not being fun. He said he'd come back later, and he vanished into the darkness."*

"Yeah, I was too much for him to handle," Paco said confidently.

"Ronnie was getting cold," Cate continued. *"I didn't want him to die. He was the only thing I had. I didn't want to lose him. I just thought about how much I wanted him to live. In a few moments, I heard him gasp for breath and cough. He wasn't dead after all."*

"Honey, I hate to tell you this," Milo said, "but I think your grandpa was a zombie."

"Oh Lord."

"I can finish the story," Paco said. "Earline told me to leave, but she did it incorrectly. She swore at me, but I didn't go. I told her that I couldn't until she dismissed me. Then, she got chains from her house and wrapped me up. I didn't fight because I was under her control. She threw me in an old sack and stuffed me in a trunk."

Cate skimmed the pages. "Yeah, but she only did it because she thought you caused everything."

"It was still hurtful."

"I can't believe Grandma had you for all those years."

"I guess I was her skeleton in the closet, er, attic," Paco said.

"But, Cate," Milo began, "why did your grandma leave you the trunk? Why even keep it at all? Why not drop it in a river or something?"

"That's not nice," the skeleton said.

"Maybe, deep down, she knew something was going to happen," Cate replied.

"What?" Milo asked.

"I have no idea. I just have a bad feeling." She walked over to Paco and pulled off the chains.

"Hey!" Milo said. "What are you doing?" What about your bad feeling? Your grandma chained him up for a reason."

"You heard Paco, and you heard Grandma's story. Paco tried to protect her. He's not here to hurt us."

"I'm not as sure of the skeleton's intention as you are," her husband replied. He sat on the carpet among the boxes and pictures

"What are you doing?" Cate asked.

"I'm going to watch Paco."

"Why?"

"There's a talking skeleton in my house, Catie. I want to make sure it doesn't do anything."

The shadows in the living room grew as Cate and Milo watched the skeleton sit in the trunk. She stood.

"Where are you going?" her husband asked, looking up at her.

"I'm hungry. I'm going to get something to eat." She walked into the kitchen.

Milo followed. "But-but-Paco!" he yelled, pointing toward the living room.

"If he was going to do anything, he would've. I'm tired of waiting." Cate opened the refrigerator. As she surveyed the plastic containers filled with leftovers, a strange feeling, like nervousness, washed over her. She now felt hot and nauseated.

She closed the refrigerator and looked out the window above the sink. Wind blew outside, rustling the leaves of the large oak in the backyard. A man wearing a black suit and tie with a white dress shirt stood beneath the tree. He was unnaturally tall and thin, like he was a distorted reflection in a funhouse mirror. His white hair was cropped close to his scalp.

The man raised his head. Horrible black circles hung under his dark eyes. His skin was pale, almost gray. The man stood in stark contrast to the green lawn and flowering plants of Cate and Milo's backyard. It was as if someone had placed him there artificially. He smiled widely at her, not in happiness or in greeting. His upper lip curled in aggression.

She gasped.

Milo moved to go outside to confront the man.

Cate caught his arm. "No," she whispered. "I think this is the man Grandma wrote about." She glanced outside. The man was about five feet closer to the house. She ducked away from the window, crouching in front of the sink. Milo still looked out. She grabbed his arm and pulled him to the floor next to her.

"Come on out, Catherine. I know you're in the house," the man said coldly.

Milo crawled over to a closet in the hallway, opened it, and grabbed a baseball bat. He walked back into the kitchen and turned to go outside.

"What are you doing?" Cate asked.

"I'm going to say hello to our guest," he replied. "Stay in the house."

"No, I'm coming with you. He knows who I am. He knew Grandma. I need to find out who *he* is."

"I don't want you to get hurt. Just stay."

"Damn it, Milo. You know how stubborn I am. You're not going to change my mind."

Milo sighed. "Okay, fine, come on. Just stay behind me."

Cate stood behind her husband as he slowly opened the French doors that led to the yard. Milo held the bat up, ready to defend against an attack.

The stranger waited for them. Clouds covered the sun, darkening the landscape. It was as if he sucked all the color out of the world.

"Hello, Catherine," he said.

"Who are you?" she asked. A faint, musty smell, like stored clothing, hit her nose.

"You don't know me, either?"

"I'm supposed to?"

"Your grandmother didn't know who I was when I visited her, oh, about fifty years ago. My, how time flies in the land of the living."

Cate glared at him.

"Oh, I should stop blathering on."

"Who are you?" she asked again. "What's your name?"

"Silly girl, I'm not giving you my name. Don't you know that names have power?"

She stared at the man. Two dark figures appeared on the hill overlooking the yard. As they approached, she could smell death.

She thought they were recently deceased, because they weren't yet rotted, but they were bloated and gray. They were slow, but didn't shuffle like movie zombies. They moved in halted, jerky motions, as if their lifeless limbs resisted whatever force propelled them.

"Where are they coming from?" Milo asked.

Cate thought for a moment. "The cemetery over the hill?" she wondered.

"That's impossible," he whispered.

"There's a talking skeleton in our living room."

"Good point."

They watched as the two corpses moved closer to their backyard. The dead came to the wooden fence that marked the edge of the property.

"The fence will keep them out, right?" Milo asked.

"It didn't keep me out, did it?" the man in black snarled.

Four undead hands clasped the top of the fence. The two risen creatures pulled themselves up and over it. They fell to the ground with two squishy thuds. The corpses stood up awkwardly, like grotesque marionettes, and stood behind the man in black. Their eyes stared ahead but didn't focus on anything.

Cate heard a clacking sound behind her. She didn't turn around. "What are you doing, Paco?" she asked.

"I figured you needed help," he replied.

So I do, she thought. She grabbed the bat from Milo and walked toward the man.

"Wait, what are you doing?" her husband asked.

"I'm going to fight him."

"Let me do it," he said as he reached for the bat.

"No," Cate said, jerking her arm away. "This is my fight, apparently. Hopefully, three years on my high school softball team will help me."

"Weren't you the equipment manager?" Milo asked.

"Shut it."

"You'll fight me on your own?" the man asked.

"No, I have a friend, too. Come, Paco."

The skeleton walked behind her. "Do with me what you will, Mistress."

"That sounded kind of dirty."

"I'm sorry. That was not my intention."

"Do you really think you can beat me with just a dusty old

skeleton?" the stranger asked.

"She's got me!" Milo yelled. He stood by the water spigot, holding a green water hose in one hand. He turned the spigot with the other and sprayed Cate, the man in black, and the undead creatures. Water dripped from the cadavers, soaking the lawn. The spray parted over the man in black, and he remained dry.

"Really?" Cate asked.

"I thought they might melt."

"That's witches, honey."

The corpses shambled toward her. She froze. *What do I do?* she wondered.

Paco jumped between Cate and the reanimated bodies. "Go get the man in black!" he yelled.

As she ran toward the stranger, Milo flung open the shed door.

"Paco, catch!" he yelled.

Out of the corner of her eye, she saw Paco seize a rake from the air. "A rake?" he asked.

Milo ran over to him, holding a garden hoe. "Hey, man, it's all we have." He saw that she looked in their direction. "Never mind us, we'll be fine," he said.

The man in black stood a few feet away. Cate swung the bat at him, and he deftly dodged. She swung a few more times and missed the darkly clad stranger each time.

"Well, this isn't going to work," she muttered.

"Got one!" Milo called out.

She glanced over. One of the corpses lay in pieces on the lawn. Its limbs still twitched, but it was mostly harmless. No bodiless hands crept toward her husband. No headless body continued its pursuit.

"I guess I'll have to remedy that," the man in black said. Two new corpses fell over the fence and shambled toward Milo and Paco.

"Get them, guys. I'll take care of this one," she said.

"You haven't taken care of me yet, Catherine," he drawled.

"Give me time. I'm just getting started." She swung the bat and connected with his side. He hissed in pain. She swung twice more, hitting him in his other side and in his right arm. *I need to go for the legs*, she realized. *If I can get him to the ground, maybe I can finish him.* She aimed a blow for his left thigh. He stumbled.

"I guess I won't go easy on you anymore." He reached out

with his long arms and squeezed her neck. His strength belied his frail appearance. He lifted her into the air, choking the life from her.

She struggled against the man. Her eyes bulged, and tears ran down her face.

"I can call up legions of the dead, and your face me with one measly skeleton and your pretty-boy husband?" He snorted.

Milo rushed behind the man in black and hit him in the head with the handle of the hoe. The man dropped Cate and clutched the back of his head.

"The pretty-boy husband can do enough," Milo said.

Cate was hunched over, struggling to catch her breath.

The man in black stared intently at Milo and smiled.

"Don't you dare," Cate growled.

The man shrugged.

"Get out of the way, Milo!" she screamed. "I don't want a zombie husband!"

There was something new about the man. He now emitted a strange aura. He's like Scruffles, Cate realized. He's undead. Cate ran from the man, thinking quickly. *Can't I just send him back?* she wondered. She stopped and stared at the man, concentrating on sending him back to death. She tried to remember how she had sent her dog back when she was a little girl. She strained, but the stranger just glared at her.

"Don't try too hard, Catherine. I wouldn't want you to hurt yourself."

How am I going to beat him? she wondered. He's been doing this a lot longer than me.

Don't you know that names have power? the man's voice repeated.

She gasped. "Why didn't I think of it before?" she muttered. She stopped and stared at her opponent. "Stay right where you are, Samuel."

The man froze, arms hanging at his sides. "How do you know my name?" he snarled.

"My grandma told me. Although, I didn't think of it earlier because I assumed you'd given her an alias. Why did you use your real name, anyway?"

"I didn't think she would figure out how to properly use her powers. She knew nothing of her family's history, so I believed she would know nothing of its magic."

"And you would take advantage of her ignorance?"

"Of course."

She remembered what he said earlier. "Wait, what was so special about my grandmother's family?"

"They're necromancers. Well, at least the women are."

"You've known them for a while, huh? You have some sort of quarrel with them?"

"You could say that. One of your ancestors...I think her name was Hortense or something...didn't take too kindly to me raising the dead and making things interesting. She thought I should be like her: to have a gift and never use it."

"What did Hortense do?"

"She killed me."

"Oh. Well, you didn't stay dead. Who brought you back?"

"I did." He grinned.

"What?" she squeaked. "How is that even possible?"

"As I descended into the land of death, I saw the thread tethering me to the living world grow thinner. Normal people don't even see the thread, so they don't have the opportunity to pull themselves out of it like I did."

"Tell me what you did after you came back, Samuel."

"Hortense was gone. I suspect she sensed my resurrection and fled. Can't say I blame her."

Cate squinted. "Have you been hunting her—my—family all this time?"

He clamped his mouth shut, trying to stop himself from saying anything else. Cate's power was stronger. "Yes. You ladies hide well."

"My grandmother was the first one you found?"

"Yes. I thought things would be pretty fun with your skeleton friend around, but I realized she knew absolutely nothing. It wouldn't be fair to fight someone who's completely unarmed, would it?" He had a look of false concern on his face.

"You killed my grandfather."

"Well, it didn't turn out too badly, did it? You're here."

"You should have killed my grandmother when you had the chance," she sneered. "I send you back, Samuel. Your soul shall return to the land of the dead, and your body will once again be lifeless. Never to rise again."

A white light emanated from Samuel's eyes, mouth, and

nose. The light intensified, enveloping the undead man. Cate shielded he eyes. The light continued to grow brighter until it burst like a supernova. The force of the explosion knocked her to the ground, and the world went from light to dark.

Cate awoke to the smell of damp earth. She couldn't see anything. *Oh God, I'm blind. No, wait, it's just my hair* she thought. She pushed the hair out of her face and looked around, expecting to see Samuel waiting to attack her again. There was no trace of the man, other than a scorched patch of grass and the remnant of his undead soldiers on the ground.

Something touched her back. She jumped and turned around, hitting Paco in the head with her bat. "Sorry," she said.

"I apologize for scaring you," he replied, adjusting his skull so it sat properly on his spine.

"Where's Milo?"

Groans came from another part of the yard. Cate crawled to her husband. "Milo, are you okay?"

"Yeah, I'm fine." He slowly sat up.

"Are you sure?"

"Pretty sure. Where's the man in black, Samuel?"

"He's gone. I sent him back to the land of death," she said quietly.

"You killed him?" Milo asked.

Cate shook her head. "He wasn't alive like you or me. He already died once. I just sent him back."

Milo stood, then offered his hand to help his wife off the ground. She let him pull her up. They surveyed the damage to their backyard. The oak tree was now missing many limbs. There were large ruts in the ground where the combatants had dug in their heels while fighting. The flowering bushes near the fence were also partially destroyed.

"My azaleas," Cate said mournfully.

"We're going to have fun cleaning this up," Milo muttered.

"Well, it's good that I still have this rake," Paco said, holding out the garden implement.

Cate walked over to the skeleton and touched his right radius. "About that," she said. "Thank you for helping us fight, Samuel."

"It wasn't a problem. It was what I was called to do."

"Do you want to stay here, Paco?"

"It doesn't matter what I want to do. I am under your control."

"Paco," she said more sternly. "Do you want to stay here, in the living world?"

"Well, I was awake in that trunk an awfully long time. I think I should like to go back to sleep."

"Okay," she said.

"What are you going to do?" Milo asked.

Cate turned to her husband and smiled. "I just realized why Grandma couldn't send Paco back."

"Why?"

"He needed a name." She turned back to the skeleton. "I dismiss you, Paco."

"Thank you," he replied softly. The skeleton then fell apart. The bones crashed to the ground, clattering like a bamboo wind chime. The rake fell into the grass with a soft thump.

Milo grabbed Cate's free hand and held it while they stood in silence, staring at the bones on the ground.

"I'm going to miss Paco."

"I'm not," he grumbled.

"Aw, why?" she asked, nudging Milo in the side. "You two were brothers in arms."

"Meh."

They were quiet again.

"How did you know to send Samuel and Paco back?" Milo asked.

"Honestly, I just pulled them out of my ass, but they seemed…right."

"Another question: why didn't Paco get all explodey when you sent him back? Samuel did."

Cate shrugged. "I'm not sure. I'm kind of new to this."

Milo snorted.

She continued. "I think the reaction was so powerful because Samuel brought himself back. It must take a lot of power to do that."

"Yet, you defeated him," her husband said, smiling.

"Yeah," she said, smiling in return.

"So, what do we do now?"

"Well, we have to return the corpses. I say we go to the cemetery, find the disturbed graves, and hope for the best. Then, we need to rebury Paco and clean up the yard. I don't know the location of his original grave, so I guess I'll bury him here," she said.

"Can't we just chuck him over the fence?" he whined.

"A person's skeleton commands more respect, doesn't it?"

"I guess so," Milo replied. "What do we do after that?"

"We live, I guess."

"That was kind of cheesy."

"Yeah, I know," she replied. She picked up the rake and handed it to Milo.

"What's this for?"

"Get to rakin', pretty boy. I'm going to find a box to put Paco in, and then you're going to fix my azaleas." She walked into the house while Milo tried to put things in the yard back to normal.

Kristina R. Mosley lives in Kensett, Arkansas, a tiny place no one has heard of. When she isn't working or writing, she's wondering if her Google searches have landed her on a watch list. Her work has been featured in numerous publications, including Undead Living, Micro Horror, Fiction on the Web, Dangerous Dreams, *and* We Are Dust and Shadow. *She has a languishing blog, but she tweets too often at twitter.com/elstupacabra.*

THE SNOUT

By Matthew Pegg

It was October 1898 before I visited my friend Jon Darkness again. The Affair of the Dangling Turret had unnerved me and for some months I avoided the gatherings where he recounted his experiences in the realm of the outré. It was not until the nights closed in that I braved the winter chill and ventured out to see my old friend.

A frosty breeze blew along the Bloomsbury Street where Darkness lived, sending respectable ladies and be-suited gentlemen scurrying for the warmth and safety of home and hearth. I strode up the steps to my friend's door and rang the bell. Moments later, I heard measured footsteps approaching. Jon's man Broughton opened the door. A short, rotund fellow, his red face was surmounted by white hair that stuck up in tufts, despite Broughton's attempts to smooth it into a respectable shape.

"What ho, Broughton!" I said, cheerily, "Is Darkness here?"

"Aye sorr," said Broughton. "He's in yon liebrary. Proper mustulated he be. I cor do nuthin with him!"[1]

"Very good, very good!" I said, pretending I had understood.

A strange aroma, redolent of the seaside wafted from the doorway. I coughed and my eyes began to water.

"What is that appalling smell?" I ejaculated.

Broughton viewed me with a pained expression.

"It's me sorr. Hair tonic exsperrymunt 65: eel guts and

---

[1] Broughton had hand-built his peculiar accent, using dialects purloined from sixteen counties.

creosote in honey!" he explained.

"Ah, lovely. Any good?" I managed to ask.

"No sorr. The hair has its own will as you can see. And in addition I am followed every whichplace by cats." He shook his head in sorrow. "Wunt do nohow!" He shuffled off down the corridor and beckoned me to follow.

Broughton fulfilled the roles of butler, chauffeur, handyman, cook and maid. He wore a variety of eccentric apparel depending on what he was creating in the cellar workshop. Today it was an all-enveloping suit of black, rubberised material. Around his neck was a pair of large goggles with dark lenses and his hands were encased in huge gauntlets. Heavy leather boots rounded off the outfit. A fluffy pink feather boa round his neck struck an incongruous note.

"Is that the reason for the exotic garb?" I enquired, "Your hair experiments?"

Broughton looked down at himself as if surprised to discover what he was wearing.

"This old thing sorr? Oh no. I jus'.... likes to wear it on occasion. For old times' sake." he confided. "Reminds me of my Da."

He stopped at the library door and cleared his throat.

"Jus so you know sorr, Mr. Darkness.... ain't quite hisself at the moment."

"Who is he?" I mean what's wrong with him?" I asked.

Broughton shook his head. "Tisn't not my purlace to henquire. But somethin' is a preyin' on his mind as you might say. Somethin' *worse* than normal!"

He ushered me into the library and closed the door behind me. I heard his footsteps recede as he returned to his lair in the cellar.

My eyes took a few seconds to adjust to the crepuscular darkness. The only illumination came from a small fire that sputtered testily in the grate. The familiar room was lined with cases containing my friend's collection of supernatural trinkets: an Amulet from sunken Atlantis, the skull of a were-marmoset, a box of cursed legumes, and in pride of place a set of soiled undergarments once worn by Dr John Dee. Tall shelves housed books on aspects of the occult. The walls bore engravings and paintings of a mystical nature along with a couple of sentimental studies of kittens.

There was a movement near the fireplace and I realised that

my friend was sitting in an armchair, still as a sphinx. "Ah Jackson," he murmured, "Sit down." He gestured to the sofa.

"Why are you in the dark?" I asked.

"I must have lost track of time. By all means put the lights on, old fellow."

I switched on a lamp[2] and warm illumination chased away the shadows.

At first glance, my friend seemed every inch his normal, avuncular self. He wore a brocade smoking jacket and his sandy hair was neatly combed. I noted the familiar deprivations of his chosen profession: the left eyebrow, lost during the case of the Deptford Vampire, the mangled earlobe nearly chewed off by the terrible Purple Worm of the Terrible, and the missing little finger, forfeit to an aggressively starched collar as he dressed for the premiere of Benzigger's operetta *La Pucelle Français et le Cardinal*. There were no new deprivations from his battle against the denizens of the night, no further bits missing. However, the side table held three empty bottles of liniment and a morocco case containing his pipe, tongs, and speculum, his only weakness in moments of turmoil.

"How are you old, fellow?" I asked.

Darkness stared at me. The pause was so extensive that I wondered if he might have suffered some kind of mental collapse, but there was no drooling or gibbering, the signs that clearly denote madness.[3] Just as I was about to stifle a yawn, Darkness finally spoke.

---

[2] The house was lit by an electrical system devised and constructed by Broughton: carbon filament lamps powered from some kind of Voltaic pile in the basement. In turn, this was charged by what Broughton called a 'hydramalectric system' which involved a complex series of paddle wheels installed in the sewers beneath the house. Darkness allowed Broughton his fancies whilst quite rightly discouraging him when he stated an intention to patent his system. I didn't think it would ever catch on; after all, electricity is chancy stuff and there are endless supplies of oil.

[3] Had there been such signs I would have seen to it that he was immediately conveyed to an asylum for the insane. There he would be chained to a wall in a stone cell, hosed down twice a day with iced water, hourly beaten with birch rods, force-fed watery gruel and deprived of the excessive stimuli that had undoubtedly brought on his madness, such as comfy beds, sunlight, fresh air, fruit and vegetables and the carefree, happy laughter of innocent children. Thus would he be incarcerated until he recovered his senses. Nothing but the best modern treatment would suffice for my dear friend.

"I am not myself, Jackson old fellow. I have... had a grievous shock." His voice tailed off and he stared at me with something akin to panic in his eyes. I was taken aback. Darkness always related his exploits with an offhand manner which suggested that they were mere nothings. I have seen him deadly serious, frivolous, gay, sombre, morose, pensive, playful, satirical and wry, but never before, rattled.

Bolger's Common Ailments suggests that the remedy for mental imbalance is to receive a strong shaking and if that seems ineffective, a manly blow to the chin. I was just preparing to administer this curative action when Darkness spoke again.

"I apologise for my manner, Jackson. Not what you expect from me."

"That's fine old chap," I said, "But what has disturbed you to such an extent? You, who have wrestled giant rodents on three continents, and defeated countless denizens of the dark realms?"

"I shall tell you the story," he replied, "And you will understand the horror of it. Bring the decanter and two glasses."

I did as he requested and poured two generous helpings of brandy. Thus fortified, I sat down to listen to my friend's tale.

"It was August this year," he began, "The foul business began innocuously enough. I received a letter which Broughton delivered to my bedroom, by means of his pneumatic tube system. When I had blotted the paper cut on my brow I opened the letter which was addressed from "H_____ House, Lincolnshire.

My Dear Mr. Darkness,

I hope you will forgive my writing to you in this unseemly fashion, without the normal thirteen introductions from members of society. I am suffering considerable distress. You helped my cousin Charles in the affair of The Green Opium Kettle and I think you may be the only person who can offer me succour. I cannot offer any details in a letter that may be perused by members of other social classes. If you can visit in person then I promise I will explain all. Be assured that this is a problem that only someone with your special knowledge can hope to solve.

I remain yours in Eager Anticipation,
Lady Jane H_____

"It was the work of moments to leap from my bed, dart down the stair and into the street. Then the shocked glances of a cabby and some nuns brought me to my senses and I returned to the house to put on a tie.

"By ten o'clock, Broughton and I had boarded a train for Lincolnshire. Broughton wore his normal travelling attire: vulcanised galoshes and marquetry overcoat. I wore my beloved Dover Sole hat and the red weskit and spats, aware of Lincolnshire's reputation for precipitation but still cutting rather a dash. We stowed a substantial trunk in the guard's van, containing Broughton's equipment as well as the large bottle of succour I had asked him to make up for Lady H_____. Then we made ourselves comfortable in our compartment where we whiled away the journey with a game of Unction, which I am happy to report, I won, taking all Broughton's aces and three of his marbles, leaving him only a lone castle with which to defend his poodle."

"I will not bore you with the minutiae of our journey. Should you wish to gain a flavour of our travels I suggest you consult Jottingley's Comprehensive Rail and Dog Cart Almanac, which is full of the incidental detail which attends the modern traveller. Suffice it to say that by the late afternoon, we arrived at the small station and were conveyed by carriage to H_____ Hall, an elegant seventeenth century building of honey-coloured stone, set in extensive grounds.

"As we approached the hall, I looked in vain for any of the usual signs of outré activity: statues in suggestive postures, hooded figures on the brows of hills, rabbits looking too innocent, crows, ash trees and so forth, but no such portents were evident.

"At the front door, a butler directed Broughton to the tradesman's entrance and then escorted me to a well-appointed library lined with tall shelves of the best plywood.

" 'Mr. Darkness,' announced the butler and withdrew. The sole inhabitant of the room rose from her seat next to the fire. Lady H_____ was of medium height and somewhat younger than I had expected. She wore a severe black dress and a veil concealed her features. She took my proffered hand.

" 'Welcome, Mr. Darkness,' she said in the kind of voice termed 'melodious' in penny novels. "I am so grateful that you could come. I am Lady H_____." She drew back her veil and smiled at me.

Her features were fine, her eyes grey and candid. A maid brought a tray containing tea and laudanum cakes. We sat. As she poured the tea, her hands shook.

" 'I must explain why I asked you to come. Yet I hardly know where to begin. Something haunts this house, something terrible and evil.'

"I patted her arm gently. 'Have no fear,' I exclaimed, 'I have had many experiences both terrible *and* evil. I am sure I will be able to help. Now please, explain what is wrong.'

"With an effort she pulled herself together.

" 'I will show you,' she declared, and led me through a door onto the terrace. 'There lies the cause of all our problems.' She shaded her eyes and pointed to a small crenelated tower above the east wing. It seemed innocuous. As we returned to the library I glanced up at the windows expecting to see a strange pallid face peering down at me. No such apparition appeared, and as a result I left the terrace with a considerable sense of unease.

"Once we were again seated, she told me her tale. 'Two years ago I was but a simple governess to a respectable family in London. Lord H_____ and I met by accident during a fancy dress party. Due to a number of unlikely coincidences, I mistook him for a mere costermonger while he believed me to be third in line to the Duchy of Schleswig Holstein. We discovered the truth and were married a scant two weeks later. At first we were happy. We travelled in Europe for six months and then returned here to his family home. But then things began to change horribly. The tower room had been boarded up for many years. My husband had it opened to see if it might be useful for storing servants or orphans. But afterwards he became distant and strange, spending time alone in there, doing I know not what.'

" 'Have you considered onanism?' I suggested, needing to eliminate any normal explanation for her husband's behaviour.

" 'Since he died I have,' she said, blushing, 'The nights are long when one is alone in the world!'

'I meant your husband,' I corrected gently and was rewarded with another pretty blush.

'I did wonder if an inexperienced girl such as myself could wholly satisfy his needs,; she confided, 'We only performed the act of sexual congress four or five times each night. But he did have access to the maids and indeed the footmen: a tradition in this part of

Lincolnshire.'

"I found this information startling but bade her continue.

'When I asked him what he was doing in the tower, he became angry. One day he was away on business in Grantham, selling a gross of villagers to an iron foundry. I went upstairs. The tower room was locked. Though I possessed a key and it turned in the lock, I could not open the door. It was as if some *thing* was on the other side, resisting my efforts.'

(As you know Jackson, many of the creatures which inhabit the void between worlds like nothing more than to hold doors shut in this way. Pretty silly behaviour for vast inhuman intelligences I've always thought but there's no accounting for it.)

"Lady H_____ continued. 'Then a foolish urge persuaded me to place my ear against the door.'

" 'What did you hear?' I asked, holding her hand for medical reasons.

" 'Nothing!' she declared dramatically. 'But then as I withdrew there was a horrible *scratching* sound from behind the door.'

"Mice?" I suggested.

"She turned her face away from my gaze. 'There are no mice in Lincolnshire,' she declared. 'It is a little known scientific fact.'

"I stood and stared out of the window. I saw Broughton and one of the maids in the grounds. He carried a tub of goose grease and a bicycle pump. They went into a picturesque classical folly down by the lake. I was glad to see he was making himself useful.

" 'Pray continue, Lady H_____,' I said.

" 'A few days later my husband was gone from our bed when I awoke. He was not at breakfast so we searched the house. He was found in the tower, sprawled in the corner, quite dead, on his face an expression of horrible horror, as if he had witnessed something so unspeakable that his soul had simply run away.'

" 'Is there anything else you can tell me?' I asked, testing her pulse by slipping my hand down the front of her dress in the approved manner.

" 'The police searched the room but found nothing.' she said. 'Doctor Thrashington believed that his heart simply stopped due to excessive *droit de seigneur*, a condition rife in this area. But I cannot believe that. *Something* caused his death. Mr. Darkness, something not of this world. I hear dreadful sounds in the night; a snuffling, a terrible, terrible snuffling! Oh please, please help me.'

" 'I will do my best,' I said patting her on the patella. 'Do not distress yourself.'

"I stood to leave, but at the door I turned back to her.

" 'I am curious. Why do you attempt to conceal your identity by spelling your name 'Lady H_____'?' I asked, 'Surely it is a very outmoded literary conceit?'

"I was alarmed to see tears in her eyes. 'It is no attempt at anonymity! My name... was eaten away by whatever haunts this house! One morning I awoke to find two letters missing and it has got steadily worse! The servants have been affected too. Many have left for fear of losing all! For a while, I concealed my affliction by using capitals, but eventually they too vanished. I am reduced to a single letter. When that goes, I will have no name at all. You are my last hope, Mr. Darkness! If you do not help, all will be lost!'

"With that she swept from the room, leaving me alone to consider what eldritch force could consume the very letters that make up our identity.

"I collected Broughton from below stairs. He emerged from the butler's pantry wiping olive oil from his fingers with a piece of fine lace.

" 'How are the servants, Broughton?' I asked.

" 'Proper mussified they be,' replied the stout fellow, 'The Maids are all traddled and the cook's got a case of the drivvers proper bad. Yon laddyship is like to be on her owners come Mickletide, Sorr!'

"I decided to examine the tower forthwith. We were directed by the third under back footman, a tall fellow who gave the impression of a lack of height by walking with knees bent and shoulders hunched. His hair was perfectly white and his hands shook as he handed us the keys to the tower room.

" 'That fellow has suffered the effect of whatever blights this place,' I whispered to Broughton as we watched the footman totter off down the corridor.

" 'Yes Sorr. An' he only ninety eight years old,' nodded that stout chap, pursing his lips.[4]

---

[4] In a fellow of my own standing I might have considered this tantamount to sarcasm, but since this was forbidden to the lower classes by the Lower Forms of Humour Act of 1867, it could not be so.

"Then together we ascended the dread stair to the tower.

"Unless this manifestation involved one of the twelve great horrors recorded by Cornelius Holzapfel in his *Pueri Libri Monsters Horrendus*[5], I was confident we were in little danger during daylight. Still, we were not without protection. I wore Broughton's Clockwork Oscillating Amulet, patent refused. You will recall, Jackson, the Affair of the Whistling Owl where, I fully believe, Broughton's device saved my life and, more importantly, my immortal soul and my best trousers. Broughton himself wore his liver suit and the occult purple slippers of Count Cagliostro.

"We came to a stout wooden door which I unlocked. The room beyond was rectangular and empty of furniture. Windows in two adjacent walls gave scenic views of the grounds.

"I took a careful step over the threshold, but experienced no unusual sensations. We sounded the walls, paying special attention to the one with no windows, but found no secret entrances. We took sweepings with the Portable Cyclonic Cleanerator. Broughton pedaled and I aimed the flexible tube into the corners of the room.[6] Dust often suggests the nature of a manifestation; for example, particles of bandage can indicate a beastly infestation of foreign gods from around the Nile. Exotic unguents, bone fragments, tea leaves, and opium have all been found in dust samples and have been helpful in determining the cause of etheric disturbance.

"We examined the dust under the propelling microscope.

" 'Standard British dust, type 143, Sorr,' exclaimed Broughton, consulting *Fisher's Almanac of Detritus*, 3rd Edition, 1895. 'Nothin' contrarywise there.'

"Peevishly I prodded the sample with a pencil. We might be dealing with a case such as The Affair of the Shuffling Annoyance, wherein ingenious criminals fabricated a plague of zombies to cover up an ambitious forgery enterprise. Perhaps Lord H_____ had met his end at human rather than supernatural hands?

---

[5] *'Boy's Own Book of Horrible Monsters'*

[6] The machine was another invention that Broughton had wished to patent. Darkness discouraged him, pointing out that if it ever came into widespread use, his invention would make obsolete the hordes of maids, under maids, behind maids and over back maids currently employed in every household, leaving them no recourse but ruin and early death in the stews and brothels of the East End.

"I uncovered a small flat item in the sample. Broughton peered at it. "Tis nobbut but a oat, Sorr."

" 'Dash it all, Broughton,' I exclaimed, slamming down the pencil, 'This case is darned tricky.'

" 'Could be a infestishun o' mice,' suggested Broughton, 'The can make an 'orrible big racket in an owd place.'

"I stared at the fellow with irritation.

" 'Can't you come up with a better theory than that?'

" 'Mebbe yon laddyship is makin it up sorr?' he said. "Coverin' up the 'orrible murder of her 'usband.'

" 'When have the British aristocracy ever stooped to murder?'

"Broughton opened his mouth to reply, but I cut him off.

" 'And why would she then call me in to investigate? It doesn't bear consideration. Best leave the detective work to me in future old chap.'

"There was nothing else for it. I would have to spend the night in the room."

"I ate supper in a pleasant panelled dining room, watching the sun set outside and shadows envelop the park. Broughton was entertained in the servants' hall by the cook, two maids and an under footman.

" 'An then we ate a pie an' som ale too,' he told me, smacking his lips.

"After that we carried our heavy equipment into the tower and spent an hour setting it up.

"Broughton left an emergency sandwich in some greased paper and bid me goodnight.

"Alone, I placed oil lamps at each corner of the room. Then I adjusted the Chicken Influx Device. This was inspired by the practice of taking canaries into mines to obtain early warning of noxious gases[7]. Eight small wire pens each contained a live chicken. Broughton had discovered that of all fowl, chickens were the most sensitive to demonic forces. A chute beneath each pen led to a

---

[7] The practice had been abandoned when some canaries escaped and bred, infesting certain mines with flocks of large, aggressive, sooty birds, in effect making them unworkable.

—

58

receptacle, linked to a panel of coloured vacuum tubes. In response to an influx of the outré, the chickens would lay eggs in a particular order. This would trigger a sequence of colours on the panel, a crude early indication as to what species of horror we were dealing with. The device always caused inappropriate hilarity among the ignorant, but I believe it had saved my life on two separate occasions and we always had fresh eggs for breakfast.

"Having ensured that the chickens were alert, I placed a chair inside the Pungent Pentacle[8] and sat down to wait."

"The hours passed slowly. Chickens clucked. The oil lamps burned steadily. Nothing unusual happened. The room was cold so I was able to stay awake without difficulty. I amused myself by performing imitations of farm animals. Time crawled by.

"Hours later, the sky outside began to lighten. I resolved to stay until dawn broke and then give up my vigil.

"Then, I noticed that the room appeared to be darker rather than lighter. One of the lamps went out. The other lamps flickered and died, one after another. A chicken gave a squawk and an egg dropped into the container. Blue lights flared on the panel: a warning. Shadows gathered in the corners of the room, like ink soaking into blotting paper. These pools of dark met each other and it became harder to see the walls. The panel of the chicken indicator glowed steadily but apart from that, in a few minutes, the room was utterly black.

"Two more eggs dropped into receptacles. The panel flashed red and blue, a combination indicating something powerful and dangerous. I had a lantern with me. I had not bothered to light it before, but now I did so and I am not ashamed to admit that my hands shook. The lantern illuminated the area within the pentacle, but the darkness beyond was impenetrable, as if black velvet curtains were drawn around my refuge. All I could see was the dim glow of the chicken panel through a thick veil of gloom.

---

[8] As a young man, Darkness utilised a variety of chalk pentacles and sigils gleaned from occult grimoires. Some were highly effective, but others were total mumbo jumbo and he lost his left big toe and all of his ear hair finding which were which. The Pungent Pentacle was a modern, scientific distillation of those crude methods. Scented oils from small brass reservoirs run into the glass tubes that comprise the pentacle. A system of taps and valves allow the operator to combine smells in different proportions in order to reveal, attract, or repel a manifestation.

"Then I heard a noise, a skittering, like an animal trapped behind the wainscot; but unless Lady H_____ had an infestation of buffalo, the noise was made by nothing natural.

"I adjusted the valves of the pentacle, flooding the tubes with a combination of sage and rose. I added top notes of lavender and curry. In response the noise ceased and the darkness receded a little so that I could see the opposite wall.

"What was revealed, however, was equally alarming; a stain in the centre of the wall spread and darkened as if something were soaking through from the other side. The chickens squawked in alarm. Another egg slid into the receptacle. This one appeared to be black. The lights on the panel changed to sickly purple. I had never seen that before. It didn't indicate anything wholesome.

"I noticed that the stain was swelling outwards. This increased until the whole wall bulged like a ripe boil. I began to see shapes move beneath its surface. Could that be a claw? I released fish oil and myrrh into the pentacle with no result. I stared at the wall, fascinated and appalled.

"Suddenly, I realised I had my foot raised to step out of the pentacle. Shaken, I retreated to my chair. What monstrous thing could affect my mind in that way even within my protections?

"The first rays of sunshine spilled over the horizon and bathed the room in golden light. The wall returned to normal and the shadows receded. As is often the case, the denizens of the night retreated before the dawn. I waited for long moments, but nothing further occurred. The acrid mixture of scents pulsed forth from the pentacle apparatus. All was quiet. The coloured vacuum tubes winked out one by one. I raised my foot to step out of the protective pentacle. Chickens saved me once again. One gave a strangled squawk. Three eggs slid into the receptacles and the lights flared a dull crimson. At the same moment darkness boiled into the room like a tide. The wall bulged towards me and them *something* thrust through from the other side.

"It was the snout of some rodent such as a vole or field mouse, but gigantic, filling the entire wall. The nose was the livid pink of burned flesh. Mucous dripped from each nostril. Thick, wiry hair on the snout was greyish white. Black whiskers bristled, each as thick as my little finger.

"In the pens, two birds were turned inside out like gloves and a third was transformed instantly into roast chicken with all the

---

trimmings. The lights on the panel flared puce, fused, and died in a shower of sparks.

The snout gave a couple of horrible, deep snorts, as if trying to discern what was in the room. I should have adjusted my pentacle, but fear unmanned me. I stared as the disgusting nose twitched and snuffled. Suddenly, it came straight at me. I fell, entangled with my chair. The snout actually touched me, leaving a smear of nasal secretion on my face! I cried out in horror. It had crossed the barrier as if the pentacle did not exist. This was no minor manifestation; I was facing one of the Old Dark Gods from the dawn of time. All my scientific wizardry would avail me nothing. In seconds I would be snuffed out, my soul consumed. The snout pressed further forward and now I saw its mouth, yellow teeth grinding together. The pentacle tubes began to melt and buckle.

"As you know Jackson, I am convinced some universal force of purity and light balances the unclean and foetid and that in our greatest need, we may receive help from outside. Thus it was that my hand fell on the greaseproof package left for me by Broughton. A higher power must have guided his hand, for he had prepared a cheese sandwich, though he knows I dislike dairy produce. Wildly I waved it in front of the snout and then hurled it to one side. The creature turned from me and the huge teeth snapped and worried at the package.

"I had but scant seconds of respite. With one bound, I leapt out of the pentacle and crashed through the window. It might have been better to have used the door, but bodily injury or death means very little when compared with the annihilation of the soul. Luckily the tower was festooned with ivy, and I managed to arrest my fall by clinging to the exuberant *Hedera*. A chittering roar from the room rose to a furious crescendo, and then silence fell.

"I descended awkwardly onto the roof of the Hall and thence to the interior of the house via a door in a turret. After composing myself, I sought Broughton. I found him outside the stables applying goose grease to a willing stable boy. I tore him away from this scientific demonstration. We retired to my quarters and I explained all.

" 'So I was right Sorr? T'was mice all the time?' was his response.

"Gingerly, we ventured back into the room. Our apparatus was destroyed, either chewed or melted. Only one of the chickens had survived the ordeal, but weirdly seemed quite content surrounded by the remains of her unfortunate companions. All the eggs were hard-boiled in their shells. Broughton ate one although I counselled against it, and I put my foot down when he started to eye the roast chicken.

"Apart from the damaged equipment, there was no sign that any manifestation had taken place. But now I knew what had caused the death of Lord H_____ and devoured his name."

"We examined the walls in the tower and beneath the wallpaper found a mystic circle inscribed on the wall. Lord H_____ had dabbled in the unknown and paid the price for not taking up a more appropriate hobby such as shooting exotic animals or macramé. I bade the servants remove the design and they attacked the plaster with crowbars until it was quite destroyed. I was confident the dread creature would no longer appear in the tower.

"The remaining question was: how had Lord H_____ acquired the knowledge to summon such a creature? On his bedside table I found the answer, a book, bound in mottled leather, *Arcessentes Demones pro Fun et Proficuum*[9]. A page was marked with a slip of lilac paper. I read:

Thee Terribe Shrewe or Great Srud Nigbeth, The Gnawer at the Threshold. By offeringe of oats and milke and hunney it may be persuaded to do thy wille. Butte it is a thinge of terror that wille take more than it giveth. By many names it is knowne: Owlde Scratch, or thee Devourer of Wordes.

"On the same page was an engraving of a summoning circle identical to the one in the tower.

"I consigned the wretched book to the fire and watched the paper curl and blacken."

"That afternoon I bade farewell to Lady H_____. She was writing letters in the morning room. She thanked me for my efforts but looked strained and unwell. I wondered if she would ever fully recover. Then I noticed the paper on which she was writing. It was

---

[9] *Summoning Demons for Fun and Profit*

---

the exact same shade as the bookmark in her husband's grimoire.

" 'Lady H_____ ,' I exclaimed impulsively, 'Where does your cook keep the porridge oats?'

" 'In the third larder on the fourth shelf on the right.' she said without pausing for thought. Then she looked up at me and I am certain she understood the import of my question.

" 'And honey?' I asked, 'Where is that kept?'

" 'I'm sure I have no idea.' she said deliberately. 'How should I know such a thing? If you want Cook to prepare a repast for your journey, I'm sure she'll oblige.'

"I met her gaze for a long moment until she was forced to look away.

"I departed that terrible place forthwith."

"And that is my tale," said Darkness. He filled his glass again and took a large draft of brandy, gazing at the fire.

"She did it?" I expostulated, "She summoned the creature?"

"And killed her husband as surely as if she'd shot him through the head with an elephant gun and then run him over with a traction engine. I suspect so," nodded Darkness. "She copied the circle onto the wall, performed the ritual in the book, and left an offering of oats to entice the creature into the room when her husband was there. He used the room as a study. Afterwards, she could not banish it. It began to devour her name and that of all those within the house. In desperation, she turned to me."

"You must inform the authorities!"

"No one would believe a lady capable of such a thing. And the giant shrew might also stretch their credulity. Besides, it is supposition. There is no evidence."

I stared at him. The business was appalling.

"You cared for her and she proved false. That is why this has hit you so badly?"

He nodded.

"At least you escaped with no injuries!" I consoled him, "No further loss of limbs or organs!"

"That is not so," exclaimed my friend, "Jackson, what is my middle name?"

His middle name was as familiar to me as my own. I opened my mouth, but no word emerged. I stood gaping, astounded.

"It was my great, great grandfather's name," said Darkness,

"Passed down in my family for generations. Gone! Devoured entirely during the moments I confronted the creature. Lost forever!"

He gave what might have been a sob, had he been a lady.

"I am heartily sorry, old chap!" I exclaimed.

"What if the creature returns somehow?" he continued, "What if it has acquired a *taste* for me? I could not bear it!"

I offered him all the clumsy sympathy I could muster in the form of a manly punch to the shoulder, but in truth, what comfort could I offer a man who had suffered such losses in the fight against the grotesque things that cluster outside this world?

Eventually I stammered a few inadequate words and took my leave. Broughton showed me to the front door.

"Look after him, Broughton," I said, "Treat him as you would your own brother."

Broughton stared at me in horror.

"I could never do that to Mr. Darkness sorr." he exclaimed. "But he'll come round eventual. Turpentine and beef tea, sorr, and the lib'ral application of a hussy. My mother swore by it! God rest 'er."

I bade the fellow good night. Outside, I waited for a cab, pulling up my collar as protection against the chill. *What would the world do without Jon Darkness?* I wondered. If Srud Nigbeth returned, it might devour more than just an individual name or two. What would happen if we lost some letters altogether? What concepts might we also lose and how might we suffer for it? What if there were no 'love', 'compassion', or 'courage'? Or worse still no 'd___g', '____t' or 's__w'. What would the world be like without those? Would we even realise they were gone? The British Empire would collapse, that would be certain, and the human race would become unspeakably degraded. Thank God Jon Darkness was there, standing between the world and such a fate, protecting everything we hold dear, including all 29 letters of the alphabet.

Matthew Pegg lives near Leicester in England and shares a house with a whole bunch of dysfunctional cats. He writes fiction and plays. His last play, Escaping Alice, *was about a man who doesn't want to move on after his girlfriend leaves him, so he keeps his memory of her chained up in his flat. It was produced by York Theatre Royal in 2012. Matthew has recently completed his first novel, based on a creepy local myth.*

Matthew has been an actor, director, graphic designer, drama teacher and worked as an education officer in regional theatres. His current day job is running a company specialising in street theatre, festivals and events. In 2012 he completed an MA in Creative Writing at Nottingham Trent University.

His website can be found at www.mpegg.co.uk

ALIEN DUST

By Chelsea Nolen

"Good gentles, we are now in position over Extraction Site 21287, location known as Transylvania to the natives. Please prepare for live specimen extraction," the captain's voice projected crisply from the spaceship's intercom.

Dressed in their lime-green jumpsuits, the biological extraction team stood by the antigrav unit, ready for their next specimen. Their discus-shaped spaceship floated silently in the black night above a mountainous landscape filled to the brim with dark green trees poking at the sky. A scattering of gray-white rocks, battered into skull-like shapes, peeked out below the boughs. One lone wooden structure crouched beneath the conifers, hidden in the darkness at their feet. This was the point of concentration for the team.

Their specimen should depart that structure—hopefully soon.

Hetref bobbed on his feet as he adjusted the scanner, trying to get a weight reading on this domicile. He set the parameters into his computer and tapped 'ENGAGE'. The computer returned a number, and Hetref scowled.

"Blast and bake the dung heap!" he snapped.

Two heads raised and turned his way, blinking in mild surprise.

"This building isn't living quarters—it's empty," Hetref grumbled. "Other than the specimen, there's nothing there. Not even an excrement collector. It must be one of their ancillary structures—a shed."

Tallim, leader of the survey, shrugged and turned back to the antigrav unit. Jipalt, ever more sympathetic, said, "Still hoping for a eureka find?"

Hetref sighed heavily. "We have bits and pieces of the culture, but nothing of what ties it all together. What is the center for this society?"

"You know, they might be like the Nevetine, carrying their 'center' with them," Tallim suggested.

"The Nevetine are echinoderms," Hetref replied shortly. "They are not designed to carry items. The humans, on the other hand, have our basic configuration—two arms, two legs, upright posture, sensory and intellectual capacities in the head. Every sentient species we have met with this biological configuration manifests their sociological center in at least one object. That's how they reinforce their social bonds. That's how they prove to themselves and others that they belong to the common culture."

"All right, that's enough conjecture," Tallim snapped, looking even haughtier as he tried to straighten his green jumpsuit. "We have no reason to retrieve an empty shed, Hetref; it'll be empty weight on the trip back. You'll have to satisfy your curiosity with all the other junk you've collected. Let's shake this specimen out of its lair and bring it up."

Tallim is throwing his scientific reputation in everyone's face again, Hetref snorted to himself as he continued to collect information on the shed. *What I would give to shove his face into someone else's superior credentials!*

"We have the human's signature, locking in," Jipalt noted. "Huh. The body temperature is wrong." She skimmed more commands into the computer. "Humans have an average temperature of twelve point one Agaranth…this one gives off a heat reading of nine. That's barely in the exothermic spectrum." She leaned away from the console, her mouth twisted unhappily. "The sensors must be damaged."

"Recalibrate," Tallim commanded.

This time Jipalt scowled at Tallim. "I've recalibrated the sensors twice, but I still get a nine reading. Sir."

"Then the specimen is dead." Tallim waved the problem away.

"It's still moving," Jipalt replied acerbically.

Tallim ignored his colleague's observations and directed his voice to the intercom. "Captain, we need the sensory array replaced."

The answer took several seconds. Hetref smiled a little, imagining the colorful language the captain must be using. *The captain's eyes hold fire. She stands up to Tallim on a daily basis. Such bravery!*

"Sensor array 3G is being replaced now, gentles," the captain's voice replied, carefully controlled. "We must be the beta testers this time around."

Everyone in the extraction room shook their heads in disgust.

"I'm engaging the capture sequence," Jipalt spoke quickly, before Tallim could vent on the rest of the team. "We'll just take the human's temperature the old-fashioned way."

"They really object to that, you know." Hetref moved over to her side, coming within inches of touching her. His heart jumped to double-time every time he neared her. Jipalt was grace captured in smooth, perfect jade. Somehow the green jumpsuit, which made the rest of the crew look like stalks of raw asparagus, enhanced her beauty. It suited her complexion. "And you can't really blame them. Going into their core for an accurate heat reading is downright intrusive."

"It also gives us a wealth of other information," she replied with a small smile, her eyes bright with excitement. "What they've eaten recently, water balance, what chemicals their digestive system breaks down ... all kinds of data! The stuff biologists love to know. So we'll just do it that way, even if it is somewhat unpleasant."

"Do we even have one of those older examination arrays on this ship?" Tallim grumbled.

"Indeed we do." Jipalt pointed to a deactivated console near the doorway. "This model comes with inbuilt instructions."

He snorted. "Those instructions never tell you what you actually need to know. They just dance around the important points like it's a black hole; they won't touch the vital information."

The warning klaxon sounded, and the team quickly covered their eyes with the goggles hanging around their necks.

After a moment the main tractor activated, spitting out a bright light that no one wanted to look at, even through specialized lenses.

When the light faded, a large human form nearly covered the table.

"Hetref, you're not needed here anymore. You should start classifying your garbage heap." Tallim's voice slapped the xeno-anthropologist. "Jipalt, now that our specimen is on board, you may begin analysis."

Hetref slowly pulled his goggles back down around his neck, breathing carefully as he throttled his anger and shoved it back into an obscure mental corner.

Jipalt turned her head to the immobile specimen on the table, dropping her own goggles to her neck. "Recorder on," she stated, her voice coolly professional. "Specimen 518-302 … human male. One point seven-six tegs in length … six and a half human feet. Evident secondary masculine characteristics—facial hair, large chest, minimized mammary glands. Black hair evident on the upper appendages. Skin color …" she leaned closer, blinking several times … "gray. Not human. Sensors indicate that the skin has no melatonin. None."

"An albino, then," Tallim shrugged the comment off.

"No," Jipalt spoke more hurriedly, worry edging her voice. "Temperature is still nine Agaranth. This human—this creature, should be dead."

Tallim blanched. "We brought up a corpse?"

The human grunted at that point, clenching his fists. It opened red eyes and glared at them.

"That's not dead," Hetref's voice trembled as he backed toward the door.

"That's not—humans lack the genetic sequence for red eyes!" Jipalt's voice reached the upper ranges; her fingers nervously activated the restraints on the examination table. "What—"

The specimen growled and raised its lips, exposing long pointed fangs.

Jipalt trilled in distress. "Those aren't human teeth! They're nothing like the human teeth we've collected to date!"

"It must be a new species," Tallim decided, his voice squeaking in excitement. "An entirely different species coexisting alongside the humans! We've never seen this before!"

The specimen struggled against the energy restraints, slowly managing to sit up.

"Ship emergency!" Hetref shrieked before the specimen fully escaped. "Escaped specimen! Maximum restraint!"

The room brightened as the computer sought the specimen. The light slid right across the alien's broad back. The creature rolled off the examination table, breaking through the energy restraints. Its feet barely touched the ground before it leapt at Tallim.

"No, no!" Tallim shouted. "It missed him! Temperature lock on nine Agaranth! Nine—eeeee!"

A long hairy arm whipped out and snatched hold of Tallim's goggles. The goggle's strap held firm as the scientist was yanked violently toward the monster; he shrieked as he flew through the air.

The creature landed on his feet and rolled his arm overhead. Held captive by the goggles, Tallim followed that trajectory until he slammed into the floor with lethal force. Hetref heard the bones break—Tallim's face, his skull, his neck.

"No, no, no!" Jipalt screamed.

The creature turned its face toward Jipalt and exposed its teeth further, growling low in its chest. Then it glanced down at Tallim's corpse at its feet, his eyes as blank as river rock, blood dripping from his open mouth and chin. The creature touched the pooling blood with his finger and sniffed it, scowling at the odor. It wiped the residue on Tallim's suit.

"How do you live with such sludge in your veins?" The human-thing spoke with a deep voice, lisping slightly around its fangs.

Jipalt and Hetref fled the room.

Hetref peeked around the corner. The specimen remained standing, carelessly wiping green blood off his hands.

"Emergency seal on Extraction room, effective immediately," Hetref commanded shakily. The doors slammed shut, the nine locks clicking into place. The two survivors stood there for long moments, trying to breathe.

"Humans can't even scratch the doors. A Nevetine can't pull them off their tracks. Even the acidic Trolph can't breach it. So we're safe, Jipalt. We're safe." Hetref turned to comfort Jipalt, but she wasn't looking at him. Her eyes widened as she stared at the door.

Hetref turned. He gawped at the grainy dark dust as it trickled into the hallway from around the edges of the door. The dust swirled about the door, defying the air currents, defying logic. More and more dust escaped the room, collecting into a swirling column that widened and lengthened with every moment.

When enough accumulated, the dust consolidated into a single form—the specimen the xeno-anthropologist had locked behind the doors.

Hetref dashed down the hall. Jipalt zipped past him as if he was standing still. He heard the specimen's heavy footsteps behind him, encouraging his feet to move even faster. Despite Hetref's panicked flight, the sounds grew nearer by the second.

By the time the anthropologist found himself at the Cultural Artifacts bay, he could feel the thing's foul breath on the back of his head. Hetref dodged and ducked, opening the bay doors and rushing in while the creature slid to an awkward halt. The bay doors shut and sealed behind him. His feet pattered an insane tempo as Hetref looked blindly around. Human artifacts surrounded him—a chest of dark red wood, a padded seat for several individuals covered in dark leather, a Laz-E-Boy™ seat and footrest that reclined in several positions, an overly large computer monitor. The objects from a Hollywood mansion, three Galveston beach houses, two mid-west farmhouses, one post office, and a rusted-out trailer from West Virginia were compacted into this single bay.

The anthropologist dashed among the treasures from the world they circled. "They have to know," he muttered to himself, turning and surveying everything nervously. "They have to know. They live with these—toothed monstrosities. The humans must know how to deal with these—them!"

The bay door shuddered as the creature assaulted it. Hetref began a frantic rush through the furnishings and appliances, clambering over satin-sheeted beds, opening dresser drawers and armoire doors, strewing the items wildly about. "It would be easy to see," he spluttered, "easy to handle. Quick and simple, something even children could use. Small. Lightweight. Colored for quick identification. Look for green—no! Their emergency color is red! Red like their blood! Small, easy, red, marked. Marked with what? Marked with what?"

A triangular object caught his attention, small enough to hold in his two hands, lightweight, red. He read the label.

"Dustbuster™ ," he translated aloud.

Hetref clutched the vacuum to his chest and crawled into the smallest space he could fit. He panted with anxiety, his heart pounded. The monster couldn't reach him here—not without first turning back into dust. *Please go away please go away ...*

He saw tendrils of black dust floating under the four-post bed, between the slate-gray storage bins and the maple entertainment center, over the square herringbone coffee table. *It's looking for me,* he realized in mounting horror. *It can detect things, even without eyes. I have to collect all of the dust to stop it.*

He glanced down at the vacuum. *This thing isn't airtight. Why isn't it airtight?*

The dust started collecting in thicker whorls just beyond his reach. Hetref cowered as far back in the small enclave as he could, struggling to find enough courage to turn the machine on.

When the dust began consolidating into a thick tower, Hetref clicked the on button and leapt forward onto the coffee table with a wild shriek. He waved the vacuum madly about, sucking in as many of the granules as he could. He jumped about, wailing like a lost soul every time his slippers crunched down on grit.

The vacuum choked when he finally collected all the monster's bits. Hetref clutched it tighter, scared to let go. "I-I-I need a container, a box with a lid, something airtight! Maybe red?" He swiveled around, his feet pounding his frantic heartbeat against the floor. *Plastic ... red ... YES! The humans have these containers in all their houses! The main part is red—it must be for emergencies like this!*

He yanked the Coleman™ cooler from the gray shelves, flipped the lid off, and dumped its contents over the four-post bed before slamming the vacuum into its depths. A tube of instant glue made the seal between the cooler and the lid airtight. Hetref hunted through the other contents of the cooler, finding the thick clear tape from the post office, providing an additional layer of sealant.

Finally he put the container in a metallic wagon that was small enough for him to maneuver. *It's almost the same size as this box, but it has edges that should keep the beast in. And it's red. This must be its function.* He found a highlighter and covered it in bright green warnings.

DO NOT TOUCH, STAY AWAY, LETHAL

Pulling the cart behind him, Hetref staggered out of the artifact bay and collapsed in the hallway.

The crew gathered around the Little Red Wagon™, everyone careful to stay well outside its range of motion. The cooler quivered and jumped, banging against the side of the cart.

Hetref sat on the floor, staring at the other side of the hall. Jipalt crouched next to him, holding his hand, rubbing comfort into his arm as she secured a small patch to the back of his hand.

"You'll be fine," she crooned to Hetref, before standing up to address the rest of the crew. "It's just shock. We got to him in plenty of time. He'll be back on his feet by tomorrow."

"Good," the captain replied. She pointed at the wagon. "We need to get rid of that thing. It is NOT staying on my ship. It is NOT coming home with us."

The navigator objected. "We have to. It's a valid specimen. Our superiors won't believe us if we don't have proof."

"We can't take it home, it's too dangerous!" Jipalt cried out. "I don't want to touch it; I don't want to examine it. I just want it out! Throw it out the airlock!"

"No one will believe us if we don't bring it back," the navigator raised his voice.

"We have the ship's records. We have the results from the examination room. It will have to do. That thing is too dangerous to be brought back to our home." The captain stood like a rock.

The crew nodded agreement. Everyone turned back to the still twitching container.

"But where do we leave it?" the navigator asked.

"We give it back to the humans," Hetref finally spoke up, his eyes clearing. "They've been dealing with this type of monstrosity for millennia; they'll know what to do with it. I'm sure we've wrapped it up in a way they can't mistake. I'll even label it."

An electric pulse annihilated Budapest's electrical systems late Monday night. The ship landed in near total darkness next to an outlying branch of the city's postal service. Silence crawled down the streets like fog, thickening the darkness, filling the spaces between buildings.

A small patch of light appeared in the darkness as the ship lowered its ramp. Hetref bravely inched out into the dark street, eyes darting from car to building to car, the Little Red Wagon™ creaking faithfully behind him.

Jipalt deserves a brave companion. I can be brave for her. I can be brave...

When he reached the sidewalk, he crept slowly and carefully up to the door of the post office. He coaxed the wagon forward until it rested next to the doors.

Hetref knocked for a few moments, stopped, and knocked again. *I don't want to be here ... please answer ... that thing is behind me.*

After long moments, the door cracked open and the security guard ogled him through the door, a cigarette dangling from his lips, his strange blue eyes perfectly round. The weapon in the guard's hand shook.

Hetref carefully presented him with the handle of the Little Red Wagon™. Next he presented him with a clipboard. "Sign please."

"S-s-sign?" the human spluttered out, the burning tobacco filling the air with a vile odor.

"We are civilized people. This was picked up by mistake. We wish to return it."

The guard wriggled his arm out the opening, picked up the pen, scrawled some indecipherable squiggle across the bottom of the form, then jerked his arm back behind the door.

Hetref took two steps back, turned, and raced back to the ramp of the spaceship.

Darkness returned to Budapest's streets.

The security guard stood for some moments, staring at the strange contraption he'd just signed for. He approached the cooler cautiously, playing his flashlight about the item.

Taped to the top, a large piece of paper drew his attention, the message written in big block letters:

CONTENTS: ONE DUSTY ALIEN. PROPERLY CONTAINED. DO NOT OPEN.

As he reached out to touch it, the cooler twitched and shifted. The guard dropped his cigarette, jumped back into the post office, and slammed the door shut.

Chelsea Nolen has been in programming and testing for most of her working life. To get away from the tedium, she writes things— odd, off-the-wall ideas that come to her at irregular intervals. When this is not enough diversion, she cares for her dogs, cats, and 5 family members. Chelsea et al live in Oregon (they appreciate her sense of humor here).

OUTSOURCING

By Gary Piserchio & Frank Tagader

Barb smiled and looked relieved when I entered the second-floor lab. "Thanks for coming by, Steve. I need to talk to someone."

"Anything for you," I said. My friend looked tired. No, more than that. She looked exhausted. "You okay?"

She shrugged. "Well, maybe. That's what I wanted to talk to you—"

I glanced at my phone. "I gotta head in 10 minutes for lunch."

"Oh, sure. Sorry. I need to talk to you about Bill." She motioned toward the containment room, a medium-ish room with thick windows. They used the room to perform some of their more potentially dangerous testing.

I glanced in and frowned. "What's up with him? He doesn't look so good."

"Yeah, I don't think he's feeling very well right now," said Barb, fidgeting with the sleeve of her white lab coat.

I tapped on the window. Bill shuffled in our direction. "What's wrong? He got the flu or something?"

"Or something. Listen, I think—"

"Why's he licking the window?"

Bill stood—swayed—on the other side of the containment room window licking the glass and staring at me, his tongue a giant gray slug leaving a slime trail.

I grimaced and said, "Oh, that's just gross."

Barb looked at him with concern on her face. "Just let me tell—"

I tapped on the window and raised my voice. "What are you

doing?" Something was wrong with his face. It wasn't as gray as that freaky slimy tongue, but it sure looked like he could use some sun. He leaned forward, both hands on the glass as he stared at me with a kinda pervy and creepy intensity, all the while that gray slug of his worked the glass. His eyes looked fouled with clam chowder.

"Ah, man, that's just disgusting."

"Pay attention. I'm trying to tell you what's wrong with Bill."

I gagged a little before yelling at Bill, "That's grossing me out. You don't know what's on that glass."

Barb grabbed my arm. "Look at me, Steve!"

I grimaced before turning. "Really gross."

"I know," she said. "Bill and I are working on a bio-reactive agent and he accidentally ingested a small quantity. It's something we're making for one of our foreign customers."

"Is it Tunisia? We're developing a software system for their healthcare infrastructure. We're calling it TunaCare."

"Bill and I were—"

My gut burned. "We're behind on bug fixes, though. We have beta in a few weeks and Derek won't give me the right people to get the system fixed."

"That doesn't matter right now. Bill was—"

"Derek is such an asshole. I wish he would—"

"Shut up! The stuff Bill ingested was part of the genetic-remediation project."

"Genetic-whatsit?"

"You probably heard our tagline: Turn decay into pay? No? Anyway. The agent turns dead biologic matter into something—less dead."

"And what's that mean for Bill?"

"I don't think he's quite living anymore," said Barb.

"Huh?"

"He's sort of a—"

"I didn't catch that."

She mumbled some more.

"What?"

"A zombie!" she yelled.

I blinked at her a few times. "What?"

She pulled up the sleeve of her lab coat. There was dried blood and teeth marks. "He bit me. I think he wanted to eat me."

Shocked, I looked back into the containment room. "Really?" Bill shuffled over to the technician's computer. He sat/fell into the chair and started typing. "What's he doing?"

She shrugged. There was drool oozing from the corner of her mouth.

"You feeling okay? You look pale."

"I—" she swayed and put her hand against the containment window. "I don't know. It's getting hard to think. Like I'm really brain dead."

"You should lie down."

"I'll be fine."

I looked back at Bill. "He's really going at it on the computer. Typing gibberish, right?"

Barb went to the containment room door and opened it.

"Wait, where are you going—ah, crap." I hurried to stop her but she shuffled in. I tiptoed behind her and took hold of her arm to stop her. She nodded toward Bill and gave me a look of *go see*. I nodded toward the containment room door and gave her a look of *let's get the hell out of here*. She nodded toward Bill again. I rolled my eyes and eased around to look at Bill's computer screen. Holy cow, he was working—coding some statements for a database table. His gray fingers were flying over the keyboard. I looked at Barb and pointed at Bill's screen. Her eyes were almost closed and she swayed sideways too much and banged her hip into the desk. Bill whirled on us, snarling like a wild animal. He pushed up from his chair and lurched toward Barb, furiously chomping his teeth. I mean, really chomping them. Making a loud clacking noise. It was terrifying and unsettling.

Barb just stood there. She looked too tired, too exhausted, to even raise her arms to fend him off. I yelped and jumped between them. Bill clacked his teeth next to my face. It was horrible, his breath smelled like old roadkill. I shoved him backward, took Barb's arm, and hauled ass out of there, slamming the door shut behind us.

"Wow, Bill's really not doing so good," I said.

"Yeah. But he calmed down the first time after I gave him a brain."

"Beg pardon?"

"When I first put him in the containment room he started asking for brains."

I felt queasy. "But you didn't—"

Barb nodded.

I shuddered. "Ew, now *that's* gross. Where the hell did you find a brain to give him—any chance it was Derek's?"

"Holy crap that's a lot of brains. Are they human?" Barb had led me across the parking lot from our office building to the huge company warehouse next door. We stood on the concrete floor of one of the gigantic rooms. Before us were row upon row of squat glass cylinders with wires and gizmos erupting from each, making them look like something from an old horror movie. Barb should have been rubbing her hands together and giggling maniacally. Each cylinder held one grayish-pink brain.

"There are about 10,000 living brains here. Kangaroo brains. We're keeping them alive for an Alzheimer's project."

"Kangaroo brains?"

"One of our Australian subsidiaries was testing kangaroos in their mutagenic farming systems, pumping them full of different experimental chemicals. When they were finished, they slaughtered the kangaroos, selling the meat to fast food companies and sending these over here."

"That's both disgusting and cool at the same time."

Barb nodded, scratching at her arm. "It's getting itchy."

"You should put Neosporin on it."

Barb looked at me for a moment, swaying. "Steve, I know this is going to sound sick, but brains kinda sound good right now."

I took her by the arm. "Okay, you've been around Bill and brains too long. You're a vegan, for crying out loud. There's an empty office next to mine, you're going to rest."

Barb shuffled alongside me. "Maybe your brains."

I grabbed a cot from storage and set it up in the empty office next to mine. Barb was turning a sort of gray, like a color photograph fading to black and white. Dark circles—trenches—were forming around her eyes. She dropped down on the cot with a grunt.

"Brains?" she said softly.

I shook my head. "No, Barb. Just get some sleep, okay?"

I closed the office door behind me. This wasn't good. At all. Should I get the company nurse? There was a thump against the door. Then another. Faintly I heard Barb say, "Brains."

"Ah, crap." I suspected it was too late for the nurse.

"Is someone in there?"

It felt like I jumped a good foot or more and my heart tried to escape out my mouth. "Oh, hi, Derek. You, uh, you startled me." I shook my head. "No. No one's in—"

"Steve, walk with me."

"I'm kinda busy—" *freaking the F out.*

Derek started off down the hall. He was taller than me with dark hair that was almost shoulder length. He was rail thin everywhere but his pooch of a belly, like he was smuggling an extra-large hot-water bottle under his shirt. "Have you seen the latest bug report?"

"I was just getting to that." I hurried to catch up.

"No real surprise, but your team has the most defects to fix."

"Well, you see, the team isn't exactly—"

"You are aware that there are only three weeks until beta. Right?"

"Yes, but the team—"

"If you don't have those bugs fixed by beta, I'm afraid the whole department will be outsourced, including yourself."

I stopped and Derek kept walking. I could have sworn a smile spread across his face as he turned the corner up ahead. I went cold. Three weeks wasn't enough time. I needed to talk to Barb, she'd know what to—I'd momentarily forgotten she was sick. Maybe she wasn't too far gone, though. I plodded back to the office next to mine. As I put my hand on the doorknob I could hear her moaning, "Brains," over and over.

"Oh, this is disgusting." The goo inside the glass cylinder threatened to spill on me. The pinkish brain inside with all the wires sprouting from it looked like a techno-nightmare daddy longlegs doing a wobbly dance. I opened the office door and Barb was standing right there. Except that it was no longer Barb. There was no life left in her eyes, her face expressionless.

She took a tottering step forward, reaching out. "Brains."

Maybe after she ate a brain she'd be more normal again. I could hope. I pushed her back into the office and closed the door behind me. Some of the goo sloshed down the front of my shirt. "Great. Just friggin' great. Now get back, Barb, and stop trying to bite me! See what I got you?"

"Roo brain." She grabbed it from the cylinder, getting more

goo on me. She smashed as much of the brain into her open maw as she could, chewing and swallowing and smashing in more. Brain and goo oozed out from between her fingers and even out her nose.

It was horrifying and amazing to watch. "You used to eat, like, a pear and a diet D.P. for lunch. Uh, yeah, just keep cramming that baby in there. You might want to remove the—no, you just go ahead and eat those wires. How's that goo taste? Good? Mmmm, yes, that's some tasty goo."

She had almost as much brain smeared across her face as she had crammed into her mouth.

I pointed to my cheek. "You have a little something—" then I tried not to vomit. Swallowing the spit flooding my mouth, I took a deep breath. Calmed myself down somewhat—calm being a loosely used term. "Geez, Barb, I'm really screwed. There's no way my crappy team is going to get those bugs fixed in three weeks. I doubt they could do it in three months. What can I do, Barb?"

"Brains?"

I shook my head. "Derek is going to can my ass. He's outsourcing my team."

"Outsource?"

"Yeah, outsource. I mean, don't get me wrong, I don't give a crap about my team, but he's outsourcing me!"

"Outsource?"

"Yes! Outsource!" She had always been so helpful before, offering good advice. Always willing to lend an ear. She could literally lend me that ear now. I regretted that thought as soon as it popped into my head.

"Outsource!" she yelled, her voice like gravel, her goo-covered eyes unblinking.

I backed out of the office and shut the door.

"Oh, God," I said, breathing hard and resting my forehead against the door. My shirt and pants were goo-drenched. "Does this stuff even come out?"

"Hey, man, I'm not feeling so hot. I think I'm going to head for the day."

I turned toward Ned. "Did Bill bite you?"

Ned scrunched up his grizzled face, "What, man?"

I looked at my watch. "It's 1 o'clock."

Ned nodded, looking bored. "Yeah. So I'm going to head, okay?"

"How many software bugs did you fix today?"

Ned looked over at his cube as if counting. "Oh, hey, I didn't get to any bugs today. You know, man, stuff and meetings and stuff."

"No fixes? Beta is in three weeks and we still have 70-plus defects to fix."

Ned looked back at me, I could see the No Vacancy sign in his eyes. "What?"

"Get back to your desk and work on some defects."

Ned nodded. "Yeah, man, first thing tomorrow. Hey, you spilled something on yourself."

I started to say something else but Ned was already walking away. Freakin' hippie freak. Derek had forced the burnout on me and wouldn't let me fire the guy. I looked over at the twenty cubes that made up my team. A little tan maze of chest-high faux walls. Most on my team were rejects foisted on me by my boss. "You *suck*, Derek."

I was going to lose my job because of the idiots on my team. I felt sick. Queasy. Headachy. I'd just bought a new car. My heart ached at the thought of having it repossessed. And my apartment downtown? Oh, God, I'd have to move back in with my parents. I shuddered and looked over at my quadrant, imagining the deadbeats behind those cubicle walls. Then a thought occurred to me. Huh. I felt a sliver of hope.

"Okay, people," I said, standing in front of the conference room whiteboard. "Here's where we're at." Why hadn't I thought of this earlier? When in trouble, call a meeting. I'd inspire the troops. They'd rally to my side. Together we'd overcome this—this opportunity for improvement—and stick it up Derek's ass.

On the whiteboard were the defect numbers with the name of the team member assigned to each. I looked at my team of nineteen, with Ned having gone home. They sat around the long conference table. I beamed at them, the embodiment of optimism. This would work. They stared back at me blankly. Heather had nodded off. She drooled, her face planted on the table. That was okay. After I explained our predicament, even Heather would be marching by my side. The Marines' Hymn was running rampant through my head. I turned and slapped the whiteboard hard, hurting my hand. "Heather! has fifteen bugs to fix in the next three weeks." She didn't flinch. In fact, she snored softly.

Mark raised his hand.

As leaderly as possible, I said, "Yes, Mark?" Questions were good. Inquiring minds were a sign of deep thought and intelligence.

"Why isn't Ned here? I don't see why he gets to miss this meeting."

I stared at him for a moment. That's. Okay. I took a deep breath and forced my jaw to unclench. "Ned's not important. We need to focus. Buckle down. This is serious, guys. Derek talked to me just a little bit ago, and he wants these bugs fixed before beta." Then I dropped the bomb. This would get their attention. "Our jobs are on the line."

I paused, waiting for the impact to sink in. This was it. They'd see they were up against it and they'd rise to the occasion. *Come on, team.* At least a minute went by without any change of expression from the people in front of him. Finally, Mark raised his hand.

I blinked at him once or twice. Surely— "Yes, Mark?"

"What's all over your clothes?"

Anger erupted like napalm in my gut, burning away any sick or panicked feeling I had. I looked at my team. "Don't you get it? We're done for if we don't get TunaCare in the can by beta." I looked for some spark in their eyes. But most had their heads bowed as they not-so-surreptitiously texted on their phones. I pictured the room in flames, my team melting like wax. I mind felt fuzzy. Disconnected. Floating in angry goo. Could goo be angry?

Mark raised his hand.

"What!"

Mark pointed at the whiteboard. Was this it? Was he going to step up? "Why do I have more bug fixes than Heather? That doesn't seem fair."

Heather snorted and looked up, bleary-eyed. Then she stood and walked out of the conference room without saying a word, leaving a puddle of saliva on the conference table. In my mind, I used a flamethrower on her. But even afire she continued toward her cube at her turtle pace.

Mark raised his hand. I blinked and Heather returned to her not-on-fire self. Pity. I looked back at my dismal team. It was like trying to talk to a room full of zombies. Suddenly Barb's undead voice rang in my head, "Outsource!"

I stood deep in thought for several minutes as Mark waved

his hand spastically. When I snapped out of it half my team had already walked out.

"You're dismissed," I said.

Mark looked crestfallen and slowly lowered his arm. The rest of my team lurched from their chairs. Mark was the last one out.

"Mark, walk with me."

Mark looked scared, like a child caught in a lie, with one hand in the cookie jar and the other cradling his brother's broken toy.

I walked toward my office. "You're the only one on my team I can trust. I need you to help me so that we can help the team. I'm going to try a new program. It's kind of like outsourcing, but you'll get to keep your job."

"Okay," said Mark, "I don't understand what you're saying."

"That's fine. Don't worry about it. I just need you to meet with someone. She's going to explain it all to you."

"Okay?" said Mark.

I paused with my hand on the doorknob of the office next to mine. I heard—or maybe felt was a better word—a swarm of bees trapped inside my head. Buzzing and buzzing. It wasn't unpleasant. Maybe I'd get some honey out of this, or some tasty goo. Everything was going to work out.

"Do I get an office?" said Mark.

I smiled and opened the door. "Mark, have you met Barb?"

Barb looked like undead hell. Her hair was matted with goo and bits of brain. Eyes sunken. Skin a leathery greenish-gray. Her undead gaze flitted back and forth between Mark and me.

"Outsource?"

I nodded. "Yes, Barb, outsource."

"What?" said Mark.

I got behind him and shoved, propelling him into Barb's waiting arms. I slammed and locked the door. Mark's screams were louder than I thought they'd be. Panic raced like steel-toed rats through my body. "Oh, crap. I'm going to need chains."

I set the cylinder down on Mark's desk. With a rattle of chains, Mark grabbed for the brain. He wore a studded leather dog collar around his neck with matching leather cuffs on his wrists. All three cuffs were attached to chains. I had picked them up at the Crypt, the S&M place down on Broadway. Chains ran from the dog collar and wrists to a leg of the desk, preventing the undead Mark from wandering off. There was, however, enough chain length for Mark to reach the brain, which he squished greedily into his mouth, and to reach his keyboard. I pursed my lips. I needed to get some kind of cover to keep the brains from clogging up the keys.

I pushed the cart loaded with 20 cylinders of brains covered with a green tarp through the building's foyer. I'd made a lot of trips between the warehouse and my quadrant of cubes over the past four days since outsourcing my entire team. The cylinders thunked together under the tarp as if a handbell choir had fallen down a well and were dauntlessly playing for help. I pushed the cart onto the elevator, but before the doors closed Derek stepped on.

"What the hell's that?"

"Brains."

Derek shook his head. He looked pissed, his face red. "So what's gotten into your team? They've closed 56 defects since Monday."

I almost said brains again. "Oh, I gave them a pep talk."

Derek started to say something else as the elevator doors opened on our floor. Without waiting, I pushed the cart out, down the hall, around the corner, then stopped suddenly, the cylinders thunking together as the handbell choir fell atop one another. Undead Ned shambled in my direction. The dog collar and wrist cuffs were still on, but the chains dragged behind him. He looked like a kinky version of Marley's ghost. He was coming up behind Nancy, a member of the Quality Assurance team. She was doing something with her cell phone, too engrossed to notice the sound of rattling chains behind her. Ned extended his arms and opened his mouth wide for optimal brain consumption. Panic sparked through my body with the same feel as a 9-volt battery on my tongue. I grabbed a cylinder from under the tarp, nearly knocking over the whole thing. Goo sloshed down the front of my clothes. I hurried toward Ned and Nancy.

She looked up and frowned at me. "What are you doing?"

I tried to smile. "Nothing. Hey, Ned. How's it going?"

Ned's undead eyes locked on the kangaroo brain that I held up. My zombie changed its course. Nancy jerked away. "What the hell? You scared the crap out of me, Ned. Why are you dressed like that?"

"He's trying out his, um, S&M zombie Halloween costume."

86

"In August?"

I shrugged, holding the brain out of my zombie's reach. "You know Ned."

"And what the hell is that?"

I looked at the brain floating in the goo. It kinda looked like a giant wad of bubble gum. "Uh. Bubble gum?"

"Really?" She reached toward the cylinder.

"Whoa, there, grabby. You have to sign a shitload of waivers before you can even look at it. New top secret stuff from the labs."

Nancy lowered her arm. "Why's it say 'Kangaroo Brain' on the side?"

"To keep people like you away. Now come on, Ned, let's let Nancy get back to work." I led Ned back to the cubes. He looked like a toddler after a cookie, arms outstretched with hands trying to grab. I set the cylinder down on Ned's desk and while he gorged himself on brain, I hunched down under the desk to reattach the chains. As Ned grunted and slobbered above me I found the problem: the S&M chains weren't that strong. Two links had twisted and snapped off. I re-secured Ned as best I could. I needed to buy thicker chains.

As I walked back down the row of cubicles, my team began to moan for brains. A lot of them tried to stand up. "Oh, pipe down, your brains are coming."

I walked back to the hallway and froze. The cart was empty. The tarp was on the floor and all of the cylinders were gone. My insides pretty much liquefied and threatened to gush out onto the carpet. What the hell? I ran to Nancy's cube. She was gagging and spitting out a chunk of kangaroo brain. "That's disgusting." She looked up at me. "This is terrible bubble gum."

"And where's the rest of the bubble gum from the cart?"

"Well, I may have sent out an email that there was free bubble gum."

I nodded slowly as I broke into an itchy panic-sweat. Perfect. Then I said, "Keep eating it. It gets better the more you try."

"Really?"

With the empty cart in front of me, I rammed the building's front glass doors, not caring if I broke them. They didn't break, but I nearly broke my wrists. My heart raced. My stomach churned. Upstairs, my team was restless and pulling at their chains. If I didn't get more brains up there they'd break loose and eat everybody and I'd lose my job for sure.

I clattered across the parking lot toward the warehouse next door. It was like one of those telescoping hallway shots in a horror movie. Each time I looked up the friggin' warehouse seemed farther away. And each time I did that, the skittering cart careened out of control. With much cussing, I kept it upright and moving forward. When I glanced up again, the cart flew sideways and took a five-foot-long gouge of paint off the side of a black BMW. I smiled. It was Derek's car. I might have done that on purpose. Then, finally, the warehouse loomed in front of me. But in looking up, I lost sight of the sidewalk curb. The cart wheels struck it hard and did a cartwheel, with me holding on like an idiot. The world spun around in slow motion as I sailed up and over, landing hard and awkwardly on the sidewalk.

"Ow."

There was applause behind me. In pain, I stood up as best I could. I'd twisted my right knee and skinned myself up pretty good. Turning, there were six people standing in front of the warehouse door. With a strained voice, I said, "What's up, guys?"

Still clapping, one of them shrugged. "The card reader is broken. We can't get in. We're waiting for Facilities to show up and fix it."

I stopped breathing and stared at the small black box on the warehouse wall next to the door. The rest of the world seemed to disappear. "Are you kidding me?" I moved forward, limping and pushing the empty cart, which wobbled erratically. I'd broken one of the wheels. With hollow satisfaction, I bashed a few co-workers' shins along the way. Getting to the door, I grabbed the handle and pulled and grunted. "Open!" I banged on the door. Maybe someone on the inside could open it.

"Dude, it's not working. Facilities'll be here in a bit. Enjoy the break!" said a smiling bald man with thick glasses. I almost punched him.

"There must be another way in, right?"

"Well, sure, but it's all the way in the back."

I grabbed the cart and tried to run. It wasn't pretty. My lungs burned, my knee throbbed, and my heart felt like it really would explode. It didn't help that the warehouse was so friggin' big. I had to stop, not even a quarter of the way there, and catch my breath as sharp pain stabbed me repeatedly throughout my body like I was someone's voodoo doll. Derek's, no doubt. I didn't think there was a part of me that didn't hurt. From behind me, the bald guy yelled. "Door's open!"

"You gotta be—" I turned, sucking air with lungs that didn't work anymore. The asshole smiled and waved at me. I tried to run back, but my knees buckled. Hanging onto the cart was the only thing that kept me from doing a face plant.

Limping and half jogging at a pace slower than my usual walk, I pushed the fully laden cart into the elevator once again. I punched the floor button repeatedly, even after it lit up. It would have been satisfying to see the button shatter, but I only managed to cut one of my knuckles.

After an eternity, the doors opened on the fourth floor. I shoved the cart before me, cussing the entire time under my breath. I hadn't bothered to cover the cart. Goo slopped out onto the floor, making a trail of slime that I slipped and slid in. Without any traction, my legs barely worked at all now. As soon as the elevator opened, I heard the chains rattling and my team moaning. I rounded the corner near my quadrant.

There was Derek standing halfway down one of the cubicle rows.

"Fuck me," I said, gamely pushing the cart forward until I was only a few feet from my boss. Derek turned, confusion on his face.

"What's going on here? What's with the chains and—moaning? What are they saying?"

"'Brains.'"

"What?"

I shrugged. "It's all part of my new team building project." Mark suddenly popped up behind Derek, chains flying. With a sick feeling of adrenaline, I jumped between the zombie and my boss. Mark chomped his teeth at me. I held him away.

"Something's wrong with Mark's face," said Derek. "It's gray, isn't it?"

I nodded. "You could say that."

"And his eyes—"

"Like clam chowder."

"Is he sick?"

"Weren't you going to tell me something?"

"What? Oh. Yeah. Well. I have some good news."

I braced myself for the worst while bracing against Mark's relentless attempts to eat my face.

"Seriously, what's wrong with Mark?"

"Nothing a little Neosporin won't help. But you were saying?" Come *on!* I couldn't hold this zombie forever.

"Right." He stared at Mark, unable to hide the disgust he felt for Mark's current look. "I'm not outsourcing your department."

I must have heard him wrong. "Huh?"

Derek slapped me on the back. "I was never going to outsource your department. I knew if I motivated you a little you'd rise to the occasion."

"Huh?" My thoughts tumbled together like a child's tower of blocks slowly imploding. I tried to make sense of what I was hearing.

"I knew you could do it."

I thought I would spontaneously combust. "Are you fucking kidding me?"

He shook his head and laughed. "You did great." And he looked at me with this genuine joy on his face. This look of *how awesome am I?*

"You friggin' asshole."

He looked stunned. "Huh?"

I felt dizzy and my head spun. "You dick. You total and absolute dick."

He took a step back, the smile on his face melting. "Huh?"

I glanced at Mark. "Fuck it." I let him go, giving him a nudge past me. The zombie snarled and grabbed Derek.

"What's he doing? Stop that." Mark sank his teeth into the side of Derek's neck. "What are you— ow. Ow. Ow! Stop biting me!"

Heather stood up next, followed by Ned. I shook my head and walked past Mark and Derek as they danced.

"God, stop that!" yelled Derek. Blood oozed up around Mark's dark, slimy teeth as Heather grabbed Derek's head and bit down on his ear. My boss jerked away from both of them. The top half of his ear was pulled away from his head. His neck had a six-inch strip of skin hanging from it; blood spurted from the wound, drenching the collar of his white dress shirt.

———

90

Derek turned on his assailants. "Are you nuts? What the hell are you doing?" Ned slammed his open mouth into the back of Derek's head. The undead hippie knocked out all of his front teeth. Undead or alive, he wasn't the brightest bulb. Then one after another of my zombies broke free of their chains, popping up like undead prairie dogs. Derek was screaming now as Heather and Mark went in for seconds. With what teeth he had left, Ned bit at the back of Derek's neck. He didn't do much damage. I picked up a brain from the cart and handing it to Ned. At least he could gum it.

Derek's screams had brought attention to my quadrant. A group of people were huddled up in the hallway looking our way. That got my zombies' attention and they shambled toward them. The people—the living people in the hallway—just stood there. That is up until the first zombie bit into someone, spurting blood and causing general mayhem from the huddle group.

I handed out brains to Mark and Heather to get them to stop munching on Derek. He wasn't very grateful, glaring at me but unable to speak because one of them had done a job on the front of his throat. He fell to his knees. He'd lost a lot of blood. I knelt in front of him, put a hand on one of his bloody shoulders, and looked him in the eye. "I'm afraid I've had to outsource you. But you can feel some solace in knowing—" his eyes rolled back in his head and he keeled over, dead for the moment. That wouldn't last long.

They—whoever "they" are—actually traced the zombie outbreak back to Bill. No idea how, but they said that he was Zombie Zero, and that it spread from him. Some surmised that someone inadvertently left the containment room door open and that's how he got out and started the fairly short-lived outbreak—it only lasted a couple of weeks before they were all put down. I actually saw, on the news, them shooting Ned in the head. I doubt that lessened his intelligence. The stories often wondered what happened to Bill's lab partner, Barb. The most repeated theory was that he ate her. All of her.

Truth is, after the zombies went crazy in the Development department and everyone ran from the building, I felt sorry for Bill. So I let him out. The news outlets assumed he'd gotten out before then, but I was about to refute their stories.

And after the outbreak was traced back to Bill and the company, it went under pretty quickly and so it turned out I was out of a job after all. But that didn't last long. I started my own software consulting company. I had top-notch programmers. I made sure to only hire single people without immediate family in the area. Loners. They were always a delight to work with, especially after their one-on-one with my HR manager.

Gary Piserchio and Frank Tagader have written fiction together for more years than they can remember, though their co-output tends to be a story every 5 or 10 years. Both live in Denver. Both are technical writers. Both are working on solo fiction projects. Frank shares a home with a couple of terriers, a lot of books and movies, and just about any kitchen gadget you can think of. Gary wonders if he has too many Batmobiles (the answer is no). This is their second published short of the co-written variety.

THE DEMON OF CITY HALL

By Rosalind Barden

To her face they called her, "Yes, ma'am," or "Of, course, ma'am," and if she was boring her eyes into them with particular intensity, "Immediately, ma'am." Among themselves, they referred to her as "Miss Ann."

Their largely forgotten unit in an obscure corner of City Hall had been without a director for some time, since their unit had a reputation as a dead end. There was even a rumor that once there, no one ever left unless they were dead. One man supposedly sped up this process by killing himself in his office, but Marabella knew better. He only went mad, deciding he was a budgie, and a female one at that, but that is an entirely different story. So, forgotten, ignored and neglected, Marabella and her co-workers had been left to do their work in peace.

Upon the abrupt departure of the Mayor, their peace came to an end. The new Mayor, of course, had his own friends who needed jobs, so the old Mayor's friends were cast adrift. One drifted to their obscure corner. That was Miss Ann.

She was immediately displeased. She complained about being on the 13th floor, though it was actually the 8th. She complained her office hadn't been dusted and organized for her arrival. Her artwork was not hung, coordinated desk accessories not ordered. Instead of a sunny expansive view outside her window, it looked upon an airshaft. The little people shuffling papers and huddled at their computers infuriated her. She demanded they give her "bullet point" lists explaining themselves. These she did not read and instead bellowed, "I do not understand!" to the cowering employees at her weekly, and then bi-weekly Team Achievement

Understanding and Quality Sessions, or TAUQS for short.

It was difficult getting work done, with her storming about demanding timelines and bullet points, though fortunately she was busy with her own life so only darkened the office upon occasion and then only long enough to be on the phone scheduling more amusing pastimes with people she deemed far more worthy than her unit. Of course, she squeezed in the half hour, or less if she was running late from lunch, for the TAUQS.

When she was in, she took a particular dislike to Marabella. Miss Ann's dislike seemed to grow and twist when she raised the issue of the dark, closet-like office across from hers. "Why isn't that office used for something? That's inefficient. I don't understand! I should have an assistant sitting there!"

"No one uses it because it used to be Mr. Hubert's," Marabella advised her.

"I don't understand! That's no excuse!"

Being that this was in a bi-weekly TAUQS, all the staff was sitting nervously around the conference room table. At the mention of Mr. Hubert, their trembling visibly increased, and Miss Ann's glowering frown deepened.

"You!" she waved her foot to point the pointed toe of her too high-heeled shoe at Bims, the listless man who handled New Applications. "What is the problem? What is *your* problem?"

He jerked back as if attacked. But he settled himself, and said to his hands, "Mr. Hubert shot himself in there. That's what we heard. He shot himself in the throat because he said the human voice was no longer important. There was blood everywhere, that's the story. Council had special cleaning people come and clean it all up and take away his stuff overnight. So they say. By the time we came back in the morning, it was empty. Dark and empty."

"I don't understand!"

"I think what Bims is saying," Marabella smiled, "is that Mr. Hubert is dead. Stone cold." Of course he wasn't really, he was being a budgie in a nice rest home in Malibu since his family came from money, but dead is what Bims did indicate, so in that way, Marabella was accurate.

"I don't understand!" and Miss Ann's voice raised and her foot shod in the pointed shoe waved in an agitated fashion.

"No pulse. I believe that is standard. Never to see the sun rise again. Never to walk the earth. Ten feet under, etc. They say his blood is yet here and there in the gaps of his desk, the cracks in the walls, betwixt the very carpet fibers," and the assembled shuddered since these stories had been circulating in whispers since Mr. Hubert disappeared.

"You are impertinent! You will immediately, and I mean immediately, give me a bullet point timeline on what you will do – personally – about this!"

Her annoyance was further fueled by the sudden shadow of Mr. Clarence, the cleaning staff assigned to the 8th floor, as he paused in the conference room doorway. "Um, uh, 'twas a demon snatched his soul. I heard him, making bird sounds before he vanished. Birds draw the demons. My nana from Louisiana said so herself."

It should be noted that this juncture that Mr. Clarence and his relations for many generations going back hailed firmly from Pasadena, which can hardly be mistaken for Louisiana. Marabella was aware of this. Mr. Hubert, also from Pasadena, had advised her of this when he was still deigning to use human speech. Likewise, she opted not to remind anyone that a decade ago, Mr. Clarence was convinced City Hall was, "ripe with aliens," though over time the concept of demons featured more attractively in his thinking. She kept silent because Mr. Clarence was most effective in spreading rumors about Mr. Hubert.

"Uh, um. Demons," and he walked slowly away, pushing his dust mop along the carpet as he always did, since the city decided vacuum cleaners use too much electricity.

Miss Ann stared after him with an incredulous, twisted expression before she stormed off and went on a long shopping expedition that lasted into the next day.

On this next day, Miss Ann was in a cheerier mood, surrounded by the debris of her shopping, including Santa-themed wrapping paper and ribbons. On the phone was the theater where she was in the process of booking a show, which she would attend with select persons she deemed important after eating at a particular of-the-moment eatery, the website of which was displaying enticing images of menu selections, rotating fashion, on her computer screen. Abruptly, her cheeriness ended with the appearance of a small mousy man with little hair.

She noticed him standing in the doorway to her office. He wasn't facing her, but turned to look behind at Mr. Hubert's dark closet-like space. He turned back. "That where the guy died, huh?" he said to her, and appeared about to say more in hope of eliciting interesting gossip about the rumored ghastly happening, when he was struck silent by her small glaring eyes and deep frown.

She said nothing, and continued frowning, so he mumbled his purpose, "Um, I'm from next door, in Ethics? Our copy machine is jammed, so we were going to borrow your machine, for maybe about an hour? We have these reports due."

She shook her head. "Unbelievable. No. Absolutely not."

"Um. We usually borrow it, when ours breaks. And if the one here breaks, you guys use ours. It's been like that for a long time. I think you're new, but . . . ."

She cut him off. "Don't you shine me up with your talk! I am not responsible for you dropping the ball! If you want an extraordinary request of my unit, you must submit it in bullet point format, with a timeline."

"But . . . ."

"We have work to do. Do you need help finding the door?"

His eyes scanned the wrapping paper, the elaborate dishes pulsating on her computer screen, and just then the theater agent began chirping from her phone's speaker about the "most excellent grouping of seats!" The little man from Ethics left mumbling, "No wonder he killed himself."

All this was reported breathlessly by Evengiline who had been there in person, hands deep in wrapping paper, because Miss Ann drafted her for the task, as well as decorating Miss Ann's office for the festive holiday season.

Evengiline also let spill about the little troll doll she spotted on Miss Ann's desk. This gave Marabella an excellent idea. As 5pm came around, and the office emptied, Marabella slipped into Miss Ann's office. Miss Ann had been gone some hours, since the moment Evengiline completed her wrapping assignment to specifications, so Marabella knew she was safe.

There it was on the desk, as Evengiline had reported: grinning, wild black hair, and the name of a desert casino printed diagonally across its bulging belly in lurid colors along with a smiling cactus plant logo. This explained at least some of Miss Ann's extended lunches, being as the casino was two hours away.

The next day, as anticipated, Marabella heard shuffling about in Miss Ann's office. "Evengiline! Get in here!" and then the friendly mumbling from Evengiline, followed with, "Give me my troll back! Now!" Now more tearful mumblings and "You are lying!" before Evengiline fled.

Marabella felt guilty, not anticipating Evengiline would become the scapegoat, but she was in too deep now to stop. Miss Ann stormed out of her office, then paused, possibly noticing what Marabella hoped, that the light in Mr. Hubert's office, the light that was always dark, was suddenly on. A stifled gasp, then more yelling: "Who did that?"

Bims peeked around the corner about the time Marabella casually wandered over, along with others drawn by the ruckus. There it was, the troll, on Mr. Hubert's desk, facing towards Miss Ann's office with its ridiculous smile. Mr. Clarence came by sliding his dust mop. "Um, uh, that's the demon. At work."

"That's no demon. That's my bingo troll!"

"Um, uh, you oughtn't bring such devil's toys in here. That nigh on summoned the demon. Um, uh," and he pushed the mop past Miss Ann's speechless face and out the door.

She recovered herself after he was gone to fix her anger on Bims, her nearest target. "You," Bims flinched, "you do something about that man. Fire him! Now!"

"But, he doesn't work for our unit, I can't fire him, I . . . ."

"Then go to whatever incompetent person is his boss and tell him to fire that incompetent cleaner person!"

"But, the cleaning people are in the basement. It's dark down there. I don't want to go down there in the dark . . . ."

"I am tired of your excuses! You give me a bullet point list now!" She furthermore ordered Evengiline to remove the troll from Mr. Hubert's desk, which prompted her to sob at the prospect of entering that demon-infested den. "I'll remove it," Marabella offered, hopefully in recompense for getting Evengiline in trouble. She strolled into Mr. Hubert's office, picked up the offending troll, and deposited it in Ms. Ann's hands.

She gave Marabella's smile a deep, penetrating stare. "You're up to something." But, shopping and long lunches (at the casino again?) were calling, so she was out the door in two shakes of a budgie's tail.

Over the next several days, Marabella noticed Miss Ann looking at her with a triumphant smile. Um. During one of Miss Ann's absences, a long lunch from whence she never returned,

Marabella was in her office depositing the latest bullet point timeline, "explaining your bad attitude and what -- exactly -- you are going to do about it." She was pondering the growing layer of dust atop the pile of other bullet point timelines from herself and her co-workers slumbering in Miss Ann's in-box, when her eye caught a red blinking light emanating from beneath a shopping bag on Miss Ann's book shelf.

"I think Miss Ann has a spy camera in her office," Marabella reported to Bims and Evengiline.

They came up with a strategy to deflect Miss Ann's suspicion, of which Evengiline worried she was the focus. Standing just outside her office, Evengiline said loudly and happily, "They say she's such a hard worker and we're so lucky to have her!" Bims replied, also loudly, "So, right! Grover Cleveland could do no better."

The result was an annoyed email from Miss Ann to Evengiline and Bims demanding, "what is this grover [sic] Cleveland!" along with her command to generate a bullet point timeline on what they intended to do about it, including proof they contacted the City of Cleveland for "feedback."

Marabella came up with a better strategy. She tarried late that afternoon. When she was certain everyone had gone home, she crept close to Miss Ann's office door, careful that her shadow did not betray her. She moved about a small pocket mirror to catch the office light and make reflections.

"Evengiline!" screamed this time from Miss Ann the following afternoon after she arrived. "Get in here now!" Marabella heard Evengiline burst into tears and run to Miss Ann's office, then more shouts of, "What is that! What do you see on the screen!" and more sobs from Evengiline. Mr. Clarence, hearing the fuss, pushed his dust mop into Miss Ann's office and took the liberty of peering at her computer screen playing the recording of odd patches of light dancing about in front of Miss Ann's office door.

"Demon. You woke it up now. Um, uh," and then he pushed his dust mop out again.

Miss Ann leapt up and proceeded to wave her arms and shout at Evengiline and the other peeking faces, "Get out! Get out!" She scooped up her shopping bags and hurried on her way. "But we have a TAUQS scheduled for now," Bims pointed out. That only resulted in more, "Shut up! Get out of my face!" from Miss Ann before she vanished for the day.

On the morrow, about 3pm, Miss Ann returned. She was more calm, looked like she'd had her hair freshly done, but still tension vibrated just beneath the surface. Marabella picked up her phone to Miss Ann's voice ordering, "Get in my office now!"

"You," Miss Ann scowled when Marabella appeared, smiling, "you do a bullet point timeline on this demon thing and what you are going to do about it. You do it now, or I will write you up for insubordination." Miss Ann sat back, arms folded, with challenge in her eyes. "Immediately, ma'am," Marabella replied.

Marabella's bullet point timeline was in the form of a memo to the Mayor, and all members of the City Council. It went like this:

To: The Honorable Mayor, The Honorable Members of Council
From: Director of the Applications, Submittals and Processing Unit
Re: The Demon of City Hall

Because of the ongoing demonic activity on the 8th floor, which appears to be centered in the office across from mine, previously occupied by a former and possibly deceased employee by the name of Mr. Hubert, I demand the following actions on the following timeline:

* *Hire paranormal investigators right now.*
* *If there are no funds in the budget for this purpose, sell the Ethics Unit's photocopy machine within 2 days.*
* *There is a perception the Ethics Unit does no work, so this should not be a problem.*

Because this demon is interfering with my ability to have TAUQS with my staff, and otherwise do my work, I will only come in occasionally until you properly handle this emergency. I will expect all of you to give me daily bullet point timelines on your progress and I will tolerate no excuses.

Marabella also cc'd Ethics, as a courtesy, since their copy machine was involved.

The next day, as Marabella's draft memo reposed with the growing pile of dust-collecting bullet point timelines, Miss Ann again summoned her into her office. "Well? Where's your follow-though?"

"Immediately, ma'am," and taking what Miss Ann said as the go-ahead, she distributed the memo to all parties, Ethics included.

The next morning, Marabella came upon Evengiline, Bims, and the rest of her co-works, clustered around Miss Ann's office. It was utterly empty. No shopping bags on the bookshelf, no spare pointed shoes under the desk. Even her dusty inbox was empty of the dozens of bullet point timelines.

Mr. Clarence pushed by with his dust mop. "Yup. Mr. Hubert snatched that woman straight down to hell with him. Demon told him to do it. Um, uh," and he pushed away once again. Marabella thought it more likely Security had cleared away her things, rather like they had boxed up Mr. Hubert's office late one night after Marabella coaxed him from the air shaft window, where he had been chirping and flapping his arms as if in preparation for a moonlight flight. But if demons made Mr. Clarence happy, why take that away from him?

The fear level of the staff was high. Who would the demon snatch away next? Marabella hoped to be convincing when she explained that as long as they did not taunt the demon with casino trolls, they were okay. Mr. Clarence concurred. "Casino trolls. Bad news all the way 'round."

The ex-Mayor had another friend who was without employment since his term ended. He was Mr. Tibbs ("Oh, please, call me 'Bill'," we're all informal here), the former Project Manager of the Theatrical Affairs Liaison Office. He was punctual, drifting in at 8am and staying to 5pm. Beyond that, he was harmless. He slept the day under his desk with a bottle of sherry cuddled in his arms (he was a small man). The unit settled into their old pace and were actually able to get work done.

The only problem with Mr. Tibbs was his little poodle that he brought to work daily. The poodle had a name, but Mr. Tibbs always dropped to sleep before anyone could ask, so they called it Little Bill, to differentiate it from Big Bill (Mr. Tibbs). Little Bill was as demanding as Big Bill was undemanding. This small creature threatened to upset their hard won peace, until Bims discovered he could unscrew an air vent and let Little Bill run the air shafts during the day. He always came flying out of the air shafts promptly at 5, when Big Bill magically awoke and whistled a show tune to summon "my little darling."

Before long, while the little man from Ethics was making copies on their machine, his being broken again, he nervously asked Evenilgine and Bims if they had been getting a "horrible smell" accompanied by banging and disembodied growling. Evenilgine and Bims of course knew exactly what was happening, so stammered and hemmed, which prompted the Ethics man to furtively inquire after the rumored dead man and demon. Mr. Clarence, as was his habit, fortunately pushed by with his dust mop and rescued Evenilgine and Bims from their predicament by enlightening the Ethics man. "Oh, yes, sir. It's that demon all right. Wasn't satisfied enough with that woman. You don't have a bingo troll in your office by chance?" The man, eyes wide, shook his head "no." Mr. Clarence in turn shook his head in a grim fashion. "Um, uh. I guess the demon just is hungry. Looking for fresh fat," and eyed the man's round middle.

Shortly thereafter, as if abiding by Marabella's memo timeline, paranormal investigators arrived, though fortunately without sacrificing Ethics' copy machine. The investigators determined that most positively demonic activity was brisk. A rabbi was summoned forthwith to handle the matter, and was as quickly dismissed when he suggested the possibility of a raccoon in the wall.

The new Mayor then hired a television personality who had recently gifted him with his book on "Becoming Your Empowerment now!" After sprinkling about scented oils and doing a swirling type of dance, the author/TV personality concluded that Ethics must be relocated to the 13th floor, so the good and bad "humors" would balance out. "Then their rooms must be sealed forever and visited no more by any living soul."

After Ethics gratefully moved to the 13th floor, their former offices were visited by Mr. Clarence and his fellow cleaners only long enough to dump the city's supply of typewriters and autographed books visiting authors had given mayors over the past fifty years. Marabella was amused to note one was a bullet-pointed tome entitled, "Break Insubordination with TAUQS!" written by none other than Miss Ann. Fortunately, Mr. Clarence and crew did not bother "sealing" the offices, since why would any sane person enter? This enabled Bims to open the air vents on the other end, so Little Bill could run free in the former Ethics offices. Little Bill thrived in his new environment, taking strong exception to the typewriters which he enjoyed being particularly aggressive with. The books he ignored.

Mr. Tibbs, of course, had slept through all the fuss. When advised by Evengiline about what had happened, he murmured, "Ah, yes, demons. I find sherry is quite the best cure for them."

Not long after he went on his annual theatrical pilgrimage to London. From a rambling voice mail message he left Evengiline, they were able to piece together that he reconnected with some sort of long lost love, so was never coming back: "Love. So seldom does it touch the heart. And twice in a lifetime? I am a slave utterly, and like with chains, can never leave London, but oh, my dears, such chains of velvet if I could only describe . . . ," and so on. It lasted some minutes. The upshot was that bringing Little Bill to London wasn't a possibility, so he instructed the staff to, "Love my little darling like I have loved him. Love is beautiful. Kiss him for me, because love, once it touches the heart . . . ," and so on.

The staff pooled their resources and put together a schedule assigning everyone rotating duties of dispensing dog food, dog treats, spreading down fresh newspapers, and taking Little Bill on periodic field trips to the groomers. "I think," Bims declared with wonderment one day, "this little dog may have finally solved our demon problem." There was debate over whether it was really the dog, or the author with the scented oils, but no question, no one else had since disappeared down into the bowels of hell.

Nonetheless, their unit had acquired such a reputation of being damned, that no ex-Mayor's staff members, not even the most unemployable, were willing to take the position of director. Anyone who dared come by their floor and stray too close to the former Ethics door, could count on meeting a disembodied growl. Mr. Clarence's latest theory, with science now beginning to upstage demons in his thinking, was that Mr. Tibbs "went to no London. Worm holes swallowed him up," which convinced any lingering doubters. Their unit was left finally to do its work in peace.

That spring, while visiting Mr. Hubert in his Malibu rest home, Marabella related how he had greatly helped his former co-workers with their Miss Ann problem. She was not sure if he understood, but he did chirp and trill and flutter his arms and she felt he was happy.

Rosalind Barden's short fiction has appeared in print anthologies, including Cern Zoo, *part of the award-winning* Nemonymous *series, and in webzines, such as the UK's late, great* Whispers Of Wickedness. *She wrote and illustrated the children's book* TV Monster. *Her fiction has placed in numerous competitions, including the Shriekfest Film Festival. Her darkly humorous e-novel* American Witch, *now available on Amazon.com, follows the adventures of society's castoffs in a Hollywood stripped of glamour. She lives in Los Angeles, California. Discover more at RosalindBarden.com.*

SADIE'S SELKIE

By C. A. Rowland

Sadie placed the jar of tears by her side as her knees sank into the wet sand. The waves inched away as the tide abandoned the beach it had taken earlier in the day. She'd thought it would be easy to cry simply thinking about the breakup with her long-term boyfriend, but she found no more tears would flow. Only deep heartache and emptiness remained. It had taken four hours of two movies to get the required tears. First, Steel Magnolias and then, The Notebook. It had felt weird holding the jar under one eye as she cried during the sad scenes, but she'd managed. She checked her pocket for the eye dropper and aluminum foil. All was ready.

Seven tears. Sadie wanted to be exact. After all, it wasn't every day one summoned a selkie. She smoothed out an indentation in the sand, placed the foil over it and secured it with a couple of stones. She unscrewed the jar lid and let the tiny flow of liquid roll on to the foil, pooling in the deeper center. With her eye dropper, she extracted the fluid.

She wondered if she should say something before she started. Closing her eyes, she centered herself and focused on what she wanted. Not a forever man, just someone to keep the loneliness at bay for a short time. Someone she wouldn't have to worry about clinging to her or staying too long. And something different to distract her. She'd always been fascinated by the myths of selkies. She wanted to know for sure if they existed and it seemed like a good time to try this.

Opening her eyes, she held the eye dropper over the ocean water and drizzled out seven drops. On your way, she thought. Find me a selkie. I'm waiting.

Dominic rode the waves into the San Francisco harbor. At least the water was cold here. He'd struggled to remain in the Artic but the pull had been too much for him and he'd finally given in, cruising south with the currents. Decades before, he'd traveled to this area. At that time of his life, he'd been younger and lean – lusting after the women and pleasures of being on land. *I might be a bit too old for this type of thing*, he thought. *All this swimming has worn me out.*

Dominic washed up onto the rocks of where the Sutro Baths stood. It seemed fairly deserted and in ruins. A good place to make the change. Out of the water, he shed his skin and stepped forward, the tender skin on the bottom of his feet complaining of the sharp points and unevenness. He knew humans had restrictive ideas about nakedness so he wrapped his skin around the lower part of his body and over the parts humans would expect to be covered.

He knew if people frequented the area, there'd be some facilities where he could adjust the wrapping. Once sure he wouldn't offend anyone, he could move around until he could find some other coverings. He wandered up the hill and found a lookout building. A drawing of a male on the wall directed him through a door and into a small room with a trough, mirrors and bowls. He searched for clothes. Nothing. Things sure had changed since he'd been in civilization before.

He caught the motion reflected in the mirror and stopped to look. Then glanced around. The face and body staring back at him couldn't be his. But there was no one else in the room. Thinking back, Dominic saw the years of feasting on all the small fish in the Artic and laying around on the glaciers had increased his fat layers. Wrinkles lined his face and body. His middle was pudgier than he remembered and where were his long locks of curly brown hair? He sucked in his stomach. Better. Still… I wonder what the woman who summoned me is expecting.

He moved back outside and down the hill. He'd need clothing, and taking anything would be better in the nighttime.

"Mom," Sadie said to the picture she held in her hand. "Why did you tell me all those stories were real if they weren't?" She slipped on walking shoes and grabbed her small bag with money, I.D. and the epinephrine device for her allergies and headed out. For five days, she'd made the same trek to the beachfront. Was she crazy? What was she doing? She was thirty-three and single again. Why on earth had she thought this would work? Her mother had never talked about the practical parts of the stories. Only that a selkie would come if called. How would the selkie find her? In a city the size of San Francisco, locating her would be a major job. She hadn't considered that at the time, but it shouldn't matter since they were magical creatures, should it? Just in case, Sadie thought being near the area where she sent her tears off might be a good start.

At the beach, Sadie dropped down and stared at the sea. What had she been thinking? The only people on the beach were her and a homeless middle age guy who was wandering around muttering to himself. She crossed her knees, laid her arms on them, set her head down and began to cry.

Dominic wandered the beach. He'd found the area where the tears had fallen into the ocean, but so many people had walked the area the trail across the sand was not clear. I'm really out of practice at this. I wish I had something more to go on. Worse, my skin is starting to burn and hurt.

The beach was emptying. As he walked back, he noticed a lone figure by the waterfront, a head of blond hair on her arms and her shoulders shaking. He felt a familiar draw. At last, he thought, she's come back.

Dominic approached carefully not wanting to scare the woman. "Ma'am. Don't cry. Ma'am?"

She raised her tear-stained face to him and drew back. "It's okay. I don't have a rag for your tears but my shoulder's strong." He smiled and she relaxed a bit.

He watched her note his outfit and said, "I'm new here. I travel light and we don't wear clothes like these where I come from."

"That's a strange fabric you're carrying," Sadie said.

He weighed her words. "It's not fabric. It's my skin. You called a selkie, didn't you?"

Sadie's mouth dropped open. "Oh my gosh, I didn't really believe you would come."

He frowned.

"No, you don't understand, I meant that I wanted you to come. I sent my tears. It's just hard to believe you exist, even though

I believe in you." Sadie took a breath. "I'm sorry. I'm just so surprised. And you don't look exactly like I thought you would."

"You thought I'd be younger? Taller?"

"Something along those lines."

"I'm older, and there are fewer of us these days. Most selkies live in Antarctica or, like me, in the Artic. It's a long way to travel here. And frankly, there's not much interest in us anymore so we mostly eat fish and lounge around on the ice and snow."

Sadie laughed. "I can't believe I'm actually talking to a selkie." She reached out to touch his arm and jerked her hand back. "I'm not day dreaming either. You are real. But how do I know you are what you say you are?"

He smiled again. "I can prove it. Are you comfortable moving over to that area? I need a place to slip on my skin and back off again without others seeing me."

"Okay, but not too far into the rocks."

Sadie and Dominic walked down the beach. She watched him remove the clothes, slip into his skin, dive into the water and emerge as a seal. The seal slid atop a boulder and transformed.

"Wow. A real life selkie. What's your name?"

"Dominic or you can call me Dom. And you?"

"I'm Sadie."

"So Sadie, I'm starving. I haven't been in the water to feed today and I don't have any money. Do you have any fish at your place?"

Sadie laughed. "No. My place is really small with a tiny refrigerator." She looked out at the ocean. "Can't you just get in the water and catch a few?"

Dom laughed. "I could. It's not quite that easy though. And I do only like certain kinds of fish. I am a connoisseur of sorts, you might say. I'm sure I can find something but it will take a while. They aren't just hanging around waiting to be eaten."

Sadie checked the skyline. "The sun's starting to go down. Do you want me to wait for you? Sounds like it might be a while and I don't like walking home after dark."

"No. It's late and I'm more at home near the ocean. Now that I've found you, why don't we meet up again tomorrow morning? That way, I can feed and I'll be here waiting for you. And you can get to know me better before I visit your home."

"Good plan. I'll see you here as soon as the sun rises," Sadie said. She needed time to think. Was she willing to have him in her apartment so soon? She hadn't really considered that.

Sadie woke before the sun was up. Her dreams had been of her mother walking the shores of Ireland after her father died, weeping. She was rescued by a handsome selkie who charmed her with his wit so by the end of the dream they were dancing and laughing. Her mother had seemed to be floating in the air and glistening with joy. She couldn't see Dom managing that, but she thought she'd give this a chance.

As dawn broke, she was up with the sun and out the door. Most Saturdays she slept in, so she was surprised at the number of people on the beach. Joggers and walkers seemed to be everywhere. She found her spot and sat down to wait, relishing the first rays of sun on her face.

Minutes later she felt someone sit down.

"Beautiful morning," Dom said.

"Sure is. What's it like where you live?"

"Cold and white. It's beautiful too, and I love the cold. This is so different. I'd forgotten what it was like."

"So, you've been here before?"

"Oh yes, many times when I was much younger. I've visited all the border lands with oceans that aren't too warm."

"You've never been to Mexico?"

"The name doesn't mean anything to me."

Sadie laughed. "I guess they don't teach geography where you live."

"No," Dom said, "But I attended human school from time to time. Was a bit boring and I never stayed long. I do know a bit about your history and lands, though."

"Sorry. I didn't mean to offend. It was a bit of a joke. Not a good one but I was trying to be funny. I'm curious – how did you find me?"

"I followed the trail of tears that floated on the ocean to me."

"No offense, but why you?"

"The ocean knows where the tears should go. You're a nice girl. Why did you call me?"

Sadie paused. "My boyfriend of seven years left me to take a job in another state. He didn't want me to go with him. My mother told me stories of how a selkie had helped her when my father died. I guess I thought you might help me."

Sadie's eyes clouded up with tears.

"Don't cry," Dom said, wrapping an arm around her. "It's going to be okay. I'll be here to help you."

"Thanks," Sadie said through sniffles and relishing his warmth. She hadn't realized how much she needed another's touch. "But then you'll leave and I'll be alone again."

"True. But you know I will leave. For now, I'm someone to talk to and spend time with. I will stay until you are stronger and able to move forward. Kind of your own Prince Charming for a while. Is that enough?"

"I guess it will have to be. I knew you wouldn't be here forever."

"Shall we seal this bargain with a kiss like in your fairy tales?" Dominic asked.

Sadie wasn't sure she was ready to kiss Dom, but she decided to be bold.

"Okay."

Dom leaned in. Their lips – human to magical creature – met and Sadie felt herself relax and melt into the kiss. Dom slid his soft silky tongue into her mouth. A surprise, but a luxurious one. Sadie felt herself tense. Except it wasn't her body – only her throat. A slight taste of fish lingered as she swallowed. Shellfish. Dom had had shellfish in his late night dinner.

Sadie pushed Dom away and struggled for breath. She saw surprise and then concern in Dom's face. Her hand grasped to find her bag with the epi in it before she fell back against the sand. She tried to call for help and heard the words, "Help. Help. Something is wrong with her."

Sadie held tight to her consciousness as she wheezed and tried to breathe. Her eyes sought for anything to grasp hold of and landed on a new set of eyes – the clearest, deepest green blue eyes she had ever seen. Now that's what a selkie should look like, she thought.

"Looks like she's in anaphylactic shock. Does she have epinephrine?" the man said.

"I don't know. I just got here for a visit. She was fine a minute ago," Dom said.

Sadie forced her hand to move.

"Check her bag. Wait, it's in her hand," the man said.

The man administered the device.

"Is she going to be all right? How did you know what to do?" Dom asked.

"My brother has allergies. I'm guessing she does too. Not sure what kind. She should probably see her doctor."

Sadie shook her head. She concentrated on breathing slowly and more deeply. She could feel her throat opening as the epinephrine started working.

"I don't know her doctor. Is there something else we can do? She's still having a hard time breathing." Dom asked.

"You can take her to the hospital. Do you have a car nearby?"

"No," Dom said. "Do you? Can you help her?"

"I'm okay," Sadie managed to whisper. "I need a few more minutes."

"You should really see a doctor," the man said. "My car's over there in the parking area. Can you walk?"

"I think so. If you help me," Sadie said.

"Ok. Let's take this one step at a time. First, let's get you standing up."

Dom and the man helped Sadie to her feet. She leaned against the man for support.

"Now, take a step or two. Not too fast. We don't want you to faint."

Sadie took a step, then another, all the while feeling the strength of the man's arms. She fit perfectly under the crook of his shoulder.

"I'm Sadie by the way. Thank you."

"Dave. How are you doing? Breathing easier?"

They moved towards the car and Sadie realized Dom was no longer by her side.

Dave opened the passenger door for her. "Is your friend coming?"

She lifted her arm for a slight wave to Dom. He nodded, smiling as he nodded his head.

"No. I don't think so. He only had time for a short visit. I suspect he'll head back home. He must think I'm safe with you," Sadie said as she sat down heavily in the car. She'd always wonder if that kiss was planned, or if it was a coincidence. Perhaps she'd found something better than a selkie.

C. A. Rowland is an author, lawyer, speaker and teacher. She is currently working on short stories and a humorous mystery novel set in Savannah, Georgia. Carolyn is a regular blogger on www.mostlymystery.com and has a personal blog that features Stories Inspired by Pictures (SIPs) *at www.carowland.com. She's a member of Sisters In Crime, Society of Children's Book Writers and Illustrators, Virginia Writer's Club, Inc., and Riverside Writers. Her short story, "The Gift", was a semi-finalist in the Bethlehem Writers Roundtable 2014 Short Story Contest. Two of her other short stories, "An Interview with a Rabbit" and "The Crock of Gold", were originally published in 2013 in the e-magazine,* Kings River Life *(www.kingsriverlife.com) and "An Interview with a Rabbit" was included in the anthology,* Rappahannock Voices, *which can be found at www.buybooksontheweb.com. For more information, see her website at www.carowland.com or you can follow her on twitter as @writer4993.*

GETTING A HEAD

By Joette Rozanski

"Beryl, don't forget to water the plants."

Beryl tried not to sigh as she finished dusting the gargoyle statue above her uncle's office door. The gargoyle's toothy smile mocked her.

So far Beryl's internship at the Wendigo Library of the Arcane wasn't exactly what she'd hoped. Her uncle wanted her to learn the library from top to bottom, but she wanted out.

Beryl climbed down the ladder and regarded her uncle Adam Legrande, head librarian, as he studied the pages of a large book that lay open upon the top of his ironwood desk. He was a thirty-five-year-old man who wore a navy blue suit, white shirt and burgundy tie; the light from the stained-glass window behind him lay like a cape upon his shoulders. Portraits of wizards and druids looked down upon him with stern gazes.

A century ago, her family established the Wendigo as a place of research for normals and paranormals alike. Uncle Adam thought she had the right stuff to take his place one day. Beryl was only sixteen, but he wanted her to start exploring the idea now.

She wiped dust from her jeans and green-and-white striped t-shirt. She cleared her throat, ready to tell him that he had the wrong girl.

Someone knocked on the office door.

"Come in," Uncle Adam said, not looking up from his book.

Sunny, Security Troll for the Wendigo, walked into the office. Sunny was a human-like paranormal: short, built like a fire hydrant, and covered with warts. He wore an immaculate tan uniform with green piping and a green cap perched jauntily on his head.

Uncle Adam smiled, his amber-colored eyes regarding the Troll with affection.

"Sunny! What can I do for you?" He glanced at Beryl. "Do you mind if my niece remains here? I think she could use some exposure to administrative matters."

Beryl smiled brightly. *Yuck. Arguments over time cards.*

"That'sh all right," Sunny said, nodding at Beryl. "We're buds."

Uncle Adam closed his book. "Very good. Now, what can I do for you?"

Sunny clasped his hands together. "I…I dunno how to put thish, bosh. I…I need to get a head."

Uncle Adam slapped the desktop with his hands. "Excellent! I've been thinking about promoting you for some time. We need a new bookshelf duster in maintenance…"

"Maintenansh?" Sunny asked, an appalled expression on his face. "I ain't no pretty boy! No, I need to get a head, a real head." He tapped a warty space just above his left ear.

Wow! Things are finally getting interesting, Beryl thought gleefully.

Uncle Adam's eyes grew wide. "What are you talking about?"

"You know that my shishter Daisy is getting married in a coupla weeks to that Human, Barry Amberphish, right?"

"Of course. Beryl and I are invited to the reception."

"Well, as her oldesht brother, I have to shupply a head for a…sheremony."

"You don't eat it, do you?"

Beryl nearly dropped her feather duster.

Sunny was shocked. "Huh? No! We're Trolls, not Ogres. Or zombies, I guesh. No, we don't eat it."

"Then what?"

Sunny twiddled his thick thumbs. "It'sh a wedding thing. Only happens when a Human and Troll get together. Lasht time was shenturies ago. A lot easier to get a head back then."

Uncle Adam sat back and sighed. "You need to consult with Ferentz about these sorts of requests." He scowled and his cinnamon-colored hair seemed to bristle. "But no incidents of any sort involving Humans are allowed, Sunny. The board of directors would not be pleased with such activities on the part of an employee."

Sunny nodded his agreement; he didn't seem happy.

"Beryl," Uncle Adam said. "Go with him and make sure nothing…unofficial…happens. Sometimes Ferentz is too smart for his own good."

Eleanor sat on the front counter and watched Sunny and a teen-aged girl enter the pawn shop. The girl was tall and lean, dressed in jeans, white and green striped t-shirt, denim jacket and blue running shoes. Her amber eyes were intelligent and her thick cinnamon-colored hair fell heavily across her shoulders. She looked like a LeGrande, which meant she had to be treated with respect.

Eleanor wondered what they wanted with Ferentz. No one came to him unless they wanted a solution to a very odd problem.

Beryl and Sunny sat in front of the shop counter and watched Ferentz ponder the Troll's problem. The pawn-shop owner furrowed his brow, hummed, and scratched his chin with one six-fingered hand. He was a big guy who wore jeans and a black t-shirt that read, "Dead Meat." His hair was pulled back into a stringy pony-tail.

What a strange person, Beryl thought. *Uncle said he was some kind of paranormal counselor. Must be good if Uncle trusts him.*

Evening had fallen, dipping the pawn shop in rich chocolate shadows. Beryl gazed around at the watches, bicycles, clocks and other merchandise that crowded the display tables. The place smelled of moldy clothes, old furniture and dusty carpets.

No cameras or alarms. The pawn shop owner didn't seem too worried about being ripped off.

Ferentz suddenly stood up and announced, "I have a plan."

"Oh yeah?" Sunny asked. "Is there a head in it?"

"Of course. Do you know the Headless Horseman who haunts Pinepoint Cemetery?"

Beryl had heard rumors about this particular ghost. Nobody liked him, not even other paranormals. Everyone wanted him banned from the cemetery, but were too afraid to take action.

Sunny frowned. "That jerk? He's got attitude. He won't help me."

"I have no intention of asking him to do anything for us. But maybe we could borrow his head." Ferentz frowned. "Not quite truth in advertising when it comes to headlessness, is it? Anyway, I'm certain the library's board of directors wouldn't care about a phantom body part."

He glanced at Beryl, who shrugged. "Uncle didn't say anything about ghosts."

"But...but..." Sunny crooked the fingers of his hands. "How do we grab it? Kind of not really there, if you catch my meaning."

Ferentz smiled at Beryl. "I've heard you've quite an arm, young lady. Best pitcher in the local high school softball league."

Beryl was confused. "You want me to bean him?"

"No, no, tempting as that sounds." Ferentz looked at Sunny. "An Inanimate Vampire can be quite useful in this situation, don't you think?" He turned and spoke to a brass lamp at the end of the counter. "Eleanor? Do you mind?"

The lamp dissolved into the form of a large young woman who wore an emerald green sweater, blue jeans and white sneakers. She ran her slender fingers through her long red hair and smiled at Sunny and Beryl.

"Hi, guys," she said in her musical voice. "What's up?"

Beryl smiled back at her. Uncle Adam had told Beryl about Inanimate Vampires, undead who transformed into furniture forms rather than animals. This was the first Inanimate Beryl had ever met.

Ferentz grinned and his big gorilla teeth gleamed brightly.

"Heads," he told her. "Heads up, Eleanor!"

Eleanor and Beryl lurked in the mist that wound around the headstones in Pinepoint Cemetery. They'd just come from the wedding of Barry Amberphish the Human to Daisy the Troll, held under a full moon in the ornate gazebo of Woodwild City Park. Beryl told Uncle Adam about her plans for the night and, after consulting with her parents, he permitted her to accompany Eleanor to Pinepoint. Beryl had changed from the pretty silver dress she wore to the wedding into her jeans and sweater top, for the early summer evening was cool.

"Don't you feel...odd?" Eleanor asked, pointing at the moon.

Beryl shook her head. "We don't have uncontrolled transformations in my family. We've been around too long."

Eleanor nodded. "Good. You aren't nervous?"

"Heck no! This is the first fun thing I've done since I interned at the Wendigo. I was seriously thinking about quitting."

"But your family founded the library!"

Beryl shrugged. "There are others who could take over." She smiled at the Inanimate Vampire. "But now I might stick around."

They grew quiet. A few scraggly evergreens whispered over their heads and several sparkling orbs bounced from grave to grave. A church bell rang twelve times, and at the last stroke the dark and fearsome form of the Headless Horseman and his mount reared above the long, unkempt grass nearest the cemetery gate.

The rider wore dark clothes and a black cape; from his right leather-gloved hand dangled a head by its long black hair. The head's eyes glowed red.

The enormous black horse's eyes glowed as crimson as its master's. The beast snorted and pawed the ground.

The Headless Horseman had a reputation for being a bully toward the other ghosts in the graveyard. If they could convince him to leave after this adventure…

Beryl hoped Ferentz knew what he was doing. As the Ghoul explained to her, Inanimate Vampires were ectoplasmically denser than normal, but would Eleanor have the right spiritual stuff to take on the Horseman?

Beryl sighed. *I have to believe we can solve this problem; Uncle Adam thinks I can do it.*

She put two fingers into her mouth and whistled. Eleanor transformed into a yellow ball with white stars and hopped into Beryl's right hand.

The Horseman held up his head like a lantern and looked around the graveyard until he spied Beryl, who waved.

"What would you have of me, girl?" the Horseman's head asked Beryl. Its thin lips curled into a snarl.

Beryl lifted Eleanor high and asked, "Wanna play catch?"

The Horseman's head bounced as it laughed; his body's spectral shoulders shook.

"Are…are you mad? Why would I…"

Beryl wound her arm back and blasted Eleanor directly at the Horseman's chest. "Tag! You're it!"

Eleanor unfolded herself just as she felt the Horseman's ectoplasm engulf her. The slightly thicker material of her body filled the phantom form of the mounted ghost, including its head and horse. Her body felt chilled, as if she'd fallen into an icy pond. The Horseman's eyes opened wide.

"Egad!" he exclaimed. "I am possessed!"

Eleanor's own head popped up above the Horseman's broad shoulders and she flexed her arms. She swung the head that she clutched in her right hand and tossed it toward Beryl.

"Catch!"

Beryl jumped and neatly caught the Horseman's head.

"I'll see you back at the hall!" Eleanor shouted. "I've got an errand to run first."

"All right!"

Eleanor patted the horse, which pranced beneath her and snorted. Her ectoplasm rippled through the beast and he soon quieted.

"You're a handsome boy," she soothed. "My riding lessons finally pay off, although I doubt Daddy had this in mind. Let's go to the pawnshop!"

She kicked the horse's sides and they cantered past the cemetery's main gate and onto the gravel road that snaked back toward town.

Beryl ran to Sunny's rented limo, which waited several blocks from the cemetery, and jumped in. Sunny stared at the head Beryl cradled in her hands.

"Is that who I think it is?" Sunny mocked. "Not sho tough now, are ya, Horash?"

"Horace?" Beryl asked.

"Yeah," Sunny replied. "His real name. A bogie he beat up told me."

Horace's eyes grew green, and he said in a high-pitched voice, "He's part of me, too; at least for a little while."

Sunny grinned. "Hi, Eleanor. Having fun?"

"Just doing a little shopping at Ferentz's."

"We'd better get going," Beryl said. The head felt like a slightly damp sponge in her hands and she didn't like holding it.

Sunny nodded. "Daisy's probably gettin' worried about now. Shee ya shoon, Eleanor."

The Horseman's eyes became crimson and he screamed "Outrage!" and "Bloody Revenge!" until Beryl's ears hurt. She put the head in the flour sack which Sunny brought, and sighed in relief as the Horseman's cries dwindled into muffled sneezing.

"A lovely egg tray," Eleanor said, carefully lifting the glistening ceramic object from a one-legged table. "What could be more perfect as a wedding gift?"

"Cash," Ferentz's mother grunted.

Eleanor smiled down at the slump-shouldered female dressed in a paisley muumuu. The Horseman's mount, which Eleanor had named Midnight, waited outside by the front door.

Eleanor took a quick peek through the Horseman's eyes, but saw only darkness. Maybe he was asleep. She withdrew her consciousness and turned her attention back to the pawn shop.

"Put it on my tab," she said, turning toward the door with the egg tray.

"Yeah, yeah," Ferentz's mother said. "My son's pets are bankrupting us."

Beryl and Sunny slammed past the glass doors of the reception hall and ran into the large, brightly-lit room inside. The catering crew had just finished clearing the dinner plates and the evening's entertainment had started. A five-piece band—fronted by Spring-heeled Jack, a paranormal who wore black velvet and pleather and strummed a guitar with his blue forked tail—played classic rock music on the stage opposite the lobby. Humans and Trolls danced on the wooden floor in front of the stage.

Beryl saw her uncle, parents and siblings sitting at a long table toward her right. She pulled the Horseman's head out of the flour sack and held it up triumphantly.

Daisy, dressed in her glittering white dress and veil, warts gleaming with gold dust, rushed to meet them. Her new Human husband, Barry Amberphish, looking smart in his tuxedo, followed close behind her.

Daisy saw the head that Beryl held and squealed in delight. "You got it! I didn't think you could."

Sunny gave her a quick peck on her cheek. "Of courshe. I'm your big brother!"

Barry cleaned his thick spectacles with his handkerchief and anxiously eyed the Horseman. "Is it...is it still alive?"

"I am not an it!" Horace exclaimed. "Death shall rain his doom upon you, mortal! It shall..."

The head bounced with such ferocity that Beryl nearly dropped it.

Horace's expression suddenly changed and, in a much higher voice, he said, "Hey, congratulations you two."

"Eleanor?" Daisy asked, her large black eyes blinking as she stared at the head. "Is that you?"

"Well, part of me…"

Barry cleared his throat. "Most confusing."

With a loud clatter, an enormous black horse, bearing a large red haired rider, galloped into the room.

"Here's the rest of me," Eleanor said. "Having a good time, Horace?"

The head's eyes glowed crimson and Horace gasped. "Who told you my name, wench?"

"Midnight," Eleanor said. "I learned a lot from him."

"Who in perdition is Midnight?" the Horseman's head shrieked. "And give me back my body!"

Eleanor gazed sternly at him. "Midnight is your horse." She crossed her arms. "Who you haven't treated very well. You'll get your body back when we're done here."

"Shpeaking of which," Sunny said to Daisy, "ain't there shumthing you gotta do, shish?"

"Oh, yeah!" Daisy grabbed the head from Beryl and ran to the stage where the band played. They stopped when Jack saw her gesture at them; he jumped down, spoke with her a few moments, then leapt back onto the stage in a single graceful bound, blue sparks shooting from the heels of his snakeskin boots.

"Ladies and gentlemen," Jack said into his microphone. "We'll pause the music for a bit; our lovely bride Daisy will commence a time-honored Troll tradition: the Tossing of the Head. Single ladies, please come forward."

Beryl was carried along with the crowd of female guests. She felt so embarrassed; her parents and siblings and uncle were smiling and pointing. She hunched down and looked everywhere but at Horace the head.

Daisy raised the Horseman's head high above her own. She gave a few practice swings, much to the amusement of her audience, and then let fly. The head screamed, "Bloody revenge!" which trailed into a high-pitched "Wheeee!"

Beryl couldn't help herself; instinct kicked in; she ran forward and leaped high, snagging the head by its long hair. Everybody in the hall yelled and clapped.

Horace's eyes grew green and regarded her with amusement. "I wonder if this means the same as it does for Humans?"

"About me getting married next?" Beryl asked; she felt her face grow warm.

Spring-Heeled Jack took the microphone again.

"And now, according to Troll tradition, the lucky lady holding the head may take her pick from the wedding gifts on the table to her right."

"The egg tray is very nice," Eleanor suggested.

"Maybe later." Beryl thrust the head at Eleanor on the horse. "Here. You can have this."

Horace's eyes glowed red and rolled around in their sockets. "Can...can...we go now?" he asked piteously.

Uncle Adam approached Beryl after she returned from the dance floor.

"I hope you didn't mind this last assignment," he said to her. "You did really well. I wanted you to understand that there is so much more to being a librarian than shelving books. I hope you'll remain at the Wendigo."

Beryl smiled. "I didn't like it at first, Uncle, but I'm willing to give it another try."

Uncle Adam returned her smile and gave her a quick hug.

Eleanor, astride Midnight and paced by Sunny and Beryl in the Troll's limo, arrived at Pinepoint Cemetery just before three o'clock in the morning. Sunny parked near the front gate; he and Beryl hopped out of the limo, stopping near the closest mausoleum.

Beryl watched Eleanor pat Midnight one last time. The Inanimate vampire sneezed; her ectoplasm, once again in the shape of a yellow ball with white stars, dropped to the grass below. She rolled toward the mausoleum and transformed into her human shape.

The newly-restored Horseman pulled back on Midnight's reins and flourished the head he gripped in his gloved right hand.

"At last!" the Horseman's head keened, red eyes aglow. "Revenge shall now be mine!"

With one powerful kick, Midnight threw the Horseman off

his back and, with a triumphant neigh, dashed through the cemetery's front gates and ran freely into the night. The Horseman lost his grip on his head, which bounced toward the plots in the wealthier section of the graveyard, a rolling lawn dotted with large obelisks and intricately-carved crypts. The Horseman's body got on its hands and needs, its fingers groping blindly through the grass.

"Should we help him?" Beryl asked.

"Nah," Sunny said. "Let'sh go back to the reshepshun. I don't wanna mish the dollar danshe. If the headlesh body had any shensh, it would follow the horshe."

Beryl, Eleanor and Sunny walked to the limo. Beryl doubted the Horseman would be much trouble to cemetery creatures in the future.

Far in the distance she heard the Horseman's head bellow, "Marco!" The Horseman's body stood up and shrugged.

"Marco, curse you!" the head screamed.

Beryl looked back in time to see the Horseman's body trip over a grave marker. Horace, both parts of him, was in for a long night.

Joette Rozanski lives in Toledo, Ohio and works as a desktop publisher. Her hobbies are photography and, of course, writing. She loves the humor of Donald Westlake and his Dortmunder caper stories and P.G. Woodhouse's adventures of Jeeves and Wooster. Her favorite genres are science fiction, fantasy, and horror. She's been published in zines, small press and the anthologies Such a Pretty Face *and the* Sword and Sorceress *series (*XIII *and* XVI*). She hopes to see more humor in these genres; instead of whistling past the graveyard, we need to laugh.*

FOLKESMUIR (THE TOWN THAT COULDN'T UN-DIE)

By John Grey

The dark coach, pulled by four even darker horses, rattled down the even more dark forest trail. The faceless coachman drove the steeds remorselessly, slapping their naked thighs with a whip darker than the coach but slightly lighter in shade than the horses. He was dressed from head to foot in dark shoes, dark coat and dark top hat. And he was in a dark mood.

The woman inside the coach was heavily veiled. Only her deep crimson lips were visible to the mirror in her small vanity case. There was something very strange about that mouth, otherwise you wouldn't be reading this. When she parted those lips, she revealed glistening white teeth, a rarity in that part of England where dentistry was considered the devil's work. Two of those teeth were longer than any other two of her teeth. According to Romanian weights and measures of the time, any tooth over three inches in length from root to tip was designated a fang.

Faster and faster sped the coach. But the speed worried neither the driver nor the passenger. They were approaching hellhound velocity but neither batted an eye. The driver in fact, had no eyes but, just in case anyone was watching, he didn't bat his featureless visage.

Unfortunately, earlier in the evening, a tree had fallen in that forest, despite the sound of it crashing to earth being outside of anyone's auditory senses. It collapsed across that very trail down which horse and coach raced. The animals saw the obstacle and leapt accordingly, but the wheels of the vehicle were not so flexible. They rammed into the tree-trunk and the vehicle capsized. The woman inside, crimson lips and all, was flung through the open window by the impact. She slammed into an ancient oak whose pointed branch pierced her chest. Dead and shriveled to a prune within moments, her first visit to the English countryside had not been all she'd hoped.

The coachman righted his vehicle, gave each of the horses their nightly painkillers and, after whipping the poor beasts into the thickest, whitest lather this side of an S & M club, beast, man and coach flew off into the night.

The port of Grimsby, on the east coast of England, is a well-known transit point for vampires travelling back and forth to the continent. The dock-workers who load and unload the ships handle coffins filled with unconsecrated dirt and the occasional dozing denizen of the undead on an everyday basis. Lids creaking open, skeletal hands sliding out, don't bother them in the slightest. They're true professionals.

Unfortunately, on a bright sunny day (the first in five years) in August, the dock-workers union struck over the issue of their new health benefits failing to cover plague. Management had replacement workers on the job before you could say, "I don't drink…wine."

Ernie and Clive were no different from any other Ernie and Clive who'd been rousted out of their favorite pub, the Bucket of Blood, to earn a pound or two down at the wharf. The ship *Vlad the Impaler* was in port and the captain was chained helplessly to the wheel as an albatross poked out his eyes. Aside from that, he was anxious to be rid of his cargo and their accompanying swarm of non-paying Norway rats.

"Bloody queer lookin' boxes," quipped Ernie.

Each took one end of a coffin and toted it toward a waiting van.

"You know what this is, don't yer," said Clive. "It's a coffin, that's what it is. My Uncle Harry nicked one off the back of a lorry once to bury Aunt Gracie. And she weren't even dead yet. It was her fault for always complainin' about how sick she was."

:"Bloody, 'ell, A coffin. Give me the creeps, it does."

Ernie began to tremble which, in turn, caused him to lose his grip.

"Watch out!" he screamed.

The coffin crashed to the ground and broke apart. A body rumbled out of its cozy bed of dirt and rolled onto the dock.

"Oh my God," said Clive.

"It's a dead 'un."

The corpse was of a man dressed in a long black cloak with a wide collar like bat's wings. His face was sickeningly pale but for his sensual red lips. And his hair was black. Blacker than a black coach but not as black as a black horse. The sun's rays shone hot and bright on skin that hadn't seen the light of day since Henry VIII's first bachelor party. The body began to crumble right before the stunned eyes of Ernie and Clive.

"Well, will you look at that," declared Clive.

"The undertakers what done up this body must have been shite."

"They pumped gallons of that thermalda-whatsis into my Aunt Gracie. She looked so good after that my Uncle Harry wanted some."

Before Ernie and Clive could decide on a plan of action, the body was nothing but dust.

The foreman strode by, snapped, "Why don't you two sweep up that mess you're making?"

"But it's…"

Ernie decided against trying to explain the situation to their boss. He and Clive grabbed brooms and brushed the remains of one of the most notorious blood-suckers in all of Eastern Europe into the North Sea.

"You think we oughta say somethin'?" asked Ernie.

"Like what."

"Last rites. You know. Like the vicar did for your mum."

"Don't be daft."

"Too bad his family couldn't be here to see him off."

"They wouldn' even have recognized him in the end. I broke an hour glass once. What a mess. Looked just like him."

Ernie and Clive loaded the remainder of the coffins into the van without any further problems.

Let me backtrack a little. It's the best way to locate the village of Folkesmuir anyhow. For those who don't know, Folksemuir is somewhere in England or Scotland. This confusion over its location has resulted in it being left off all maps of the British Isles. It was founded in 1458 by a drunken wandering Romanian expatriate by the name of Victor Antonescu, who considered the tiny dale surrounded by thick forest the ideal spot to regurgitate his prior night's meal of calf foot soup and tripe.

Too sick to move, he was soon joined by many of his old friends and even older relatives who were fleeing the eccentricities of Vlad the Impaler. A few of the more unfortunate souls arrived in their new land with stakes protruding from skulls and buttocks. Antonescu named the town after the only two people he had met when stumbling through the British Isles who could understand his thick accent. Actually, they'd assumed he was Welsh.

Because of Folkesmuir's isolation and the peculiar nature of its founding, the village that sprung up from Victor Antonescu's vomit could have been mistaken for any town in Transylvania, the home region of its inhabitants, with its tiny cottages, miniscule farms, large tavern and combined orthodox church and bee hive.

Over the centuries, Folkesmuir didn't exactly flourish. But somehow it managed to survive, thanks to various locally developed advances in inbreeding and ample supplies of beer and potatoes.

However, by the dawn of the twenty-first century, time, exasperated beyond all measure, finally decided to pass Folkesmuir by. Something had to be done, or that quaint little village somewhere in England or Scotland would fade into history where Vlad the Impaler would surely be waiting with spikes at the ready.

Realizing it was now or never, the mayor, Victor Antonescu the thirty second, called a meeting of the villagers in the town tavern, The Bloody Spike. However, outbreaks of acute drunkenness resulted in the gathering dissolving without any helpful decisions being made. It was reconvened the following day in the church.

"Something must be done!" shouted Gogu Ene.

"Something must be done!" shouted Horia Fidatov.

"Something must be done!" shouted all the men who had gathered beneath the gleaming cross and dark cloud of swarming honeybees in St Teo of the Anaphylactic Reaction Church.

But nothing would have been done were it not for young Stefan Ilie who, though only twenty one years of age, was one of the few inhabitants of Folkesmuir boasting any acquaintance with the outside world.

"Tourism," he blurted out.

"Tourism?"

The mayor eyed young Stefan with a blank look familiar to all of his constituents from those odd occasions when he disseminated policy decisions to the populace.

"Yes. That's the way into the future."

"Tourism?" The mayor was obviously flummoxed, a campaign slogan that he had run on in the last election. "But who would want to come here?"

"Last year," explained Stefan, "I went on a walking tour of England or Scotland or wherever this place is and I found my way to a seaside town called Blackpool. It was overrun with people from other parts of the country, and they were spending their money like crazy in the little shops and taverns. If we could convince them to come here and spend their money, we could all afford televisions and maybe we wouldn't have to wash our underwear in the river or undergo leeching at our annual physicals with Doctor Butacu."

Gogu Ene was the first to protest.

"I agree with the mayor. No one would want to come here. And, even if they did, we're not on the map. They'd never find us."

"So we advertise."

"Advertise what?"

"When I was in Blackpool, I went to a cinema." The others looked on Stefan in awe. "Vampires Suck Like Mad" was playing. And then I explored this bookstore. There was a whole shelf of nothing but vampire stories. They were all part of this thing called 'The Sundown Saga'. These English-Scottish people can't get enough of the undead."

Gogu was ready with a counter-argument.

"But the undead are dirty, ugly, sleazy things."

"Don't you get it? Dirty, ugly and sleazy is what sells."

The mayor looked out at the assembly, cleared his throat three times and spoke.

"Stefan has a point. I traveled to an English beach resort in my younger days. And it was dirty, ugly and sleazy. It's how the British like their fun. So what do you have in mind, Stefan?"

Stefan laid out his plans and before you could say, "Look out for that skewer", the villagers had pooled their resources and constructed a tottering castle on a hill in the middle of the forest. The shelves in the small store that once sold Bibles and honey were now stocked with sprigs of garlic, crosses and holy water. Stefan conducted classes in the tavern in what he called Hammer-ese As A Second Language.

"Okay, repeat after me," Stefan said to his makeshift class in the tavern. "Don't you be going out after dark or you'll be regretting it."

The patrons put down their tankards of ale and recited it in unison.

"I'll take you as far as the river but, after that, you're on your own."

Once again, the patrons loudly repeated the words.

They did the same for "There's something foul and ungodly out there in the forest" and "When they found the poor girl, she hadn't a drop of blood in her veins."

Stefan was proud of the progress his pupils were making. Ghita Dubre's rendition of "Come here wench and give us a kiss" replaced "What? Potatoes again?" on the town's coat of arms.

But two major stumbling blocks dropped on Stefan's plans as if they were his toes. Folkesmuir's supply of young attractive women was barrel-scrapings low. And even the handful scattered through the village hardly qualified as delectable, voluptuous virgins. Second was that the village may have had its share of hypochondriacs, reprobates, toe fetishists and avid disciples of onanism, but there were no vampires.

To resolve the first issue, Stefan advertised in all the major daily newspapers for "young, attractive, unsullied women." And for the second, it so happened that one or two of the villagers still had contacts in the old country. Advertising in newspapers was not an option because vampires are rarely up in the morning to read them. Acquiring a nosferatu or two was going to require word of mouth. This went better than expected. Within days, two résumés arrived by bat.

The hired women descended on the village in buses. At least, in the buses that had managed to successfully follow Stefan's garbled directions. Some turned left at the bullock's skull when they should have turned right and disappeared, for all time, into the marshes. Others found themselves, thanks to a loose interpretation of the old world saying 'as the vulture flies,' at the muddy bottom of the Irish Sea.

The ones that did finally make it to Folkesmuir did not quite fit the bill of the original advertisement. Most were in that stage in the flowering of youth where the petals begin to close up. And yes, they were attractive when compared to the menfolk of the village, the old and infirm ones at least, but beauties they were not. And seldom has a topic been spoken of in the long past tense so much by so many as virginity. They were barely in their new quarters before they began complaining about the cramped rooms, the diet of tripe and calf's foot soup and, most loudly of all, the lack of indoor plumbing.

Stefan was visibly disappointed with this first crop of recruits but Simu Hagi, the local priest and bee-keeper, soothed his fears.

"It's a new age, Stefan. Beautiful young virgins are in short supply. Vampires have learned to adapt. Besides, as they say, blood is all the same in the dark. By the way, can I interest you in a jar of my Stoning of St. Stephen brand honey?"

Stefan politely refused.

Luckily for village finances, the vampires they hired were willing to work for room and board which, in this case, was the castle and whatever "virgins" they could seduce and then suck dry. The Countess Aculard came well-referenced. She was also celebrated for her versatility being an eager partaker of the circulatory systems of both sexes. Count Alucard, on the other hand, was strictly a ladies' man. Both had wearied of being hounded on their home turf by crazed Catholics shoving rosaries in their faces and various members of the Van Helsing tribe disturbing their sleep at all hours of the day. They wanted a change of scenery. When word came that the far away village of Folkesmuir were hiring damnable creatures of the night, they jumped at the chance.

Stefan could hardly wait for their arrival.

When news of the fatal (?) coach accident involving the Countess Aculard reached Folkesmuir, an aura of gloom settled over the tiny burg. It didn't lift until the coffins arrived. Stefan ordered them immediately shipped up to the castle.

"I'll take you as far as the river," protested Ghita Dobre, "but after that, you're on your own."

"Save that for the tourists, Ghita," said Stefan.

All that day, the strong men of Folkesmuir toted the coffins up to their destination at the top of the hill. They were aided by the not-quite-as-strong-but-still-capable while the pathetically-weak looked on.

"I wonder which of these coffins contains the Count?" pondered a curious Stefan as the last of the boxes was delivered to the damp, cobwebbed basement of the castle. "And by the way, the dampness and cobwebs are a nice touch."

"Modeled it after me own home," spoke up Horia Fidatov.

With the coffins in place, the only step left in the plan to turn Folkesmuir into the flesh-crawling Disneyland of England or Scotland was to publicize. Stefan scraped the false bottom of the village's coffers to place large advertisements in all the leading newspapers. Each included a map of how to find "the foulest, creepiest, most God-forsaken place on the planet." Though the Blackpool Chamber of Commerce threatened to sue because of similarities to their own advertising slogan, the publicity worked. Within a week, a trickle of tourists found their way to Folkesmuir.

In the following days, the gentle folk of Folkesmuir evolved into the slightly less gentle folk of Folkesmuir and eventually the rather angry gentle folk of Folkesmuir. The old men of the village had often recounted to anyone dumb enough to listen passed-down tales of the atrocities of Vlad the Impaler. A spike through the rear end and up through the mouth for stealing a sheep, or even looking twice at a sheep, was a particular favorite. But falling foul of Vlad's peculiarities was nothing compared to having to deal with unhappy tourists.

"Where's the bloody W.C.?"

"What do you mean you don't got no pork pies? This place is shite."

"No bangers and mash? You're fookin' kidding me."

"The beer's cold. You call this a pub?"

"Where's yer dart board?"

"No TV. And it's a local derby tonight. United versus City."

There was also an on-going round of complaints that, despite much wandering through the forest late at night by one and all, there'd been no vampire sightings. The only attraction that did meet with scattered approval was the virgins.

Simu Hagi remarked that he overheard one old gentleman say to his friend as they pissed together on the church wall, thereby causing great commotion amongst the bees, "Can't remember the last time I had a bit of the other with a woman who still had all her own teeth."

Stefan felt that the lack of flushing toilets, edible food and Jacuzzis in the tiny rooms to rent over the tavern could be corrected in the days ahead or, if not, emphasized as being part of the village's charm. But the lack of a vampire after all the trouble the town had gone to acquire one was not so easily ignored.

He and a few of the other villagers hiked up to the castle to try to get to the bottom of the problem. They opened the lid of every last coffin and, to their dismay, found that not one contained anything other than unsanctified dirt.

"Maybe we could fill little bottles with this muck and sell them as genuine vampire mattress stuffing," suggested Gogu Ene.

Had Stefan Ilie a spike in his hand at that very moment, he would have driven it right through Gogu's ample chest.

My story has a happy ending of sorts. Stefan was nothing, if not, inventive. His motto was, "If it's a vampire people want, then it's a vampire they're going to get." His mother put her sewing talents to work and soon stitched together a long black cloak for her son. A coating of week's old calf's foot soup gave his face the appropriate pallor.

And so it was that Stefan Ilie became the Folkesmuir vampire. His appearances were the talk of the village. He was sighted by some tourists peering out the window of his castle. A few saw him flitting through the forest. Two came face to face with him on a moonlit night, turned and ran screaming. One of the virgins complained of something or someone biting her on the neck as she slept. However the culprit was found to be one of a party of old age pensioners who had lost their way on a bus tour of the Scottish lowlands. The truth became evident when his false teeth were found amid the virgin's tousled sheets.

What mattered most was that there had been sightings and even those who hadn't witnessed the undead first hand were satisfied. They had also concluded that cold beer didn't taste so bad after all and that, after a few tankards of the stuff, an argument could even be made for the desirability of the virgins. The tourist industry of Folkesmuir had turned a corner. The villagers had reason to believe that their quaint little burg had a future after all.

Tommy Gladding usually went to Spain for his holidays. Most of his time during those getaways was spent either sunning on a beach at the Costa del Sol or drinking the nights and early mornings into well-deserved oblivion. The most exciting thing he'd ever done was to steal the Turkish flag from atop a pole in the courtyard of that country's embassy in Madrid. Luckily, as he scrambled back over the wall, the bullets missed him.

It wasn't his idea to forgo the gorgeous Mediterranean sunshine for a tiny village in the north of England or the south of Scotland. It was his friend, Archie, who insisted. Archie was a fanatic when it came to vampires. He had the tattoo of what, in bad light, could almost be mistaken for Bella Lugosi creeping across his chest. His dingy London squat was festooned with posters of vampire movies. He slept with a stuffed bat at his bedside. He had even traveled once to Romania, but was barred from reentering over an incident in which he tried to spear an albino bus driver. It was he who urged Tommy into joining him for a week of undead fun and frolic in Folkesmuir. Tommy reluctantly agreed.

The place was worse than Tommy feared. He'd always had a soft spot for indoor plumbing, and treks to a squalid outhouse in the middle of the night were not to his bladder's liking. The novelty of a Norway rat lifting a leg to pee alongside him into an old tin bucket didn't lighten his mood any. He wanted to leave that very first night, especially after a meal of nothing but tripe and calf's foot soup. But Archie convinced him that a romp in the forest after supper was just the thing to get them in that creepy Transylvanian mood.

So after the last drop of flavor of the foot of the calf had been savored on the tongue and dropped, like a plumb line, directly into the fearfully waiting stomach, the two tourists exited the tavern, stepped gingerly around the piles of vomit left behind by their fellow diners and made their way down the vampire trail into the deep, dark forest.

The night was chilly, but they dressed sensibly with garlands of garlic and crucifixes hung from their throats. Each carried a Van Helsing autographed stake. An encounter with a real honest to goodness nosferatu was at the top of Archie's wish list. Top of Tommy's list, on the other hand, was a plate of Yorkshire pudding. But such a delicacy was not to be had in the wilds of that eerie, evil forest.

"Awesome forest," declared Archie as they trudged along the path through towering trees that blotted out the stars, the moon and all air traffic. "Very eerie, very evil. I wish I knew how they do that."

"Computer generated probably."

"Nah. This is the real thing. Any moment now a vampire's

gonna leap out from behind the bushes."

'Then what do we do?"

"We shove a stake through his bleedin' heart, that's what we do."

As the two men talked, Stefan, done up in full regalia, face painted to look like a man who's just accidentally walked in on his mother-in-law undressing, crept up slowly behind them. He had to admit he was enjoying his role as the evil denizen of the night. It was certainly far more rewarding than his day job hacking hoofs off calves.

He trailed Tommy and Archie silently, awaiting the right moment to strike. That instant would be sooner rather than later, as neither Tommy nor Archie were much in the stamina department. After a mile or so, Archie's loud panting began to frighten away the fruit bats. Tommy was about to implore his friend to turn back, when Stefan suddenly jumped out from his cover and stood before the two men in the most threatening pose he could muster.

Archie screamed, turned on his heels, and high-tailed it with surprising speed. Tommy was too weary to follow his friend. Instead, he stood his ground as Stefan moved slowly toward him.

"There's no such thing as vampires," said Tommy.

Stefan hissed.

"You know I could be lying on the beach at Torremolinos having lotion rubbed into my skin by a Spanish lovely. And here I am, on a bitter cold night in the north of England…"

"Or the south of Scotland," corrected Stefan.

"And I'm in the dark, in the middle of the woods, and my chicken-shit friend, Archie has run out on me, and I'm hungry, and as fagged out as an old age pensioner after sex, and now you come along looking like an undertaker after a lobotomy and…"

Stefan opened his mouth. A pair of fangs, finely chiseled by Simu Hagi from his wife's hair-brush, slid down over his bottom lip.

"So you're really gonna bite me, Drac old son?"

Stefan stared at Tommy. His didn't know whether to come closer to his supposed victim while looking even more menacing or just explain that he was sorry, but he'd already drunk his fill that evening and was on his way back to the castle for a nightcap. Tommy acted before Stefan had time to make up his mind.

With one swift thrust, he drove his stake through poor Stefan's heart. The faux-vampire gave him a stunned look to equal anything in the vampire deaths in all of the Hammer Horror series dating back to the late '50's. And then he toppled to the earth. Tommy was sorry he hadn't brought his camera.

He waited around for a few minutes to watch the vampire revert to dust. When that didn't happen, he retraced his steps back to the tavern. Archie, on the other hand, was never heard of or from again.

For a time, when the Folkesmuir vampire was at his most renowned, the village was finally included on a few maps. However, once Stefan's body was discovered next morning by a farmer out vivisecting badgers, the tourist industry fell on its sword or, in this case, its stake. There were no more vampire sightings. The tourists left. The virgins took a bus out of Folkesmuir and, after a circuitous route through much of Great Britain, they finally joined their sisters-in-bogus-purity at the muddy bottom of the Irish Sea. The village was removed, without warning, from those aforesaid maps.

After the failure of the tourism industry, it was announced, by mayoral decree, that the village of Folkesmuir would not be moving into the 21st century after all. In fact, there were plans underway to shunt it all the way back to the 19th. This was more than ten years ago. Owing to a successful upgrade of Ghita Dobre's still and even lower prices in the tavern, the appropriate blueprints have yet to emerge.

John Grey is an Australian born poet, playwright, musician, and Providence, RI, resident since the late seventies. He has been published in numerous magazines including Weird Tales, Christian Science Monitor, Greensboro Poetry Review, Poem, Agni, Poet Lore *and* Journal Of The American Medical Association *as well as the horror anthology* What Fears Become *and the science fiction anthology* Futuredaze. *Grey has also had plays produced in Los Angeles and off-off Broadway in New York. He is the winner of the Rhysling Award for short genre poetry in 1999.*

HELL'S WORKING GIRL

By Dan Foley

"Christ, I wish to hell something would happen to liven this place up a little," Chris said to himself as he pulled the tap to fill another pitcher of beer. As if in answer, the 'ding–ding' of the bell on top of the door rang to announce the arrival of another lost soul. After all, who else would waste a night sucking down beers in a dump like Mickey's Pub? He looked up automatically to see which one of the regulars it was, and his heart stopped. Walking through the door was the girl of his dreams. Literally, the girl of his dreams, the girl he had fantasized over since he was thirteen. She was tall, with legs that never stopped. They started at the floor, traveled upwards, and made an ass out of themselves. And what an ass it was: tight, firm, and barely contained by a flame-red, leather mini-skirt.

And tits, Jesus the girl had tits. Thirty-six D's with gumdrop-sized nipples standing up under her halter top. Short, thick, midnight-black hair, cut pixie style, gave her an impish look and accentuated an incredibly long, sensuous neck.

Every head in the place turned to watch her walk from the door to the bar. She walked like Chris knew she would, like a cat on the prowl. *Working girl*, Chris thought, *but she's in the wrong damned place. Nobody in Mickey's is in her league.*

"Shit," Chris muttered when the pitcher of beer he was filling overflowed and soaked his left hand and forearm. "Shit," he said again when he jumped back to avoid the overflow and spilled the whole damned thing.

"Are you always this coordinated?" a low, sultry voiced chimed in is ear.

Chris looked up and found himself staring into the bluest eyes he had ever seen. In the fluorescent lights of the bar, they appeared almost violet.

"Uh... what?" Chris stammered, trying to gather his wits about him.

"I asked if you're always that coordinated," the woman said with a smile.

"Uh, no," he managed to respond without croaking.

"Good," she said, "because I'd like a drink, but wouldn't want to have to lick it off the floor."

"Oooo-kay, what can I get for you?" Chris asked, his ears burning with embarrassment.

"Can you make a Slippery Nipple?"

"Uh . . ." This time Chris did choke on his words. "No." he finally managed to croak, turning redder by the second. For an instant he had wanted to say, "No, but I can make a nipple slippery," but he didn't have the balls.

"Well then," she said, obviously enjoying his discomfort, "I'll have to settle for scotch. Glenlivit, if you have it. Dewar's if you don't."

"Dewar's it is," Chris told her, finally finding his voice. "We don't get much call for the fancy stuff in here," he added.

"I wonder why?" she said, glancing around the worn and dirty interior of the bar.

Chris didn't answer; he just put some ice in a glass, filled it with an overly generous shot of scotch, and placed it on the bar in front of her. Before she could reach for it, the bell on the door chimed again, and Rocco Delucci, the neighborhood wise guy, strutted into the bar like a banty rooster.

"Whoa, what's this?" he said, raising his eyebrows and shaking his wrist in a 'hot stuff' gesture. Once he knew he had everyone's attention, he strutted over to where the woman was sitting.

"Hey, put this on my tab," he told Chris when he reached them, pointing to her drink.

"So, you're new around here, ain't cha?" he said to the woman, looking her up and down with exaggerated slowness.

"Piss off, pretty boy. I'm talking to Chris," she said, without even looking at him.

"Hey, that ain't nice, and I just bought you a drink," Rocco told her.

This time she did turn to look at him, and the smile froze on his face.

"I said piss off, you little shit," she said, poking a finger into his solar plexus for emphasis. When her finger touched him his eyes widened, a sick look came over his face, and he swallowed hard, like he had something stuck in his throat.

"Oh, now that's just disgusting," the woman said, pointing to Rocco's crotch and the dark stain that was spreading there.

Rocco whimpered like a whipped dog and fled for the door. Before he took two steps, he ripped off a loud, wet fart, and another stain appeared on the seat of his pants. He stumbled to the door, groaning and leaving little brown and yellow stains on the floor behind him. When the ding-ding of the door's bell signaled his departure, the room erupted in laughter.

"He's lucky I didn't tell him to go fuck himself," the woman said, as she turned back to face Chris.

"What?" Chris asked, not sure he had heard her correctly.

"Just kidding," she said, and picked up her drink, winked at him as if they shared some cosmic secret, and took a sip. Then she set the glass on the bar, took a deep breath, pulled her shoulders back, and stretched. Luckily, the halter top stretched with her, although it struggled mightily to contain her breasts. Chris found himself rooting for the breasts and then realized there was a similar struggle happening in his jeans. He was so captivated by the battle going on in her halter that he never heard the "ding, ding, ding, ding," of the bell on the door as his customers fled the bar like rats leaving a sinking ship.

"How about another one?" she said, tapping her glass with a crimson-red fingernail.

"What?" Chris said, coming out of his trance.

"Another scotch?" she said again.

"Sure," he answered, and filled another glass with ice and scotch.

"Whoa, big boy. You wouldn't be trying to get me drunk, would you?" the woman asked when the scotch overflowed onto the bar.

"N . . . no," Chris stammered, he face turning red again.

"You don't have to get me drunk to take me home you know. You just have to ask."

"You're fucking with me, right?" Chris asked, incredulously.

"Not yet, but I could be. Just say the word."

"What's it gonna cost me?" Chris asked.

"Does it matter?" She countered.

"I guess not," Chris answered, admitting that his, "I'll never pay for" braggadocio was just that. When confronted with a woman like this, he'd pay.

"Okay," Chris agreed. "Let's do it."

"Ding, ding, ding," the bell on the door started jumping like someone was calling the hogs for dinner. Then it fell off the wall and it hit the floor with a single, forlorn clunk.

"What the hell was that all about?" Chris asked as he stared at the bell.

"Exactly," the woman said as she slid off the stool. "And by the way, my name's Jude."

Chris watched the way her ass-cheeks moved under the mini-skirt as she walked toward the door. *Damn, I'd follow that Jude ass right to hell if I had to*, he thought to himself as he fell in behind her. Then, as if waking from a dream, he noticed that the bar was empty.

"What the hell . . . where is everybody?" he asked.

"Somewhere else," Jude answered.

No shit, he thought, but he didn't say it.

"So, your place or mine?" Chris asked as he locked up.

"Let's start with yours, then we'll go to mine," Jude answered.

"Why not just go straight to yours?" Chris asked, thinking about the unmade bed and week-old sheets at his apartment.

"Because yours is close, and mine's a hell of a walk," she said, laughing, as she took his arm in hers.

As they walked arm in arm, Chris was amazed by how hot Jude was. The night was warm, but the woman felt like she was on fire.

"You aren't sick or anything, are you," he asked nervously.

"Of course not," she answered. "What made you ask that?"

"Your arm. It feels like you're burning up."

"Just hot for you," she said, enfolding his arm in hers again.

When they reached his apartment, a two-room walkup, Chris was having second thoughts about taking her upstairs.

"Say, why don't we get a hotel room?" he suggested. "The Old Biltmore's just around the corner."

"Why bother? Your place will do fine," she told him, leading the way up the stairs. When they got to his door, Chris reluctantly unlocked and opened it, convinced Jude would bolt when she saw the mess the place was in. Sure enough, she hesitated at the door.

"Aren't you going to invite me in?" she said, standing at the threshold.

"Sure," he said. "Come on in."

Once she was in and the door was closed, Chris told her to relax on the couch while he straightened up the bedroom. Once there, he started throwing everything except the bed, sheets and furniture into the closet. He was just digging an old pair of jockey shorts out of a corner when he heard laughter in the doorway.

"I told you, you don't have to worry about that stuff," she said, and, in the blink of an eye, she was naked. He knew it wasn't possible, but her clothes just seemed to evaporate in a puff of smoke. If he had thought about it, he might have realized something was wrong, but he was hypnotized by her tits. They were magnificent – round, firm, the bright red nipples actually pointing upward. He reached for her then, but she backed away from him.

"What would you give to spend the night with me, Chris? The most exciting night in your life," she asked in a sultry voice.

"Damn," Chris said. "I knew this was too good to be true. All right, how much do you want?"

"Not money you dummy. I don't want money. I want commitment. I don't want to be just another one-night stand. What I meant was, are you willing to commit to a long-term relationship? A really long-term relationship?"

"Sure," Chris answered, so excited by the sight of her he would have said almost anything if she would just get in the damn bed.

"Say it then." she told him.

"Say what?"

"Say you agree to my terms."

"Fine. I agree to your terms. Now can we get into that bed?"

"Okay then," she said. "Get those clothes off and let's get this show on the road."

She came to him when he was naked. He reached out for her, taking a breast in each hand. Slowly, he ran a finger over each erect nipple and… "Damn!" he swore in pain and yanked his hands back. His thumbs were bleeding, a tiny drop of blood on each one of them.

He stuck the right one in his mouth, sucking the blood off. Jude grabbed the left one and pressed it onto a parchment scroll that had somehow appeared in her hand. As soon as his hand touched the parchment, sparks flew from his fingertips and a loud gong reverberated in the room.

"What the hell was that?" he demanded. "What the hell happened just now?"

"That was our contract. The commitment you agreed to."

"What? What commitment?"

"The long term commitment you agreed to have with me just a minute ago, of course."

"Who the hell are you? What the hell are you?" he said, when he looked at her closer. The nipples he had been so impressed with weren't nipples at all; they were tiny little horns.

"I'm a minion, a lower level demon," she told him proudly.

"A what?"

"A demon. You know, hell spawn?"

"What the hell are you doing here?"

"You called me."

"I called you? When?"

"Tonight. You said, 'Christ, I wish to hell something would happen to liven this place up a little.'"

"It was just a figure of speech," Chris argued. "I wasn't asking for a damned demon."

"Well you have to be careful what you wish for. Sometimes you get it."

"Well, I don't want it, go away."

"I can't, it's too late. You're mine. You signed in blood. So you might as well enjoy it," she said, holding up the parchment.

"But..."

"No buts," Jude said, pushing him back on the bed.

He started to argue but all thoughts of protest fled his mind when she mounted him. He lay on his back watching her, lost in the moment. He was just sliding into her, when something started sliding into him. Something sharp!

"Ow! What the hell is that?" he complained.

"Oops, sorry," Jude apologized. "It's my tail. Sometimes it has a mind of its own."

"Your tail. You have a tail?"

"Well, yeah. But it's not a very big one," she said, sounding embarrassed. "But size isn't everything, right?"

"Uh, right," he agreed.

"Are you sure? I mean as small as it is, it still gets the job done, right?"

"Right," he agreed, feeling sorry for her. And he had to agree, it seemed to be getting the job done right now. But then again…

When the first timid rays of sunshine poked between the bedroom blinds, a loud gong reverberated in the room.

"Oops, time to go," Jude announced, bouncing out of bed.

"Go where?" Chris asked.

"My place, of course," she answered.

"Your place? Where . . . your . . . You mean Hell?"

"Of course I mean Hell. Where else would I live?"

"Oh no," Chris protested. "I'm not going to Hell."

"Oh yes you are," Jude said, snapping her fingers.

Suddenly, they were standing in front of a large black gate. Off to one side a girl was being gang raped by a group of longhaired men. Each was carrying some sort of musical instrument.

"Help me!" the girl cried when she saw Chris.

"Ignore her," Jude told him. "We're not allowed to help her."

"Who is she? And why are those men raping her?"

"Her name is Hope," Jude answered. She's always been there, and she always will be. Those men will rape her for eternity."

"Why?" Chris asked. "What did she do?"

"I don't know," Jude answered. "It's just that there's always been a band on Hope at the gates of hell."

When they passed through the gates and abandoned Hope to her fate, Chris finally realized he was in big trouble.

"Uh…"

"What?" Jude asked.

"Uh, where are we going?"

"To the first level. That's the level reserved for the lustful. And, since you lusted after and fornicated with a demon, that's where you're going."

"Uh . . . you mean 'we' don't you? That's where we're going?"

"Oh, no," Jude said. I'm just taking you here. I don't have to stay because I'm a demon. I was just doing my job. You're the fornicator. You have to stay there."

"Forever?"

"I guess so," Jude said. "Unless you can find a loophole in the contract," she added, brandishing the scroll.

"Let's see that," Chris demanded, ripping the parchment out of her hands.

He read the whole thing through three times, including the fine print, before he found what he was looking for.

"Who wrote this?" he asked.

"I did. I always write my own contracts," Jude said proudly.

"Well, call your boss, because you fucked up."

"Duh, that's my job," Jude said, sarcastically.

"Not fucked, fucked up. Like in 'You blew it.'"

"Yeah, that's part of the job too."

"No, no, no," Chris said, losing patience with her. "You made a mistake. Call your boss. I want to talk to him."

"I don't think so," Jude said, shaking both her head and tail for emphasis.

"Just call him," Chris insisted. "I'll explain it to him."

"Fine," Jude said, stomping her foot in anger, and snapping her fingers again. Chris didn't even have time to admire the way her horns bounced before they appeared before Satan himself.

"What's the problem?" he growled, without any preamble.

"I caught this guy, fair and square," Jude said. "And now he wants out. He says there's a loophole in his contract."

"Humm," Satan said, looking at Chris.

"Did he call you?" he finally asked Jude.

"Oh, yes. He wished to hell. I heard him, clear as a bell."

"Sign the contract in blood?"

"Yes," she said, grabbing the contract out of Chris' hand and passing it over to Satan.

"Is all this true?" Satan asked Chris, who was standing before him with a smirk on his face.

"Yes, it's all true." he answered.

"Then what's the problem?" Satan asked.

"Read the contract," Chris told him.

Satan was sharp. He caught the mistake almost immediately.

"How many times did you have sex with this man?" he asked Jude.

"All night," she answered, starting to look a little worried.

"Not how long. How many times?" Satan roared.

"Including blow jobs?"

"No, not including blow jobs. Everybody knows blow jobs are not sexual relationships. How many times did you actually fuck this guy?"

"Well, let's see," Jude said, counting on her fingers. One. . . two. . . three. Yes that's it, three times."

"Shit," Satan swore. "Are you sure?"

"Of course I'm sure. Three times. I fucked him three times. What's wrong with that?"

"You fucked up, that's what's wrong with that."

"But that's my job," Jude cried as two huge demons dragged her away.

Satan looked at the contract and muttered that he couldn't believe his eyes. "Fournication. The silly bitch has been doing this job for centuries, and she still can't spell 'fornication'? That's the problem with my girls," he complained. "They're drop-dead beautiful, but they're not too bright." Then he turned his attention to Chris.

"You're the first one to find a loophole. How did you do it?" he asked.

I'm in pre-law at NYU," Chris answered. "The bartending gig is just temporary."

Satan's response to his answer was not what Chris expected. Instead of being angry, he smiled and then started laughing.

"What's so funny?" Chris asked.

"A lawyer," Satan responded. "You're going to be a lawyer. You'll be back."

Dan Foley, author of Death's Companion *and* The Whispers of Crows *has also published in various anthologies and magazines in the U.S. Canada, England and Australia. Find him at www.deathscompanion.com.*

UNIMPRESSED

By David Neilsen

The full moon glared balefully down upon the lonely and forgotten field of crabgrass. The afternoon's rain shower had churned the dirt into a particularly frothy mud which had yet to fully dry and which Horace Whitley was attempting to unobtrusively scrape off his shoes with the help of one of the many small boulders littering the ground. With a momentary sigh of regret, he silently admitted he'd been a fool to insist on wearing his $486 Alden Flex Welt Unlined Chukka Boots when the cocktail party had migrated out to the abandoned well.

Oh well, it had seemed a good idea at the time.

"This place is dismal!" squealed Henrietta Fernbush with delight. Henrietta, the reason Horace was wearing his Chukka Boots, gave one of those shivers you see excitedly-terrified women do in the movies--more for the chance to display her jiggling bosom to the men gathered around her than from any real fear, chill, or belief of dismality.

"As I explained inside, my family has not used this portion of the property since the incident occurred," said Wallace Gronk of the Saxonville Gronks in his trademark tone of nasality. "The Terror Which Lurks Below has spoilt the soil above, and nothing will grow but the crabgrass you see beneath your feet."

Horace had always hated Wallace Gronk of the Saxonville Gronks. He hated the way the man talked out of his nose. He hated the way the man's spine stood ramrod straight and caused everyone around him to feel inferior. He hated the fact that the man was ridiculously wealthy whereas Horace himself was only moderately wealthy. And he hated how the man insisted on being called Wallace Gronk of the Saxonville Gronks--as if there were any other Gronks in existence.

"My good man, are you quite certain this endeavor is worthy of our attention?" asked Bole Collins, who had been trying to talk everyone out of the idea since they walked away twenty minutes ago from the comfort, safety, warmth, and unlimited supply of cognac available within Gronk Manor. "If this terror lurking below--"

"The Terror Which Lurks Below," corrected Wallace Gronk of the Saxonville Gronks.

"My sincerest apologies. The terror which lurks-"

"It's important to call the entity by its correct name," admonished Wallace Gronk of the Saxonville Gronks.

"Yeah, OK. Got it," said Bole in exasperation. "If The Terror Which Lurks Below is so dangerous, should you be messing with it?"

Horace hid a snicker behind a forced cough. Poor Bole tried valiantly to make up for his shoddy upbringing by using an extravagant vocabulary, but whenever he grew anxious, his true breeding shone through.

"Oh, don't be a sissy man, Bole!" said Malcolm Tightenbring between sips of cognac. "I want to see a monster!"

Henrietta gave another fake-shiver combined with an intoxicatingly alluring giggle and Horace rolled his eyes. How the boorish Malcolm Tightenbring had acquired her attentions over Horace, he would never know. The man was an insult to thick-necked dunderheads.

"I would rather you not label The Terror Which Lurks Below in such a manner," said Wallace Gronk of the Saxonville Gronks. "To call it a monster belittles the entirety of its existence."

"Will you be requiring the bucket of blood, Sir?" droned Xerxes, the ancient butler who had dedicated each of the 90-plus years of his life to the care and feeding of generations of Saxonville Gronks.

"Indeed Xerxes," said Wallace Gronk of the Saxonville Gronks. "Please set it down on the lip of the well." He gestured absently to the reason for the group's excursion, the fragrantly foul stone well from which, according to Wallace Gronk of the Saxonville Gronks, would soon emerge an abomination unlike anything any of them had ever known.

Xerxes placed the sloshing bucket on the rock wall, an aggressively bored expression on his face. "If that is all Sir, I'll retire to the estate in order to better preserve my sanity," he said blandly.

Wallace Gronk of the Saxonville Gronks absently waved his aged butler away and approached the bucket of blood. "Excellent. This should be enough."

Horace looked from one intoxicated guest to another. "Is anyone else remotely disturbed by the presence of a bucket of blood?"

"Posh!" blurted Malcolm. "One can't summon a beast from Hell without a good gallon of blood at the very least."

"The Terror Which Lurks Below is the embodiment of evil the likes of which Hell hath yet ne'er vomited forth unto creation," corrected Wallace Gronk of the Saxonville Gronks absently.

"Yes, yes! Exactly!" Malcolm beamed, utterly unaware he'd just been reprimanded.

"But you're not using real blood, are you?" asked Henrietta. "From actual people? That seems so tacky."

"The Terror Which Lurks Below would not deign to respond to the visceral remains of a gerbil or parakeet, I'm afraid." answered Wallace Gronk of the Saxonville Gronks.

"What, exactly, do you do with the blood?" asked Bole before adding, "Old chum?"

At this, Wallace Gronk of the Saxonville Gronks spun around dramatically, holding his hands high to nab the attention of all. "My friends!" he began. "What I am about to do is incredibly dangerous, and the slightest interruption will call down the wrath of God himself upon us all. I must insist that each of you remain utterly silent. The slightest sound, the slightest breath of air, could have apocalyptic consequences!"

Horace rolled his eyes. Wally certainly knew how to lay it on thick.

"Would you prefer we all held our breaths?" asked Malcolm.

"Indeed," answered Wallace Gronk of the Saxonville Gronks. "That would be best."

Malcolm immediately and loudly sucked air into his lungs and cheeks. No else bothered.

Wallace Gronk of the Saxonville Gronks stood before the abandoned well and plunged both arms elbow-deep into the bucket of blood. Horace was impressed by the attention to detail.

"Hear me, Terror Which Lurks Below!" bellowed Wallace Gronk of the Saxonville Gronks. "In the name of the unholy, I call thee forth!"

He withdrew his now-blood-soaked-arms and waved them over his head like an excited two year-old, inadvertently (or perhaps completely on purpose) splattering his guests with gruesome cast-off. "Enter this realm if you dare!" he finished.

Then he grabbed the bucket of blood and dumped it into the well. The sticky substance splashed against the stone shaft as it descended, until finally dribbling into the stagnant water below.

Everyone was silent. Though only Malcolm had purposefully held his breath, everyone had stopped breathing in that haunted moment. The tension was finally shattered when Wallace Gronk of the Saxonville Gronks flicked his wrists towards the ground. "I always forget to bring a towel when I do that," he muttered.

"That's it?" asked Horace.

"Sorry?" replied Wallace Gronk of the Saxonville Gronks as he crudely wiped his hands on the side of the well.

"That was the entire production? A few choice words and you dump the bucket down the well?"

"I say, I must agree with Horace," said Bole. "It hardly seems worthy of the undivided attention of this collection of affluent and influential individuals. You promised us a horror out of time and space!"

"That was disappointingly revolting," added Henrietta.

"I held my breath for this?" piled on Malcom.

"My friends, you must show patience," soothed Wallace Gronk of the Saxonville Gronks. "The Terror Which Lurks Below will heed my call. In time."

"In time?" repeated Bole. "How long do we have to stand out here in the mud waiting? Why couldn't you have summoned this thing in the parlor?"

"I'm bored," warned Henrietta.

"My glass is empty," added Malcolm.

Horace, however, did not join in the piling on, because he noticed the rather disturbing fact that some of the blood which had supposedly just been dumped into the abyss was even now seeping back up over the rim and gurgling down onto the ground.

"Let me assure each of you," began Wallace Gronk of the Saxonville Gronks, "when The Terror That Lurks-"

"Oh stuff it!" bellowed Malcolm, waving the empty glass in his hand as an added reminder of his rising belligerence. "You promised us a monster, but instead delivered an uninspiring show a five year-old could've put together during arts and crafts!"

Malcolm stepped forward, most likely to punch Wallace Gronk of the Saxonville Gronks square in the face. Unfortunately for him (yet fortunate for Wallace Gronk of the Saxonville Gronks), before he could land a single blow, a grotesque, slimy, pink tentacle the size of an ironing board snaked out of the abandoned well, curled around Malcolm's head, and popped it right off with a violent squeeze.

For an instant, nobody moved. Nobody spoke, nobody breathed,

Then gallons of blood pulsed up through Malcolm Tightenbring's severed neck stump and the screaming began.

Looking back, Horace was hard-pressed to remember exactly what happened in those first few moments of madness. Certainly multiple tentacles reached forth from the well in search of human flesh to squeeze. Equally certain was the fact that both he and Wallace Gronk of the Saxonville Gronks dropped down into the mud faster than a single beat of one's heart. Not quite as certain was where the gun came from, nor who, exactly, shot Bole Collins in the groin. Horace was, however, fully convinced that Henrietta Fernbush remained standing in a state of permanent scream--eyes wide, mouth open, hands frozen to her cheeks--throughout the entire ordeal.

"What in God's name have you done, Wallace Gronk of the Saxonville Gronks?" cried Horace, though the words came out slightly muffled, since he was face down in the mud with his arms over his head.

"It is the Terror That Lurks Below!" screamed the host. "What were you expecting?"

The old boy has a point, admitted Horace to himself.

By now seven pink, squishy tentacles of horror had broached the aperture of the well in their thirst for human flesh to squeeze. They whipped about in the air and all around the masonry of the well in a remarkable imitation of the way Wallace Gronk of the Saxonville Gronks had waved his arms about in the air only a moment ago. One of the flailing tentacles found the toppled, headless remains of Malcolm Tightenbring and proceeded to squeeze off both of the dead man's feet at the ankles.

"Good God, man! How could you release such horror upon us all?" accused Horace.

His line of questioning was punctuated by the horrific sound of flesh being torn from flesh.

"It's never ripped anyone in half before!" answered Wallace Gronk of the Saxonville Gronks. "It must not be in the best of moods!"

Horace prepared a condescending rejoinder, but lost his train of thought when a pulpy lump of Malcolm Tightenbring's brain bounced off his back.

"Crawl away!" cried Horace. "Crawl away!"

"We cannot simply leave the Terror Which Lurks Below unattended!" cried Wallace Gronk of the Saxonville Gronks right back. "We must force it back down into its own dimension!"

"How?"

"I need another bucket of blood!"

Horace rolled his eyes again, utterly disappointed in Wally. He turned his attention to the other living male in hopes that he would prove more useful. "Bole! Bole, my good man!" he called. "Are you--"

"My manhood!" squeaked Bole. "I'm bleeding from my manhood!"

So much for Bole being useful. Pity.

"Where is my manservant, Xerxes?" asked Wallace Gronk of the Saxonville Gronks. "He would know what to do. He would bring forth a second bucket of blood! And one of the guest sheets to drape over the various unseemly pieces of Malcolm's body!"

As if to punctuate the statement, one of the repulsive, bulbous tentacles chose that moment to successfully squeeze through the former Mr. Malcolm Tightenbring's stomach, neatly severing the corpse in half and releasing a pungent wash of gore which burst outwardly in a shower of horror.

Meanwhile, Henrietta continued to scream. In fact, as near as Horace could tell, the dear girl had yet to cease her initial scream in order to reload her lungs with life-giving oxygen.

Capital set of lungs, that one, thought Horace, admiringly.

It was at this particular point in time that Horace realized with a start that if the world was to be saved from the eternal ravages of Wally's Terror Which Lurks Below, it was up to him. Wallace Gronk of the Saxonville Gronks was calling out for his manservant the way a toddler calls out for a favored stuffed onyx or emu, Henrietta was busy screaming her lungs off, Bole had been shot in the jollys and was no longer a man. Even Malcolm was useless, what with him being dead and in several pieces.

A glance back at the abhorrent scene of madness writhing up from the eldritch depths into the moist evening air confirmed Horace's worst suspicions.

More tentacles.

Easily ten or eleven by now, and Horace momentarily wondered if there was, in fact, a single entity connected to all these reality-twisting limbs or if the Terror Which Lurked Below was actually some sort of swarm of unholy tentacles.

He wasn't sure which instance he favored.

"Wally!" he called out, trying to snap Wallace Gronk of the Saxonville Gronks out of his catatonic fit. "What would you do with another bucket of blood?"

"Xerxes!" repeated the twitching host, whose mental capacity had obviously taken holiday.

"Damn you, man!" screamed Horace into his friend's ear. "Chin up! Chest out! Remember your breeding!"

Then he slapped him roughly against the cheek.

Wallace Gronk of the Saxonville Gronks closed his over-extended jaw and blinked, then turned his head to face Horace. "How dare you strike me! I am Wallace Gronk of the--"

"What would you do with a bucket of blood?" interrupted Horace.

"I would banish the Terror Which Lurks Below!"

"Could you be a little more specific?"

Wallace Gronk of the Saxonville Gronks aggressively took in a breath and held it for a moment, during which time Henrietta's never-ending scream shared time in their ears with the slobbering squishiness coming from the now-over-a-dozen tentacles writhing up and out of the well. Finally, he spoke.

"I'd dump it on him."

Horace waited for Wallace Gronk of the Saxonville Gronk to extrapolate, but the incredibly wealthy man remained silent.

"That's all?"

"From blood to blood, is the Gronk family motto."

"Well does it have to be in a bucket?"

For the second time in as many minutes, Wallace Gronk of the Saxonville Gronks was rendered speechless.

Oh, for the love of- thought Horace. Flipping over onto his back, he surveyed the state of affairs. Henrietta was screaming, but remained otherwise unharmed. Perhaps the Terror That Blah Blah Blah was sensitive to loud, prolonged noises. Bole continued to twitch and moan while cupping his hands around the dismal remains of his personal plumbing, gobs of blood seeping out from between his fingers. Perhaps if he were to convince the former man to bleed into the well... but no. Horace doubted he could coax enough blood from the lone bullet hole to constitute a 'bucket full.'

And then Horace spied the scattered remains of Malcolm.

Well hello there, old boy, thought Horace. *Here's hoping you were filled with more than hot air.*

Scrambling on all fours, Horace scurried towards the nearest segment of the former Malcolm Tightenbring- a foot. Above and around him, the various tentacles of the Terror Which Lurks Below writhed and flung themselves hither and yon in an esoteric dance of mayhem, far-flung droplets of blood raining down upon everything. Reaching the severed foot, Malcolm quickly grasped it, wincing at the slight sponginess of the flesh, and rolled onto his back to better scream at Wallace Gronk of the Saxonville Gronks- well aware that he was certainly ruining his sports jacket. He doubted even the mystical cleansing powers of Elsa, his maid, would be able to remove blood and gore from the twill cashmere-blend.

"Wally, my good man! I've got blood!" cried Horace. "Shall I just toss Malcolm's foot back into the well, then?"

Wallace Gronk of the Saxonville Gronks blinked enthusiastically, his poise and knowledge of proper etiquette swimming to the surface to replace the paralysis of indecision.

"No!" he called back. "You need to squeeze! Squeeze the foot!"

Not being overly familiar with the inner workings of the human body, Horace was momentarily confused as to exactly what Wallace Gronk of the Saxonville Gronks was driving at. "I beg your pardon?" he offered.

"Squeeze the blood out!" was the reply.

Oh, bloody Hell, thought Horace. Tossing a severed foot into the midst of this flailing cacophony of horror was one thing but did Wallace Gronk of the Saxonville Gronks truly expect him to sashay up to the edge of the well, dodging dozens of shockingly violent tentacles in the process, and drain Malcolm Tightenbring's foot of blood as if he were the pastry chef at Jean-Georges squeezing out creamy, milk-chocolate, gianduja mousse atop a hazelnut croquant?

And then inspiration cried out.

Or rather, it stopped crying out.

The lung-defying scream of Henrietta Fernbush came to a sudden and tragically horrific end. All living beings within earshot took note of the crash of silence which descended upon the field as the poor woman proved mortal after all and greedily inhaled the sweet oxygen she so desperately desired.

Unfortunately, so did the Terror Which Lurks Below, which took advantage of the break in her ear-splitting shriek to quickly wrap three tentacles around her delicate waist and twist her in half. Then, even before the shower of Henrietta's innards hit the ground, more tentacles joined the fray and neatly ripped and squeezed the once stunningly beautiful starlet into a dozen individual pieces.

Upon seeing the object of his most intimate desires torn to shreds, Horace's first thought was, *That was certainly a bit of an overkill.*

His second thought, however, was the far more useful, *Good God; her screams really were saving her life!*

He knew what he had to do.

Summoning up his inner rage, Horace let loose with a torrent of noise the sheer volume of which stunned Wallace Gronk of the Saxonville Gronks and momentarily drowned out the sounds of Bole Collins simpering like a baby. Holding the severed foot of Malcolm Tightenbring high, he rose to his feet like the second coming of Christ and ran to the rim of the well- macabre tentacles of death be damned!

To the utter consternation of Wallace Gronk of the Saxonville Gronks, the very same tentacles which had already neatly snipped two of his dinner guests into sections coiled away from the screaming Horace, as if repulsed by an energy field. Reaching the well, Horace hollered his lungs out while holding the foot upside down over the abyss with one hand and using the other to roughly massage out any and all blood he could nurse from the fractured stump. Once he felt the foot had been efficiently (if hastily) drained, Horace tossed it aside, ran back out of reach of the Terror Which Lurks Below, and doubled over with his hands on his knees to catch his breath.

"Go on!" wheezed Horace in between fresh gasps of air. "Banish your abomination already!"

But Wallace Gronk of the Saxonville Gronks could only shake his head in horror, crying, "That wasn't nearly a bucket-full! The Terror Which Lurks Below shall not be so easily vanquished!"

"Oh, honestly!" retorted an increasingly frustrated Horace. He swiveled back around and spied a manageable-sized chunk of Malcolm's torso lying amidst a sprawl of gore and viscera. After a few deep breaths to prepare his vocal systems for their workout, he let loose a primal scream and raced back into the fray.

Again, the hungry tentacles of the Terror Which Lurks Below shied away from the awful din emerging from Horace's throat, allowing him access to the blood-soaked lump of former-Malcolm. Wincing in disgust, Horace lifted the gooey mass--trying his best to contain the blood within--and hopped forward to the edge of the well. This time it wasn't necessary to squeeze the blood out of the freshly-dead flesh, as it positively rained down into the fathoms of darkness below, taking a number of internal organs with it. As before, Horace eventually tossed the remains aside and ran off. Once out of range, he crumbled to the ground and gasped for breath.

"More!" shouted Wallace Gronk of the Saxonville Gronks. "We need more!"

Of course we do, thought Horace, rolling his eyes with disdain at the tiresome bother of the whole thing.

Horace repeated his sojourn multiple times into the field of scattered Malcolm Tightenbring, selecting an arm, a leg, and a rather juicy chunk of torso to drain of bodily fluids into the well. When that still proved insufficient, he steeled his nerves, put his emotions aside, and proceeded to use the remains of the once lovely Henrietta Fernbush as well, though they did not contain the same volume of blood as the beefier Malcolm.

Finally, after coaxing a few more drops out of what had once been an absolutely stunning thigh, Horace lay prostrate on the ground, heart pounding. "Do.. tell... me..." he breathed. "Tell me... that's enough."

To his great surprise and delight, Wallace Gronk of the Saxonville Gronks found his feet, stuck out his chest, and declared, "It is time to banish this abhorrent fiend back to the depths from which it came!"

Oh, thank God, though Horace from his back, too tired to even sit up to watch the ritual unfold.

Wallace Gronk of the Saxonville Gronks was not an

unintelligent man, so he had eventually understood exactly why his acquaintance was yelling at the top of his lungs as he darted in and out of reach of the Terror Which Lurks Below. To that end, he cleared his throat, swallowed a few times to moisten and lubricate his system, and proceeded to release a cry of pure rage. Confident, he strode forward eagerly, ready to banish the monstrosity to the nether dimensions once more. As he approached, he felt a pang of regret that his heroic moment would not be witnessed by the stunningly beautiful Henrietta Fernbush. The alluring female had been the entire reason for this particular diversion, and he now felt in hindsight that summoning Pure Evil in an effort to impress a woman may not have been the wisest of moves.

Nonetheless, he stood firmly at the edge of the well, his deafening scream holding the repulsive tentacles of the Terror Which Lurks Below at bay, and closed his eyes in concentration. When he was ready, he stopped screaming and cried out,

"I banish thee!"

A few feet away, Horace was less than impressed with Wallace Gronk of the Saxonville Gronk's pedestrian ritualistic phrase. Still, he figured, it ought to do the trick.

The effect was immediate. The Terror Which Lurks Below convulsed as if stung by a wasp, with each individual tentacle rising into the air and whipping about in a dance of chaotic frenzy. A low, gravelly moan escaped from the well, grinding the teeth of both the living and the dead with waves of sonic force. One by one the grasping, clutching, squeezing arms of madness (of which there were now close to two dozen) sank back into the Stygian depths.

"Well done, old boy!" cheered Horace.

Alas, Horace cheered a moment too soon. Enraptured by his unqualified success, Wallace Gronk of the Saxonville Gronks watched the Terror Which Lurks Below vanish down the well with a proud look of satisfaction upon his face. He was so absorbed in his victory however, he neglected to scream. The last few tentacles of the Terror Which Lurks Below, free from the barrier of sound which had hitherto protected the last of the Saxonville Gronks from doom and damnation, whipped about his body and lifted him high into the air.

"Wally!" cried Horace, sitting up. He ached to charge in and save his friend, but found his will to in any way approach the sight of this climactic, Hellish chaos rather lacking.

"Help! Help! Heeeeeeelp!" screamed Wallace Gronk of the Saxonville Gronks, sounding less like a paragon of wealth and more like a whiny little girl. At length, one of the last remaining tentacles wrapped themselves around his mouth in an obvious effort to quiet the protesting socialite. Then, in an instant, the final tentacles were sucked down into the unknown abyss below, taking their summoner with them to meet his unthinkable fate.

Then there was silence.

Well, not exactly silence, as Horace could now once again hear the quiet moaning of Bole Collins as the poor sod rocked back and forth, hands weakly cupped around his bleeding genitals. However, as Collins was no longer a real man, Horace chose to ignore him.

He stood, brushed himself off, and sauntered across the well-saturated crabgrass and over to the abandoned well. At first, he gingerly picked out his steps in an attempt to salvage his $486 Alden Flex Welt Unlined Chukka Boots, but that soon proved futile.

I'm going to need a new sports coat, as well, he thought as he peered down into endless darkness. There was no sign of the Terror Which Lurks Below, nor any of Wallace Gronk of the Saxonville Gronks. It was as if neither had ever existed.

Though one look at the sheer carnage of blood and gore spread out around the well testified that they had, indeed, existed. In case there were any doubt.

"Horace..." whispered Bole, reaching a bloody hand out. "My jollys... my poor, poor jollys."

"Yes," agreed Horace. "Nasty wound you have there. I'll be sure to let Xerxes know."

With that, Horace turned and marched back to the Gronk estate, where he intended to settle into a comfortable chair and calm his nerves with a snifter of the best cognac the aged butler could find.

He absently wondered if he'd be allowed to stay on the rest of the weekend.

David Neilsen is the author of a number of slightly unsettling short stories and full-length novels in both the horror and young adult genres as well as a straight-to-DVD film he urges you not to see. In addition to writing, David is a professional storyteller whose one-man show, "H.P. Lovecraft's Call of Cthulhu", has both delighted and disturbed audiences in the greater New York region. He lives next door to the village of Sleepy Hollow with his wife, two children, and two fiendishly clever cats.

STEPHEN, THE WELL-ADJUSTED VAMPIRE

By Katrina Nicholson

Stephen drew back the curtains covering the wide living room window of his apartment, revealing a skyline of soft yellow lights against a clear black sky. With the drapes open, the new apartment looked less like a storage unit and more like a living space.

It was a small apartment--two miniscule bedrooms with a tiny living room and a kitchenette that stood just off the front door. Stephen's new neighbor, a thin, slightly airheaded blonde named Teresa, stood by the microwave clutching the bag of coffee she'd brought over as a welcome-to-the-neighborhood present.

"So, like, the university is only like three blocks away, so I thought, like, if you were a student there too, we could, like, walk together. And--"

"It's a beautiful day," Stephen said, trying to join the conversation.

"It's, like, night," replied Teresa, weaving through the stacks of cardboard boxes and joining him at the window. "Nice view, though."

Stephen winced. He kept forgetting that to other people, 'day' involved sunlight.

"Right. That's what I meant. And thank you so much for the apartment-warming gift," he said.

Stephen accepted the bag of coffee. It was half eaten and he couldn't use it, but it was the thought that counted. As far as Stephen was concerned, any thoughts a girl had about him, however misguided, were good thoughts.

Teresa smiled. Stephen smiled back. The moon was shining,

the crickets in the park across the street were chirping, and there was a pretty blonde college student paying attention to him. Maybe this time it would work out and he could actually stay in this apartment long enough to unpack all the boxes. Maybe he could call in sick to work tonight and--and then the front door slammed, ruining the moment.

Stephen was a perfectly ordinary guy. He had neat brown hair, clear green eyes, and just enough muscles to lift a box of books without giving himself a hernia. He also happened to be a vampire. His teeth were slightly pointier than average, his skin was slightly paler, and he risked spontaneous combustion if he went outside between 6am and 7pm, but for all intents and purposes he was still the same 24-year-old mortuary technician he'd always been. He paid his bills on time, he wore suits to work, and he never let his fangs down in public.

Stephen's brother, Dylan, was a different story. As a human teenager, Dylan had been skinny and pale with a head of jet black hair forced into unnatural shapes with the help of hair gel. Becoming a vampire had made him (if possible) even more morose, moody, and argumentative. For some reason, this made him irresistible to women--especially the young ones.

Dylan shed his backpack (black), sneakers (black), and leather jacket (also black) in the entryway. He gave Teresa 'the look,' the one where he dropped his chin and seemed to glower up through his own eyebrows. Stephen thought it made him look like a serial killer, but Teresa's grin widened. Then Dylan flipped up the hood of his sweatshirt (black, of course) and ducked into his bedroom.

After a moment, strains of broody pop-rock drifted into the living room.

"Ooh," Teresa drooled. "Who was that?"

Stephen rolled his eyes. Not *again*.

Just like every girl he'd ever met, his chances with Teresa were blown the minute she laid eyes on Dylan. Stephen managed to shoo the smitten co-ed out the door after enduring only three blatantly dropped hints that she wanted to do his brother.

Stephen unpacked two mugs, filled them with blood from the fridge, and went into his brother's bedroom. Dylan had already managed to paint it black, even though they'd only moved in a few hours ago. Stephen turned down the volume on the iPod dock and thrust the mug of blood at Dylan, who was kneeling on his bed tacking up his own obituary.

Dylan glared at him. "God, don't you knock?"

"Good morning, Dylan," Stephen sang. Dylan hated cheerfulness and optimism. "Did you find a job?"

"Nobody understands me," Dylan grumbled, snatching the mug.

Stephen forced the corners of his mouth down, trying not to laugh. "I'll take that as a 'no.'"

Dylan's response was to use his remote to crank the music back up.

Stephen sighed and drained his cup in one gulp. Suddenly he couldn't wait to get to work.

Work was Stephen's happy place. From his basement room at the local funeral home, Dylan removed the blood from clients' dearly departed relatives and replaced it with embalming fluid. He enjoyed it. He liked helping clients in their time of bereavement. The gleaming, white-tiled walls and concrete floor felt clean to him rather than creepy or cold, and he was comfortable with dead people who didn't talk back or cause trouble like some undead people Stephen knew. He also liked it because it saved him the trouble of hunting.

Ordinarily, the unwanted blood from a corpse went down the drain, but when Stephen worked on fresher specimens, he pumped the blood into a special 'hydration pack' he picked up at a sporting goods store. It looked just like a backpack and it had little gear pockets that he could fill with ice packs to keep things nice and fresh. Stephen and Dylan got fed, clients got pickled relatives, and nobody got hurt. He always taste tested it first, of course. No use adding 'food poisoning' to the already long list of grievances Dylan held against him.

Stephen had the tube from the radial artery of Mr. Frederick Jennings (aged 88, case of death: cerebral ischemia) in his mouth when the door opened and someone came in.

It was a short, female someone who looked to be in her mid-twenties. She was chubby, with round cheeks and short light brown hair held back by sparkly plastic barrettes. She wore a lab coat over a long blue t-shirt screenprinted with an image of a police call box. She had turned the t-shirt into a dress by adding a wide belt and leggings striped in shades of brown and orange. Stephen and this 'someone' stared at each other with wide, surprised eyes. Hers were brown. After a few long seconds, she broke the ice.

"So... um... are you a vampire?"

Stephen gulped down the mouthful of blood (it was reasonably fresh, with only a hint of blood thinners) and pulled the tube out of his mouth.

"Um... if I said 'no' right now, would you believe me?" Stephen asked, lisping slightly around his fangs.

She stared at his teeth. "Probably not."

"So... what happens now?"

"Now you finish embalming Mr. Jennings so I can work on his make up." She held up a large tackle box. "I'm the new cosmetician."

"Oh. I thought only bigger mortuaries that had a separate person for that. I mean, at my old jobs, they usually got me to do it."

That was, after all, why he chose to apply to small family-owned places - so he could have time alone with the bodies.

She shrugged. "I know. But my uncle's the owner and I needed a job."

She opened the case and started lining up creams and powders on the countertop. She noticed that Stephen was still standing there, staring at her dumbly with the tube in his hand. She raised an eyebrow at him.

"There a problem?"

Stephen shook his head. "No! I... do you mind if I... uh..." He gestured from the tube to the hydration pack.

"Nope. Everybody's gotta eat, right?"

"Right..." Stephen agreed, still not moving. He eyed her like she was a time bomb waiting to go off.

"Oh, for heaven's sake," she scoffed.

She took the tube from his hand and connected it to the pack. Then she propped Mr. Jennings on his side so the blood would drain. As she held him there with one hand, she stuck the other out to Stephen. "I'm Allison, by the way."

Stephen blinked stupidly at her hand for a second before his brain kicked into gear and he gripped it.

"Stephen."

"Dylan, what do girls usually do when they find out you're a vampire?"

162

Dylan looked up from his emo-rock magazine, surprised. The reason they'd had to move eight times in the last two years was not something Stephen often brought up.

"Usually they scream. A lot." Dylan narrowed his eyes at his brother. "Why? You got a girlfriend, Stevie?"

"What? No. Why would you think that?"

"Cause if you had a girlfriend, then maybe you wouldn't mind if I..."

"Dylan, so help me, if you go within fifty feet of a high school..." Stephen warned.

"I wasn't!" Dylan protested. "Why can't I just watch?"

"What you do is not called *watching*, Dylan, it's called *stalking*."

Dylan shrugged. "Whatever. They don't mind. I think it kinda turns them on."

"Yeah, until they find out why you don't go out in the daytime, and then they freak out, and we have to skip town! You promised," he sputtered. "You promised, no more high school girls! You--we--I--"

Stephen took a calming breath and tried to remember the good times he'd had with his brother so he wouldn't leap on Dylan and rip his throat out. Playing on the same soccer team as kids--one named after donut holes that lost every game. Jumping the neighborhood bully together to get Dylan's bike back. The way Dylan used to laugh back when he had a sense of humor.

Stephen focused on his brother's face, trying to paste those memories onto the annoying brat he was currently living with.... but he was distracted by the dark lines around Dylan's eyes. Was he wearing eyeliner?

Dylan gave him a contrite look and tried an apology. "I'm sorry, okay? It's pillow talk. It just sort of slips out."

Stephen almost choked. "You're *screwing them*?" he shouted, all calming thoughts flying out the window. "They're in *high school*!"

"It's called *making love* and it's beautiful!" Dylan yelled back, leaping off the bed.

"It's statutory rape!" Stephen countered.

"It is not, I'm seventeen!" screamed Dylan, shoving Stephen into the hallway and slamming the door in his face.

"You are not, you pervert!" Stephen yelled through the door.

His reply was mostly drowned out by angry punk music.

During their shift together the next night, Stephen kept a close eye on Allison as she applied rouge to the cheeks of Mrs. Eleanor Coughlan (aged 91, case of death: myocardial infarction). He wondered if she was acting calm because she was in shock. Maybe it would hit her all of a sudden, and she'd start screaming.

Apparently his subtlety needed work, because after about twenty minutes Allison sighed in frustration and tossed her make-up sponge onto Mrs. Coughlan's face, making a pink splotch near the middle of the dead lady's forehead.

"If you're going to eat me, would you just get it over with already and stop staring?" Allison demanded.

"Um..."

"Geez, you've got to be the worst vampire ever," Allison complained.

That stung. "Oh, you've met a lot of vampires, have you?"

"Well, no," Allison admitted. "But I can't seem to figure you out."

"Ditto," Stephen exclaimed. "I mean, you don't scream, you don't run--"

"Yeah, well you don't mope, you don't bite, you're wearing a suit for crying out loud--"

"What the hell is wrong with you?!" Stephen and Allison shouted at the same time.

They stared at each other for a few seconds, then started to laugh.

"Look, I'm not going to eat you," Stephen told her. "What you saw me doing the other day is how I feed. As for the other stuff, well, that's just what I'm like. You?"

Allison shrugged. "I guess I'm just open-minded."

"So... are we cool?" Stephen asked.

"Yeah. Can we fix Mrs. Coughlan now? We can't send her to the wake like this."

Stephen looked down at Mrs. Couglan. Her eyes were wide and bulging, her mouth open in an 'O' of surprise, and her fingers curled into claws from rigor mortis.

"She looks like she watched that tape from *The Ring*," Stephen joked, and they laughed again.

164

The next few days were the best Stephen had since he became a vampire. Probably even before that. He and Allison joked and laughed all night long as they prepared the corpses. Allison seemed comfortable around him, and Stephen was glad to have non-teenage company that he didn't have to lie to. Although Dylan still refused to speak to him because of his cradle-robbing implication, Dylan came and went at regular intervals, so Stephen assumed he had found a job.

Stephen mustered up the courage to ask Allison out after a few weeks of shared shifts. To his surprise and delight, she accepted. They went to the movies, to the park, to a concert. They shared their first kiss over the corpse of Mrs. Gladys McMillan (aged 104, case of death: pulmonary edema). On their sixth date, when Allison presented him with an opaque sippy cup for his blood so he could 'eat' when they went out to restaurants, Stephen realized he was in love.

This meant that he had to bring her home to meet Dylan, who would, of course, ruin everything.

In hindsight, Stephen realized that the eyeliner should have tipped him off. No one wears make-up to stock shelves in a grocery store.

Stephen's first clue that something was wrong came when Dylan burst into the apartment, wild-eyed and out of breath

"Quick! Tell her I'm not here!" Dylan yelled, then dove behind the sofa.

Before Stephen had a chance to ask Dylan what the hell he was talking about, the doorbell went *bing-bong*. He was surprised to find Teresa-the-coed standing in the hallway wearing a top cut nearly low enough to show nipple.

"Oh, hi, Samuel," she said. "Is Dylan here?"

"My name is Stephen," Stephen replied. "And no, he's not."

Teresa looked confused. She'd probably seen Dylan come in not two seconds ago. She tried to look around Stephen. Stephen blocked her.

"Shall I tell him you dropped by?" he asked in a tone that said 'please leave now.'

"No, I'll come back." Teresa replied. The way she said it made it sound like she had something creepier in mind than calling on a neighbor.

Stephen didn't wait for her to leave. He shut the door in her face and whirled to face his brother, who was just crawling out from behind the couch.

"What the hell was that?" Stephen demanded.

Dylan looked away. "Nothing. She just... I um..."

"You are the world's worst liar! You're sleeping with her, aren't you?"

"Um..."

Their conversation was interrupted by a knock at the door. This time it was Allison. She was wearing a Lifesaver-striped dress and bright yellow heels and looking suspiciously over her shoulder.

"Did you guys know there's a slutty blonde girl camped out in the hallway watching your door?" she asked.

Dylan glared at Allison. "This is all your fault!" he wailed, then ran down the hallway to his bedroom and slammed the door.

A second later, deafening, angsty music drifted through the door.

"Was it something I said?" Allison asked.

Stephen waved her comment away. "No, he's always like that. Can I take your coat?"

Dinner was awkward. Stephen and Allison sat at the table, her with a plate of a chicken and broccoli dish Stephen had made from a recipe he found in *Good Housekeeping* and him with a mug of blood. They ate and avoiding looking at Dylan's bedroom door, which was still emitting loud music.

Finally Allison put her fork down. "This is going badly, isn't it?"

"You haven't met many teenage boys, have you? This is about as well as it could have gone. Every time I open my mouth he seems to take what I've said as a personal affront and sulks for about a week."

"Maybe he has a chemical imbalance," Allison suggested.

"Maybe he needs to grow up," Stephen countered, mentally thanking all the deities he could think of that Dylan's inexplicable female attractive force didn't seem to work on Allison.

By dessert, Stephen had had enough.

"That's it," he said suddenly, slamming his sippy cup down hard enough to spray droplets of blood onto Allison's crème brulee. Stephen got up and stalked down the hall. He barged straight into his brother's room. It was empty.

Allison looked over his shoulder as he took in the still-blaring iPod in its dock and the curtains billowing in the breeze from the open window.

"Black. Charming," Allison said, moving past Stephen to shut off the music. Her dress brushed Dylan's mouse as she went over to the window. The screen lit up and began a slideshow of pictures featuring a pretty teenage brunette. Most of the photos looked like they were taken from a distance.

Allison stuck her head out the window. "It's a six story drop. Should we be worried?"

"No," Stephen growled, looking at the computer screen, "but he should be."

Stephen realized that dragging one's girlfriend on a tour of every high school in the city wasn't exactly one of *Cosmo's* Steps to a Stronger Relationship, but it couldn't be helped. He had two thoughts in his brain at the time, and they were:

1) Find Dylan

2) Kill Dylan

Everything else was optional. They finally found him in the uppermost branches of an oak tree on the edge of a parking lot. He was staring through the lit second story windows of a blocky brick high school a few blocks from their apartment. Inside, a group of teenage girls laughed together as they decorated the library for Literacy Week.

Stephen left Allison on the ground and clambered up the tree. "You. Are. Dead." Stephen spat at his brother when he reached Dylan's branch.

Under the circumstances, Dylan should have said something like 'please don't kill me' or 'I'm sorry, Stephen.' Stephen was caught off guard when Dylan turned to him in a panic and asked, "You didn't use the door, did you?"

Stephen blinked at him.

"To leave the apartment," Dylan clarified.

"Of course we used the door," Stephen replied. "I couldn't shove Allison out of a sixth story window!"

Dylan moaned and clutched his hair. "Nooo! Now she's going to find us! We have to get out of here!"

Dylan began climbing down. Stephen tried to get him to stop and explain, but it was no use. And anyway it was too late. Dylan froze a few branches from the ground and Stephen passed him. When he dropped to the grass, he saw that Teresa was holding a nail file to Allison's throat as if it were a knife.

"Hey Stephen, look who's here," Allison said uncomfortably, glancing at Teresa.

Teresa stared at the tree like she was expecting Jesus to descend from it.

"Dylan, there you are!" exclaimed Teresa. "I thought I'd lost you!"

Dylan reluctantly climbed the rest of the way down. "Teresa, I told you I--"

"I know, I know," Teresa interrupted. "We can't be together forever. Your brother won't let you turn me. But what if we threatened his girlfriend? Would he let you then?"

Stephen was torn between scorn (*did she really think she could kill someone with a nail file?*) worry (*what if she actually did manage to nick an artery or something?*) and blinding rage (*must... kill... moron... brother!*)

Dylan flashed Stephen the first genuinely apologetic look that had crossed his face since he turned thirteen, and began to count. "One... two..."

On 'three' Dylan and Stephen jumped. The plan was for Dylan to slam into Teresa, knocking her arm away from Allison's neck, and for Stephen to grab Allison and run. It was the same maneuver they'd used to get Dylan's bike back from Roger-the-bully when they were kids.

It worked just as well now as it had then, which was to say not at all.

Stephen stumbled over a rock and skinned his palms on the pavement. Teresa twisted away as Dylan leapt at her, scratching Allison on the neck with the nail file and sending Dylan careening past. He thumped painfully into a sign that said THIS LOT FOR FACULTY PARKING ONLY and landed on his ass.

Stephen was bemoaning the fact that being a vampire didn't give him super coordination to counterbalance his super combustibility when Allison took charge of the situation.

She hit Teresa with a combination elbow to the stomach and knee to the face, and shouted, "Run!"

The three of them fled into the darkness, leaving Teresa screeching after them that Allison was a bitch, and that her eye makeup was ruined.

They couldn't go back to Stephen and Dylan's apartment, so Allison took them to hers. It was there, on her purple couch under the light of a lamp shaped like a giant green light blob, that Dylan's story came out.

As Allison and Stephen taped garbage bags over the windows to ward off the impending daylight, Dylan told them both how his jealousy over Stephen having a girlfriend had led him back to his old habit of stalking teenage girls during their after-school activities. At the high school where Stephen and Allison found him, Dylan had discovered that Teresa the twenty-two-year-old psychology major was actually Teresa the fifteen-year-old high school student. Her divorced father had an apartment in their building. The bag of coffee she brought Stephen had been his.

"She said that destiny had brought her to our apartment that day so she could meet me, but I think she was just trying to land an older boyfriend," Dylan told them.

"Ya think?" Stephen said, thinking back to the way she'd been smiling at him.

"Anyway she has this friend, Stacey, who organizes all these fund raisers and stuff at school. I watched her for a couple days. She was so pretty and nice and stuff that I asked Teresa if she could introduce me, but she um... you know..." Dylan hedged.

"So you slept with her instead," Stephen finished for him.

Dylan folded his arms over his chest. "Well it seemed like a good idea at the time! Sleep with her, drop the v-bomb, wait for her to run screaming away from me."

"Except it didn't work that way, did it?" Allison asked.

"No," Dylan grumbled. "Instead she kept going on about wanting me to turn her into a vampire too so we could be together forever." Dylan shuddered. "As if I would. God, can you imagine putting up with her following me around for eternity? At least a human would drop dead after seventy years or so."

"Not so much fun when the shoe's on the other foot, is it?" Stephen asked.

"I guess not," Dylan admitted, picking at the edge of a polka dotted throw rug with his foot. "I guess this means we have to move again, huh?"

Stephen and Allison exchanged a look. They'd discussed what to do about Dylan over dinner. Stephen hadn't been sure he could go through with their plan, but that was before the Teresa fiasco.

"No, Dylan," Stephen said. "This means *you'll* have to move again. On your own."

Dylan looked up, shocked. "By myself!? But... but... who will look after me? Where will I get blood?"

"You'll have to look after yourself. Get a job, rent an apartment, and buy your blood at the butcher's like everyone else."

"But I'm only seventeen!" Dylan wailed.

"You're thirty-eight," Stephen corrected. "You can't stay young forever, even if you look it. You've got to grow up sometime. Do you *want* to spend your whole life as a creep who hangs around high schools trying to pick up teenagers?"

"No, I want what you found," Dylan admitted, glancing at Allison. "Why do you think I keep telling girls what I am?"

Stephen sighed. "You're a mystery encased in concrete buried at the bottom of a well to me. I never have any idea what you're thinking."

"Yeah, same here."

"But if you want to meet girls who aren't unbalanced, maybe you should try interacting face to face like a normal person."

Dylan nodded, staring at his hands.

Stephen dug some cash and a slip of paper out of his pocket. "Look, here's some money to get started and phone numbers for some decent apartments a couple hours away." He added a plastic card from the telephone company. "And here's a calling card. Check in every now and then, will you?"

"What about Teresa?"

"We can handle her," Allison told him.

Dylan took the items Stephen was offering and pushed them into the pocket of his jeans. He stood up and went over to the door. He turned back to face his brother, his hand on the knob. "Do you think we might understand each other again? Once I come back, I mean?"

Stephen shrugged. "After the month I've just had, I'd guess anything's possible."

The corner of Dylan's mouth twitched, like it was trying to remember how to smile, then he was gone, out the door and off on his own.

"Hallelujah, there's hope for him yet," Allison joked.

"If he can stay away from high schools," Stephen mused. "And remember not to go out in the daytime. And put aside enough money for blood... you know, maybe I should follow him and keep an eye on him. From a distance. Just to make sure he's okay..."

"Now don't *you* start!" Allison laughed.

A few days later, Stephen hid around the corner while Allison knocked on the door to Teresa's apartment. In her hands was a slightly dented brass urn with two handles that had been liberated from the dumpster behind the funeral home. Inside the urn was a pile of ashes. They were from the fireplace in Allison's uncle's office, but the tag on the jar read "Dylan Robertson (aged 17, cause of death: malignant melanoma)."

Teresa's father, a burly blond guy who looked like a cop, answered the door. Teresa hovered behind him trying to see who it was. Allison had dressed in a no-nonsense business suit, put on a long red wig, and changed the shape of her nose with makeup so Teresa wouldn't recognize her.

"If it's Dylan, tell him to come in! I've been looking everywhere for him!" Teresa told her father.

Her father ignored her and turned to Allison. "Can I help you?"

"I'm from MacKinlay's Funeral Home," Allison said to Teresa. "I'm very sorry to inform you that your friend Dylan passed away a few days ago and was cremated in a private ceremony. His brother asked that I bring him by so you could say your farewells, since you were kind enough to be Dylan's girlfriend despite all of his problems."

Allison held the urn out.

Neither Teresa nor her father moved.

"Problems?" Teresa asked.

"Girlfriend?" Teresa's father asked, giving his daughter the Eye of Disapproval.

"Yes, you see Dylan suffered from Xeroderma Pigmentosum, a condition that made it impossible for his skin to tolerate sunlight. He was very pale and struggled with skin cancers all his life, which led him to take refuge in the fantasy of being a vampire. Your daughter was kind enough to play along," Allison explained to Teresa's father.

"He... oh my God...." Teresa sputtered as she put the pieces together.

Allison squeezed Teresa's arm. "On his death bed, he said the night he spent with you was the best of his life."

At this Teresa's father turned purple with rage. He glared down at his mortified daughter. "Inside. Now." He said through gritted teeth, and shut the door in Allison's face.

"You are grounded for ever, missy!" Allison heard Teresa's father thunder as she walked away. There were some high pitched sounds of protest from Teresa, then an interior door slammed.

A second later, strains of self-pitying teen pop music drifted through the wall.

Allison exchanged a look with Stephen, who was leaning against the wall waiting for her, and they both burst out laughing.

Katrina Nicholson is a writer/reviewer/library clerk from Nova Scotia, Canada. She is the author of two short comedy films - iBrain *and* Double Crossed *- and 12 short stories, which you can find in the anthologies* Futuredaze, Tesseracts Fifteen, Future Embodied, *and* Kisses by Clockwork, *the Speculative Elements series, and* Carousel *magazine. Visit her website at www.katrinanicholson.com to read more spoofs, articles, and movie reviews.*

BEEHIVES OF THE DEAD

By Elizabeth Allen

I'd always held as fact that some people look better dead than alive.

Take Lorraine Duchamp, for instance. I knew her most of her adult life and she always was a homely little gal—bony arms and legs, no makeup, skin prone to rashes and her hair…well, she dealt with it herself, and it showed. Stringy and oily on top, dry as hay on the bottom. She'd come into the salon to let Maryann do her nails, but she never did let me work my magic whilst she was among the living.

As fate would have it, the morning after her 49th birthday party, I got my chance. Lorraine got zapped by a brain aneurysm, one of those out-of-left-field kinds of things. She just woke up, poured herself some Minute Maid and *bang,* keeled over onto her kitchen linoleum. She was at the hospital only long enough for them to declare her dead, and then it was off to Petty's Funeral Home. When Mr. Petty and his crew finished with the embalming, they called me.

Now, most days I cut hair at the Snip n' Polish, but when Petty's gets a customer who still has enough hair (or head) to bother with, they bring me over to bestow a final bit of grooming. The men are easy, on the whole: just a quick wash and brush through, maybe a clip here or there. The old ones tend to get a bit shaggy in their final days.

The women are different, of course. There's more work involved, but I don't mind. And when they're like little Miss Lorraine, constantly turning up her nose at the strides beauty has made over the last few decades, I consider the postmortem styling a personal mission.

When I got to Petty's, I washed Lorraine's hair and used the extra-silky conditioner. I snipped the ends off so's they were blunt and gave her the hint of bangs she so desperately needed. Then I gave her a blow-out, flipping up the ends (so cute!). And—because I am fully trained in the beauty arts—I did her makeup. A rosy cheek and bronzed lids, a bit of Crystal Mauve on the lips. I swear to you I'd never seen her look that good.

In fact, every one of my Petty's clients got some kind of makeover. Lots of the old ladies in town—Midge Johnson, Arleen Shackleford, Patricia Pringle—were Snip n' Polish regulars and they were good tippers, so I always gave them exactly what they asked for. Midge insisted that her hair be dyed the same damn clown shade, Red No. 6, "Paprika Fantasy," and coiled up with a tight perm, even when that kind of thing went way out of fashion. Patricia and Arleen demanded their big ol' layer cakes of silver-gray, teased in with extra hair pieces and pasted with half a can of hairspray over the whole shebang. And on special occasions, when I did their makeup, none of them wanted anything but light blue eye makeup and pastel pink lipstick. I delivered.

But when they died, I finally had my own way, and damn, it felt good. The late Midge got a cute little Shirley MacLaine crop cut (thank the good Lord the red had faded a bit the week she died). Patricia and Arleen got the beehives buzzed down to a modest white fluff, sorta like Dorothy Zbornak on *The Golden Girls*. Nobody who attended their funerals seemed to mind. Just the opposite— everybody told me they looked better than ever. I felt pretty good about sending each and every one of them off to the He is Risen Cemetery in style.

Then there was Miz Hightower.

Lilly Hightower was one of the richest ladies in town, and she'd been dealt a pretty good hand when it came to hair. Hers was thick with only a slight wave, and she wore it shoulder-length. She'd been a honey blonde all her life. When the gray came, instead of taking over, it just kind of blended right in.

She used to make the hour and a half drive to a salon in Raleigh, but then her husband died, her eyes faltered, and her long car trips became less and less frequent. She started coming to the Snip n' Polish instead. Maryann would lacquer up Miz Hightower's nails with the old lady's favorite shade (a trashy metallic lavender), then send her over to my chair for a shampoo, trim and style. I'd do it up nice, part it on the left and sweep it over the right side. I thought she looked like the old film star, Lauren Bacall—getting on in years, but classy (never mind the purple nails).

Each time I did her hair, she always tipped me exactly two dollars, no matter how much time or attention I'd spent on her. Then—and this beat all—I'd see her out the window of the salon walking to her car. She'd come to a dead stop in the parking lot, take those lavender claws and rake all the hair on her head the opposite way, making the part on the right and bringing it down the left side. It went against the natural lay of her hair, and it hiked up on her scalp. It looked strange, like she'd just got up from bed. But I caught her doing it after each visit. She never said anything when she was in the chair, and neither did I.

"I wouldn't cross her if I was you," Maryann said after Miz Hightower's third visit to the shop.

"I'm not crossing her," I said, grabbing the broom to sweep up the little bits of gray-blonde that had blown off Miz Hightower's shoulders onto the floor. "As a professional stylist who trained under Mr. LeRoi of Chapel Hill, I fix it the way I think it looks best. What she does with it later is her business."

"You can see she likes it parted on the right."

"It looks stupid. You know, I did that for too long—let these old ladies come in my shop and make me do their hair in ways that would make Mr. LeRoi shit in his salon smock. Well, I'm not doing it anymore. If you come to a professional stylist, you should get a professional style. If you want your hair some godawful way, you should just do it yourself."

"Haven't you heard? The customer is always right, even when she's so wrong you want to slap the lipstick off her mouth." Maryann shrugged. "I'm just surprised Miz Hightower doesn't say something to you. She's mighty closed-mouth for somebody so rich. I thought she'd be a bit pushier, but she's a sweetie."

"Hell, she ain't that rich. Just rich for a one-horse, shithole town like this."

Maryann readjusted the bottles of polish in front of her. "You see all those rings she wears?"

"Yeah, there's a couple of good ones."

"The best is the gold signet on her middle finger, right hand. I asked her about it, and she said it was special, got a picture of an

Egyptian god or something. She said her husband got it for her in Cairo years ago. How about that?"

I leaned over with the broom to chase a little tumbleweed of hair into the dustpan. "I like the big fat diamond wedding ring better."

The following winter brought a rare ice storm to eastern North Carolina. Miz Hightower, bad eyes and all, was driving to Raleigh for the day. On the way up, she got involved in a 24-car pileup on I-40. Her big old Mercedes sedan was squashed into a two-door coupe and she died, along with four other luckless souls, on that slick highway.

Petty's called at 10 the next morning, and before noon, I was staring down at the old woman's face. Her nose had been broken, so Mr. Petty had rebuilt it some, and she had a nasty gash over her right eye and another cut on her chin. I went heavy on the foundation and didn't skimp on the bronze eye shadow and Crystal Mauve lipstick. I wasted no time in parting her hair on the left and sweeping it over to the right. Even if it didn't look better—which it did—I had to cover the gash over her right eye. When I was finished, I gathered up my makeup and hair styling supplies and headed for the restroom. Mr. Petty was in the hall outside the ladies' room door.

"Hello, dear," he said and gave me that little half-smile of his. Mr. Petty always maintained his even keel. His expression never rose all the way to happy, never sunk all the way to sad. He just looked like he was concentrating real hard, like he was trying to keep a string of numbers in his head and he had to remember the right order.

"Hey, Mr. Petty," I said. "I just finished up with Miz Hightower."

"That's fine, dear. She was a lovely lady."

"Well, I think I did her justice." I grinned at him, and he gave me another half-smile and continued down the hall.

After the restroom, I wanted to take one more look at my handiwork on Miz Hightower. I ducked back into the prep area. There was an aqua brocade dress hanging on a hook on the far side of the room. Somebody'd deck her out in that now that her hair and makeup was done. She'd be looking mighty fine, considering the accident had made hash of her insides. The makeup did look stunning, but I'd thought I'd covered that cut and the hair...

_____

The hair was parted on the right.

What in the name of June Carter Cash? I looked around the room. Somebody here must have messed with it. True, there was no one near the body, but I could hear the sound of running water and a couple of the technicians talking in the other room. I whipped out my comb, leaned over the prep table and readjusted my styling with the part on the left and over the gash. Then I poked my head into the second room.

"Hey y'all, don't mess with the hair on Miz Hightower."

"We didn't touch her," the heavy-set technician said without cracking a smile. "Been in here the whole time."

"Just…don't. OK?"

"Trust us, sugar," the skinny, older technician said. "We don't touch any of these stiffs any more than we have to."

I went back to Miz Hightower to gather my stuff. Again. The part was on the right.

My stomach did a loop-de-loop. I looked around for Mr. Petty, but didn't see him anywhere. My eyes went to the old woman's arms, laid gently on either side of her. They looked no different than they had five minutes ago. I noticed all the rings on her hands, the ones Maryann had been so impressed with. The diamond ring was at least two carats, but there wasn't much shine to it. I guess Mr. Petty didn't clean the jewelry on the deceased. But the gold signet ring gleamed like a foil caramel wrapper, brighter and brighter, it seemed, the longer I looked at it.

I adjusted Miz Hightower's hair again, and watched for full-out five minutes. Nothing moved. I had other clients—breathing clients—to get to that day, so I gathered my stuff again and left the room. I waited ten seconds outside the door then poked my head back in real quick, but everything was still. I thought maybe I'd been working too hard.

Visiting hours at Petty's started at 4 p.m. the next day. Sure enough, the part was back on the right. It wasn't like I could touch her hair with all her relatives there, so I just sat in one of those wood folding chairs, staring. The makeup looked bumpy on the top of the gash and her hair was piled up like a wave getting ready to break onshore. Of course, nobody complimented me on the job I'd done on Miz Hightower. Mr. Petty stared at me and didn't even give me the half-smile.

The next day was the funeral and they'd be closing the casket after everybody left the viewing that evening, so I stuck around. As Mr. Petty ushered Mr. Hightower and Lilly's three adult children out the front door, I approached the coffin. Staring at that piled-up mess of hair for three hours straight had made me testy.

"*Look, you bitch*," I hissed. "You let it lie. You may be going to heaven or you may be going to hell, but you're going with the part on the freakin' *left*. You hear me?" I styled the hair one last time, then stood watch until Mr. Petty and the fat technician closed the casket lid. Only then did I go home.

I didn't attend the funeral the next day. The casket was permanently sealed, so what was point? Maryann went. She said the funeral at the First Baptist Church had been sad and well-attended, and that Miz Hightower had been laid to rest without incident in the He is Risen Cemetery just three blocks away on Juniper Street.

Two nights later I was at the salon late. I had a mother and daughter in for 8 p.m. appointments, and it was past 10 by the time they left. I closed up the shop and walked out to my car. True to the unpredictable winter we'd been having, the ice storm had been followed up by a spell of dry and unseasonably warm weather. There was a light breeze moving through town, and all in all, it was pretty pleasant. I swung into the driver's seat of my Corolla. The stench of rotting meat and formaldehyde hit me like a baseball bat.

There was Miz Hightower, all set to ride shotgun, wearing the aqua brocade dress they buried her in. The rings were still on her fingers; the gold signet was shining like a flashlight.

"In," she croaked.

I gaped at her. I tried to open my car door and bolt, but her arm shot out, gray and covered in dirty, loose skin, to hold me back.

"In," she said again, the sound still disturbingly deep, but coming a bit easier. "Go back in. We're coming."

This time she let me get out of the car. I turned to run up the street, but I was met by a wall of women—dead women—headed for the Snip n' Polish. They swept me along in front of them. Miz Hightower got of the Corolla and led our little party into the back door of the salon.

What could I do? I unlocked the salon door, and let everybody in. Miz Hightower shambled to a seat on the side of the room and grabbed an *US Weekly* from the magazine rack. "Lorraine," she said in her bullfrog voice. "Fix her."

Lorraine? My god, if wasn't Lorraine Duchamp. Still bony…well shit, she was pretty much a skeleton. A bit of flesh hung here and there on her, a bit of mossy green stuff clinging to her collarbone.

I tried to talk. "Well, Lorraine…I haven't…I can't…"

"Fix," she whined, bringing a bony arm up to her skull. The new hairstyle had stayed, more or less. The bangs had grown out, sure, but it still was—

"Fix!" she shrieked at me. "Like I like it! LIKE I LIKE IT!" She beat her arms up and down on the styling chair's armrest, showering little bits of dirt and grass on the floor.

Well, now, any stylist will tell you, you can't undo bangs. As Mr. LeRoi so often said, once you cross that particular Rubicon, you just have to wait 'til they grow out. But it didn't look like Lorraine was in the mood for any of that talk, so I combed all the hair she had straight down and pushed the bangs over. I would have tucked them behind her ear, if she had much of one, but I just kind of pushed into a hole in her skull. It was a gesture, that was all, but it seemed to appease her. She rose to her feet, and took a seat beside Miz Hightower.

"Midge," the old woman said in a kind of burp.

Midge came forward, clattering on a pair of heels way too high for a woman of advanced age. Except for Miz Hightower, she had been the most recent death. In truth, she was the hardest to look at. There were still strips of dark grey flesh attached to her, on her torso, arms and legs and in patches of her skull. When she took a seat, her back end made a sickly squishing sound in the chair and her limbs left a putrid residue on the armrests. The hair was still intact on her head, and as I suspected, she did not care to have it styled like Miss Shirley MacLaine for eternity.

"Red," Midge seethed. "Get the red. Curl it up."

"Yes, ma'am." I mixed up the Paprika Fantasy and got the perming solution out. It took a while to do Midge up the way she liked, but the ladies waited patiently. Miz Hightower had finished with the *US Weekly* and was thumbing through a *People* magazine. The others were as still as stones, heads bowed. I guess they were too long in the grave and had lost interest in whether this or that actress was cheated on by her husband and a tattooed porn star while she was in rehab and pregnant with triplets.

When I'd finished with Midge, it came as no surprise to see Arleen Shackleford and Patricia Pringle back to reclaim their beehives. I dug around in some drawers and found the gray hairpieces I needed, broke out the bobby pins and grabbed two cans of extra-strong hairspray from the back cupboard. Their hair had grown some, so it was just a matter of pinning the extra hairpieces in, teasing the whole mess up, and pasting it with the spray. It was nearing 2 a.m. when I finished; each skeletal lady had gained nine inches of height. They no longer bowed their heads but took their places on the seats around the salon, proud as princesses.

Now all of the dead looked at their queen, at Miz Hightower. She laid aside the *National Enquirer* she was reading, and rose. She approached the chair, but instead of taking a seat right away, she jabbed a gray, waxy hand at me and the gold signet on the middle finger flashed like a little bit of lightning, right there in the Snip n' Polish.

"By the power of Osiris, the great Egyptian deity, god of the afterlife, lord of the underworld, I command you, fix me!"

"OK, Miz Hightower, OK. Just have a seat and—"

"Silence! Fix me, and no more perpetrate your will in opposition to that of the living or the dead!"

"But, Miz Hightower—"

"Swear this, or be struck down."

I guess you could say I was not in a position to argue. I agreed, and the old woman took her seat. This was an easy fix, but the most painful of the bunch. I took the hair, parted it on the right and scooped it up over her scalp onto the left side. It still looked stupid.

As I looked at her in the styling mirror, I noticed the bronze eye shadow, the cheek color and the Crystal Mauve lipstick I'd applied at Petty's were still hanging tough. "You want me to take the makeup off, Miz Hightower?"

"No," she said and the waxy mask of her face seemed to soften a bit. "No, I like it." She slid off the chair and stood. All the other ladies got to their feet too. Miz Hightower dug a gray hand into the side pocket of her aqua brocade and pulled out two crumpled dollar bills. "For your trouble," she said, handing them to me.

I took the money, and watched the ladies leave the salon by the back way, still shedding little bits of dirt and grass. When I was sure they had left the building, I ran to the back door and watched them head back to Juniper Street in a solemn, single-file procession. They were almost out of sight when a figure emerged from behind a tree not far from the group's path. Whoever it was carried a shovel and followed the women, I'm sure, back to the cemetery to cover them up once more.

I was too tired to leave the salon and too perturbed to sleep. I took some Barbicide disinfectant and wiped down the styling chair and all the seating around the salon. I swept up the dirt and grass bits that were spread around the floor. I found some clean linen scent air freshener and sprayed a whole can's worth around the salon, trying to get rid of the stench of the visitors. When I was convinced things were almost normal, I took a seat.

I woke to a bright salon and Maryann nudging me. "Did you stay here all night?" she murmured.

I stared at her stupidly for a moment. "Yeah, I…I was just real tired."

"I know, me too," Maryann said from her nail table. Her hair was still wet from her morning shower. She set a travel coffee mug down and pulled on her pink Snip n' Polish smock.

"That coffee looks good. I need some of that." I went to the salon's back room to get my purse, and that's when I saw the shovel. It was leaning up in one of the corners of the room, caked with dirt at its tip. I poked my head out of the room. "Where did this shovel come from?"

"I borrowed it from Dave Shackleford. He said he'd come by to get it sometime this afternoon."

"And what were you doing with it?"

Maryann took a sip of her coffee and looked at me. "You know what I was doing with it. You shouldn't have crossed her. You shouldn't have crossed any of them."

"How did you—"

"It's that ring. The gold ring. That's some bad mojo right there. She told me about it when I did her nails. And after she died, well, she came to me. I mean, freakin' came into my house, at night! She said the ring let her rise from the grave any time she wanted to, but she couldn't, you know, cover herself back up when returned. She said she needed my help."

"So y'all thought you'd teach me a lesson."

"She didn't really give me a choice," Maryann said.

"Jesus crackers. 'Member how meek she was when she was

alive? She's a stone-cold bitch now."

"I know. And I ain't gonna cross her."

"Well, I don't suppose I will either," I said. "Do you know what she made me promise? Any damn thing anybody wants in here—half-shaved heads, green hair, beehives, anything!—I have to do. 'Cause if I don't, that old woman'll come back and mess me up good."

"Do you think I wanted to do that purple polish on her when she was alive? I know it's trashy. But you know, the customer is always right, so…"

"Might as well change our name to the 'Bow n' Scrape.'"

In the end, we did change the name of the salon. It's now Osiris's. Doesn't exactly roll off the tongue, but it seemed appropriate, given the circumstances. Every customer who comes in gets exactly what she wants, whether it's hair or nails, whether she's old and set in her ways or young and full of bad choices, black or white, rich or poor, ornery or nice.

She might be living or she might be dead, but she will always, *always,* be right.

Elizabeth (Betsy) Allen is a writer with 30 years of experience in professional communications. She has toiled in a variety of modestly compensated, reasonably interesting jobs—magazine copy editor, PR manager, corporate communications specialist, freelance journalist and editor—but frankly, none of those things is as much fun as fiction writing.

Allen holds a bachelor's degree in journalism from The Ohio State University and a master's degree in English from George Mason University in Fairfax, Virginia. In fall 2014, she began her MFA program in fiction writing at George Mason. She currently favors the short story format, but also is revising her first novel, The Sons of Necessity. *In addition, she is the co-author of a graphic novel trilogy (*The End of Gath*) with her brother, Ben Small.*

At home in Alexandria, Virginia, Allen lives with her husband and two disobedient but (lucky for them) adorable dogs. She is a member of Pennwriters and the Round Hill Writers Group, and in her spare time, frets about her two grown children and her grandson. If you'd like, find her on Facebook, follow her on Twitter (@WriterMuse) or write her at ballenbrs@aol.com.

———

THE OTHER HALF

A. Steven Clark

When Fred Staines walked into my office and I saw what shape he was in, I nearly choked on the raspberry jelly donut I'd been nibbling on.

He smiled at me, that wide, toothy hillbilly grin of his that I hadn't seen in years, then he burbled, "Gus!" as a flood of brown bile came spilling out of his mouth, pushing between the gaps in his teeth. Shortly thereafter, as he crossed toward me, I noticed his left leg dragging across the floor, as it if were attached to his torso by a few loose threads.

"Evening, Fred," I said. "Looks like you're having a problem with your leg there?"

"Shoot, Gus, that ain't even the worst of it." He paused, touched his chin a moment, then asked, "Would you prefer I call you Dr. Shumacher?" More bile gushed out as he said my name.

"Most people just call me 'Doc' these days," I told him.

He snickered and said, "Hard for me to imagine you as a doctor. I remember when we went fishin' together as kids. You was squeamish about cleanin' your own fish, so I had to do it for you. Now look at you… all growed up and doin' surgeries on people."

"I'm not a surgeon, Fred—just a general practitioner," I corrected him.

"Well, whatever kinda doc you are, I 'preciate you seein' me at night like this," he said. "By tomorrow I mighta been a real mess."

"We have regular evening hours at this clinic. I'm not doing you any special favors in that regard. Now, you want to go ahead and climb up on the table and I'll take a look at you." I patted the examination table, which I'd already covered with three extra layers of paper. Based on the symptoms my old friend had shared with me over the phone, I was certain I already knew his diagnosis—and there was no mistaking the external signs really—but as a rule I never reached my final conclusion till after completing the full exam.

As Fred climbed up onto the table, his left leg fell out of his pant leg and flopped onto the floor. Glancing downward, I wrinkled my nose at the thing as it lay there, oozing brown goo and pink pus all over the white-tiled floor. The detached leg twitched a couple times, then became still.

"Gosh darnit!" Fred snapped. "I had that sucker duct-taped on real good, too! Sorry about the mess, Gus. I mean Doc."

Doing my best to ignore the rancid piece of meat that now graced my office floor, I began my examination. After donning a pair of latex gloves, I took up my otoscope and pressed the speculum into Fred's left ear. Deep inside the ear I could see maggot larvae—not a good sign at all. As I pulled the otoscope away, the outer part of Fred's ear came loose, tumbled down the side of his body and plopped onto the exam table a couple inches to his left.

Fred looked down at it and grimaced. "Shoot! That happened this mornin' when I was cleanin' it out with a Q-tip. I used some Krazy Glue to put it back on, but I think the tube mighta been expired."

"I'm sure a fresh tube would do the trick," I said as I watched Fred pick up the ear and stuff it into his shirt pocket.

With my instrument I detected a number of unsavory things growing in his right ear. In addition to maggot larvae, there were at least two different varieties of fungus and an odd fleshy growth that resembled a miniature Eiffel Tower—not to mention a tuft of bristly, wax-covered hair that stuck out of the ear like weeds poking through a sidewalk crack (my guess was the hair tuft had been there for some time and was unrelated to his current diagnosis).

After making a few notes, I used the otoscope to look into Fred's nostrils (which, in all honesty, was a part of the exam I'd been dreading). But aside from the fact that his mucus was the color and general consistency of chocolate pudding, everything looked normal enough inside my friend's nasal passages.

"Do you think it's The Virus, Doc?" Fred asked me bluntly.

"I can't answer that yet. I've not finished the examination."

"You know, Doc, the insurance company won't cover me if it is The Virus."

"I know, Fred. None of them are covering it. They found some legal loophole."

"Maybe if you could come up with another diagnosis—any other diagnosis—they might be willin' to pay something."

"I won't charge you for my exam, since we're old friends," I told him. "As for the rest… well, we'll have to wait and see."

Setting the otoscope aside, I took a tongue depressor from the jar and unwrapped it.

"Say ahhhh."

When Fred said "ahhhh" a fresh flood of bile came pouring out of his throat and down the front of his already-stained bib overalls. The stench produced by the bile struck me like a violent slap to the face; it smelled to me like roadkill roasting in a vat of battery acid. A man with a weaker stomach would have certainly lost his last meal within seconds; to me, the stench was merely an unpleasant inconvenience.

After the last of the bile had dribbled down Fred's chin, I was able to see clearly into the back of his throat. There I spotted a number of small perforations, little dime-sized holes—as if flesh-eating mites had infested his digestive tract. The holes were a tell-tale sign. If I'd had any doubts about his diagnosis to begin with (which I hadn't really) they were completely gone now. Still, more out of habit than anything, I decided to finish the exam before delivering my final verdict.

"You gonna have to check the opposite end now?" Fred asked as soon as I drew the tongue depressor away from his mouth.

I cocked an eyebrow at him. "Opposite end?"

"You know . . ." He pointed toward his backside.

I shook my head quickly and emphatically. "No, Fred, that won't be necessary."

He blinked at me, mildly surprised. "You sure, Doc? I saw something crawl out of there this mornin'—"

"I really don't need to hear those kinds of details—"

"But, Doc, I think there might be a family of mice livin' up there."

"Please, Fred—"

"Although they could be voles. Most people've never heard of voles. You know what a vole is, Doc?"

"Yes, Fred, I've heard of voles."

"Well, I think I might have a family of them livin' up my hiney."

"Fred, stop!" I said, raising my voice without quite shouting.

"I won't be looking up your hiney today! It's not necessary." I paused, taking a moment to gather myself; then, lowering my voice, I added, "I just need to check one more thing and then I'll give you my diagnosis."

"Don't you need to draw blood, Doc?"

"No. That won't be necessary, either."

"My blood ain't red no more. Now it's all brown and grimy." Fred paused and made a chortling sound before he went on. "I used to call myself a red-blooded American male. Guess I cain't do that no more. Not unless you can fix me up, Doc."

"Fred . . ." I looked him in the eyes and sighed. "You know there's no cure, right?"

"I know," he replied in a small, deflated voice. "But you ain't told me yet if I got The Virus or if it might be something else."

Swallowing a lump in my throat, I put on my stethoscope and pressed the chest piece up against his shirt.

I didn't need to listen for long.

The fact was, I didn't really even need a stethoscope. I could hear a human heartbeat from two hundred feet away. I had always liked stethoscopes, what they represented... the symbolism. The instrument reminded me of Dr. Grayson, my doctor as a child and the man who'd initially inspired me to pursue a career in medicine. He was the reason I liked to wear a white lab coat in my office; he was the reason I used a stethoscope even though I had no need for one; and Dr. Grayson was the one who'd inspired me to carry along a vintage black medical bag when I made my house calls at night. Somehow, the trappings—the coat, the stethoscope, the medical bag—made me feel like a real healer.

After listening to his chest for a few moments, I cleared my throat softly. "I don't know how to say this, Fred..."

"You don't hear it?"

I shook my head. "I don't hear a thing."

He licked his lips nervously. "Nothing? No faint little thumpedy-thump at all?"

I sighed. This was the part of being a physician I disliked: the part where I had to share bad news with my patients. "No thumped-thump, Fred," I told him. "Nothing. Just... silence. Like an empty oil drum."

Fred's disappointment showed all over his maggot-ridden face. His shoulders slumped forward and after a few seconds he said,

"Well, I knew it. I was hopin' it wasn't true, but deep down I already knew it."

"I really am sorry, Fred. Really I am."

"You don't have anything to be sorry about, Gus. I mean, Doc. It ain't your fault. You didn't create The Virus. It ain't your fault half the folks in town are turning into zombies."

"No, Fred, what I mean is . . . I'm sorry I didn't get to you sooner."

"Get to me sooner?" Fred wrinkled his eyebrows in puzzlement. "But I just called you and told you about my symptoms earlier this evenin'. You didn't know I had The Virus, so how could you have—?"

"I haven't seen you in a while, Fred," I interrupted him. "Honestly, you sort of fell off my radar. You're not even my friend on Mugbook."

"I know we've fallen out of touch, Gus. But what's that got to with my situation now?"

I sighed again. "Fred, have you wondered why half the people in town have been affected by The Virus and the other half haven't?"

He shrugged. "I figured they must have it, too, or something like it. Heck, those folks sleep all day, seems like. And they all look so pale, like they could all use a coupla days in one of Jamaica Jack's tanning beds. They must have some kind of zombie disease, too . . . maybe another strain of it."

"It's not a zombie disease, Fred. Those people—the other half—will never be affected by The Virus. Only human beings can become zombies... the medical community now knows that with certainty."

"But they are human..."

Fred's voice trailed off when he saw me shaking my head. "No, they're not humans," I said. "Not anymore. There's something you don't understand, Fred ..."

My old friend listened intently as I explained to him that I'd been a very busy doctor lately; that every night, for the past couple of weeks, I'd been travelling from house to house, treating as many people as I could.

"I began with those closest to me and then went on to more distant acquaintances," I told him. "That's why I apologized to you. If you hadn't slipped my mind, I would have come to see you as well."

Fred lowered his eyes as what I was telling him finally began to sink in. After a few moments, he glared up at me and, in a voice thick with bitterness, said, "You have a vaccination and you didn't let me in on it? That really hurts, Gus. It really does. I thought you and me was friends from way back."

I had already apologized to him; at this point there was little more I could do to ease the sting. I watched as a sullen Fred Staines—or what was left of the man who was once known as Fred Staines—slid down off the exam table and hopped on one leg over to where his other leg lay.

Bending over and picking up the leg, he slung it over his shoulder like the handle of an axe, then hopped on over to my office door.

Fred jerked the door open and, pausing there in the doorway, pivoted back toward me.

"Go to hell, Gus," he said, leaking more bile through his teeth. While delivering his insult Fred attempted an obscene gesture—the Italian one where one arm is raised while the other is brought down against the bicep. Because of the leg he was holding, the gesture didn't come off exactly as he'd planned. When he tried it his left hand flew off the end of his wrist and sailed across my office, landing just a few inches short of the wastebasket on the opposite side of the room.

He coughed—a phony-sounding cough that was meant to distract. Then he said, "Er, Gus... would you be so kind as to toss me my hand?"

With some reluctance (since I'd already peeled off the latex gloves), I picked up the hand from where it had landed and carried it over to him. He took the hand and shoved it into the front pocket of his bib overalls and it sat in there with the fingers poking out at the top, as if the detached hand were waving goodbye.

"As I was sayin'... go to Hell, Gus," he repeated, spewing bile in more ways than one. Then, turning abruptly, he hopped through the open doorway and slammed the door shut behind him. A moment later, I heard something plop onto the floor right outside my office door (I was pretty sure Fred had used too much force to yank the door shut and in doing so had pulled his arm out of the socket). I heard him mutter a curse word, presumably as he was picking his arm up off the floor, then I heard him proceed—*hop, hop, hop*—

down the long hallway.

I stood for a long moment staring at the door, shaking my head slowly from side to side. I felt truly sorry for my old friend. He had a right to curse me. If I hadn't forgotten about him I could have saved him, like I'd saved so many others.

Like I'd save the other half of the town's citizens.

The half that now sleeps all day and only comes outside after sunset.

The half that will live on, that will populate the town, long after Fred and his kind have turned into globs of brown jelly on the street.

The half that are now my kind.

Heaving a sigh, I reached for my medical bag... and for just that moment, I saw Dr. Grayson standing there in my office, a foot or two behind my examination table. I began to smile at him, but the image—which had clearly been conjured up by my imagination—quickly vanished. I knew I had no choice but to go on. Were he actually here, Dr. Grayson would have encouraged me to continue making my rounds. Despite the weariness I felt deep in my bones, there was more work to be done. I still hadn't covered the outskirts of town, the farthest populated areas. By all accounts, The Virus hadn't reached those areas yet. The people who lived in those parts were the sort who rarely came into town, and that's why they hadn't yet been exposed.

But the walking dead—those without heartbeats, who limped and hopped and dragged themselves from house to house seeking to spread The Virus—were beginning to make their way into the woods at the edge of the town limits. Soon, I had no doubt, The Virus would reach those far-flung residences, those less sociable citizens who still, as of this date, clung to their humanity. Soon, I had no doubt, The Virus would blanket the entire region, infecting and eventually killing everyone in its path.

Unless I could get to them first.

Opening my medical bag, I took out my metal file and, working with my usual careful precision, began to sharpen my lateral incisors.

Began to sharpen them in preparation for another round of house calls.

Another long, bone-wearying night of house call after house call...

As the town's oldest doctor, and the only physician in the area not infected by The Virus, I consider it my professional obligation.

I am certain that Dr. Grayson, were he still alive, would do the same.

A. Steven Clark writes in the sci-fi, horror and Western genres. He has published numerous short stories and articles in various anthologies and periodicals. His first novel, The Guerrilla Man, *was nominated as Best First Novel in 2012 by the Western Fictioneers. Clark, who formerly worked as a radio disc jockey, teaches economics and performs as a professional storyteller and children's musician. Songs from his* Parents' Choice *Award-winning children's CD have aired on dozens of radio stations across the U.S. and overseas, including appearances on two nationally syndicated programs. He lives with his wife in St. Charles, Missouri.*

DEAD TO WRITE

By Chantal Boudreau

Andrew Teller stared in frustration at the latest rejection letter. He could have wallpapered his office with them, but he was not alone. He had seen pictures on the Internet from other writers who had done exactly that. He crumpled the paper into a ball and tossed it across the room with a heavy sigh.

He could not figure out what he was doing wrong. Everything he had accomplished up to this point suggested that his work had some serious potential. He had done well in several writing competitions. He had placed second in a couple of lesser contests, ones set up by local venues, and he had even had been awarded honourable mention status in larger, more prestigious affairs. He had sold multiple short stories and articles to magazines, journals and anthologies. His test-readers loved him, but that was as far as his success went. He had tried desperately to secure an agent for his three completed novels, that were all sure to be bestsellers, or a smaller publisher that would allow him to skip the agent altogether. So far, it was no go.

It would have been much simpler for Andrew had there been something specific he could have latched onto that required improvement. He was open to criticism, and ready to improve in whatever way his critics deemed necessary, even if it meant they would eat him alive. The problem was that the criticism often opposed itself, sending him in two completely contrasting directions at the same time. Like this last one – this letter complained that his manuscript was too sparse in its description. He had gotten back a separate rejection letter for the same version of that manuscript from a different source claiming it was too verbose and overly descriptive.

He just couldn't win.

Andrew laughed quietly, a sad laugh of defeat, and allowed his shoulders to sag.

If only, he thought, he could write like his idol, Sherralyn Lewis. He stared at the many copies of her bestsellers sitting atop his shelf. She'd had more success than Andrew could possibly dream of, and even the harshest of reviewers seemed to like her. One of his writer friends had suggested that Andrew mimic her style until he was well-established and could return to his own ways of doing things. Andrew had tried that, but he hadn't been able to make it work for him. The stories he had written this way had come across as bad Lewis knock-offs and would never offer him entrance past the gatekeepers. No, he had to find another way in.

Steeling himself for the next rejection, Andrew reached for the following envelope on the pile. That was when his computer chimed to let him know that a new e-mail had arrived. He sighed again. No doubt yet another rejection, an electronic one this time.

But it wasn't a rejection; in fact, it was possibly the big break he had been waiting for. It was an e-mail from the goddess of fiction herself, Sherralyn Lewis. On a whim one day, a desperate ploy, Andrew had sent her the manuscript of his latest novel, a well-researched thriller based on voodoo practices involved in raising the dead and creating zombie slaves. He had praised her work and begged her for some pointers, something that might help him get published. He wasn't sure why he had bothered. She was a very busy woman, and was not getting any younger - too busy, he had assumed, to spend time helping him. He had been wrong. Something about his correspondence had appealed to her. She *had* read his manuscript. She would be making an appearance at a local bookstore for a reading and a book signing, and then she would drop in to see him, to discuss it.

All of this was to be hush-hush and confidential for the moment, she had told him. She didn't want outsiders knowing she would be there, since her presence had been known to draw an unruly crowd. She intended on keeping things quiet on her end as well. Her agent had complained that she wasted too much of her time taking on "pet projects and charity cases." She enjoyed mentoring new authors, she wrote. It kept her feeling young.

Andrew read the e-mail several times over before believing it. Sherralyn Lewis was going to come to his house – his house! She was willing to mentor him!

Andrew whooped and shoved the remainder of the unopened envelopes aside. This news was incredible. It was truly his lucky day. He wasn't sure what he had done to deserve this, but perhaps karma was finally working in his favour.

Drawing in a deep breath, Andrew glanced frantically around him. He would have to make sure the house was spotless, bring in her favourite foods and drink, and whatever else it would take to make her comfortable. He also worried a little about the fact that she would be coming to him. He didn't live in the best part of town. His unsatisfying day job didn't make him much money and with his writing, he was lucky to land a sale every now and then that paid him anything beyond a contributor copy, at least with his shorter works. He afforded what he could, a squalid little townhouse in need of some serious renovations.

Andrew decided he couldn't worry about that now. He had to focus on what kind of impression he could make on Sherralyn, and not fret over things he couldn't control for the moment. He would gather together his research catalogue, his reference material and even samples of the various components used by the villain in his book in the creation of a zombie. He would show her he meant serious business, not taking the endeavour of being a writer lightly.

He spent the week that followed in hasty preparation, ready to expose everything he had to offer to his favourite author. It was a dream come true, and his obsession with having everything just right for her actually managed to counter his usual drive to write in ridiculously prolific quantities. Andrew's mentor-to-be would merit perfection.

Early afternoon of the day in question arrived and Andrew fumbled around his home, sweaty and on the brink of hyperventilating. When the doorbell finally rang, it almost made him jump out of his skin. He let his gaze drift across his living room. It looked like the lair of a voodoo witch doctor, or at least one expecting guests. He hoped Sherralyn would appreciate the ambiance.

When he opened the door he was surprised to find the woman to be much older and frailer looking than he was expecting. She was resting against the door frame, hunched over and short of breath. Her skin was pale and clammy.

"M-Ms. Lewis? Please, come in. Are you okay?" Andrew

asked.

"I don't travel very well, and my agent booked me in to five signings in the last three days. I don't know what she was thinking. I consider this visit a welcome break. Just point me to a chair so I can sit and check my e-mails on my laptop. Then fetch me some tea. I'll be fine," she wheezed, frowning slightly.

He led her to a chair in his living room. She seemed oblivious to his efforts to set the scene surrounding his research, focused on her laptop and looking horribly peaked. Andrew left her there, fiddling with the machine as he exited to the kitchen.

When he returned to see if she took milk or sugar in her tea, the living room was very still and quiet – too quiet. Andrew's mentor-to-be was hunched over her laptop, open to an e-mail from her agent that she had apparently been reading. She wasn't moving, not even a twitch, and she wasn't blinking. When he got close enough, by the grey cast to her skin and the blueness of her lips, Andrew could see that she also was not breathing. Sherralyn Lewis was dead.

In denial at first, Andrew made use of his best first aid knowledge, which wasn't all that great, to test that theory. Despite her lifeless staring eyes and her death grip on her laptop, he wouldn't want to be wrong. He called her name loudly, gave her a less than gentle shake and even tried putting a hand-held mirror up to her mouth to look for subtle evidence of breathing. As opposed to what she had suggested upon her entrance, she was not fine. By the time he was done, he was certain that today was the day that Sherralyn Lewis had perished in his living room. He slouched in an opposing chair and stared at her.

In his panic, Andrew hadn't bothered to call 911. What could they do for her at this point anyway? The voodoo decor that surrounded him seemed to intrude on his thoughts, as though fate had somehow foreshadowed this and was laughing at him. It had dangled pleasing bait before him; what looked like good fortune that had finally come his way, only to be yanked cruelly out of reach again. His opportunity to be mentored by one of the greatest had been stolen from him.

Or had it?

Ogling Sherralyn's corpse, without responding in any other way to his morbid circumstances, did strange things to Andrew's mind. The voodoo paraphernalia seeped into his thought process, tainting it. He wished he were his villain, capable of raising her from the dead to perform his bidding and forcing her to do what she had come here to do after all. He knew the rituals. He had all the components. He imagined her serving him from beyond the grave, grunting almost incoherent responses to his questions. He laughed – a crazy, desperate laugh, loud and shrill.

And then the laugh faded. What would it hurt to try? It wasn't like anybody knew where she was, and he could even make it seem like she had disappeared of her own accord. She had admitted that she had been overworked and over-tired...

Andrew began to scheme. Sherralyn was about to go on a prolonged and well-deserved vacation, as far as the publishing industry was concerned. He half dragged, half carried the dead woman up to his office, planting her cooling body into his computer chair and propping it into an upright position. He located her cell phone in her purse and a box large enough to accommodate both it and her laptop. Then he sent a reply to the e-mail that she had opened before death had taken her. It was a "I've had enough – I can't take it anymore" kind of e-mail, that concluded with a "don't try to reach me" and a "I'll be in touch when I'm good and ready."

To suggest she was extremely serious, Andrew packaged up her laptop and cell phone and shipped them off to her agent. This, he had decided, would also deal with the possibility that her agent or worried friends or family might be able to convince the authorities to track her via GPS. He had no doubt that she had the most current devices that technology could offer. She could certainly afford it, and by the way she had plonked down and started into checking her e-mail, without asking if Andrew had wifi, supported that theory.

These minor details addressed, Andrew now turned to making his primary plan happen. The first thing he made sure to do was to bind the corpse to the chair with various restraints. If the voodoo magic actually worked and he could reanimate Sherralyn, all his research suggested she would be craving living flesh and would try to bite him. Her bite would transfer the zombie curse to him, and if that happened it would make all of his efforts rather pointless.

It then took Andrew hours to get everything ready for the ritual, including scrawling the necromantic symbols onto the floor in goat's blood, and mixing up the necessary concoction that included mandrake root and puffer-fish toxin. He even looked up the proper pronunciation for the words in the incantation, to make sure that he would get them right. He had always been obsessive about even the smallest of details. If the spell didn't work, he wouldn't be the one responsible.

The chanting was a lengthy process as well, done as he burned the necessary mixture of herbs. Andrew was seriously dizzy by the time he came to the end of the incantation, and the smell of blood, sweat and scorched weeds was making him nauseous. When he was done, he dragged himself over to the window and took great gulps of air, trying to restore his senses. After a couple of minutes of sucking back cool, damp and only slightly polluted breaths, he turned to face the immobile figure tied to his computer chair.

"Well, that was a giant waste of time," he sighed.

And then she moaned.

Andrew was so startled he jostled the window, which almost slammed down on top of his fingers. He hadn't actually believed that it would work, but he had been so desperate not to lose this opportunity, he would have tried almost anything. She shuddered slightly and moaned a second time. He felt that this was sufficient confirmation that his addled mind hadn't just imagined that first moan.

Releasing the window, Andrew approached hesitantly.

"Sherralyn? I made a couple of improvements to the manuscript since I sent it to you. I was hoping to get your opinion..." he mumbled, deciding there was no point in being formal anymore and sliding a stack of paper into the zombie's view. Her response was incoherent, less so than Andrew had hoped for, as she gnashed her teeth in his direction and strained against her bindings.

Andrew's dreams were momentarily dashed. The full critique he had been anticipating wasn't going to happen, even if he had managed to raise her from the dead. He flopped into a sitting position on the floor, what would have been just out of reach had she been free to flail about. He was exhausted and just about the most disappointed he had ever been in his life.

"Damn – I knew this was a crazy idea, but I was hoping no matter what had happened to you, the writer in you would never die. I guess I'm fucked. Karma wins again."

The Sherralyn zombie strained in her chair, but this time she didn't seem to be reaching for Andrew. She was leaning towards the computer.

"Wrrriiiitte," she groaned.

Devoid of all scepticism now that he had seen the dead rise, Andrew was ready to test any wild theory that rose to the surface. Zombies were supposed to be creatures of animalistic habit, ones that ran on basal instinct. But what if Sharralyn Lewis had spent so much time writing that it had become an integral part of her being, as natural as the urge to feed? Maybe he could get her to type in a critique despite the fact that she was undead, if he freed up one of her hands.

It took several minutes for Andrew to build up the nerve to get close enough to loosen the ties on her right arm. She hissed at him, and shrieked as she tried to bury her teeth in his flesh, her jaws snapping shut less than an inch away from his exposed fingers. Once her hand was no longer bound, Andrew pointed at the computer.

"Write," he agreed.

She typed slowly, her gestures jerky and sporadic with the single hand. Overwhelmed by fatigue, Andrew left her to work and crawled back to his bedroom. He was asleep before his head hit the pillow.

Andrew called in sick the next morning, despite the fact it meant sacrificing a day's worth of his meagre wages. After slogging around in his kitchen in a daze until early afternoon, and sloshing back half a pot of coffee to steady his nerves, he headed up the stairs to see if the Sherralyn zombie had produced anything worthwhile.

Andrew faced yet another disappointment. Sherralyn had not addressed his manuscript changes at all. In fact, it looked as though what she had produced was a short work of fiction, much like her typical work. He shoved the wheeled chair away from the computer in frustration. Useless! The zombie stretched in her seat, alternating between trying to grab for Andrew and the computer. It was too bad that he was not an agent or publisher, as opposed to a mentor-seeking aspiring writer, Andrew thought. If he could profit from her work, her zeal to write would earn him a mint.

That was when it hit him – why couldn't he profit from that compulsion? Nobody would know that this was a Sherralyn Lewis original, not if it wasn't publicly identified as hers. His friends had encouraged him to get his foot in the door by mimicking his favourite writers. Andrew could just put his name on the manuscript and claim it as his own. He could be the next James Frey. What better way to mimic than to plagiarize without anyone knowing? Andrew wasn't even sure if you could count it as plagiarism considering the author was already dead when she wrote it. This would force them to recognize his talent. There would be no more floundering; the gatekeepers would finally let him through.

Leaving the zombie to flail in her chair in the corner, Andrew began to format the new story and consider the various pro-rate venues that might be a good match for the piece.

The move had been difficult, but once he had accumulated enough wealth and fame, Andrew could hardly justify remaining in the grungy townhouse where he had gotten his start. He had arranged for a two level flat uptown. It wasn't a penthouse apartment or a luxury condo -- he was still a rising star -- but he had definitely improved his circumstances. He knew he would have to make sure everything was in place and spot on before he threw his house-warming party. He would be inviting industry bigwigs: top agents, experienced editors, bestselling authors and acclaimed critics. This was as much a "break out" event for him as anything else.

The most challenging part for Andrew was transporting his Sherralyn zombie without anyone discovering her. He had already begun treating her with formaldehyde to control the rot. It hadn't stopped it altogether, but it had kept it to a minimum, with only the occasional shred of skin falling away or cloudy discharge of rank bodily fluids. One eyeball lolled a little, she drooled continuously and her exposed flesh had a scattering of oozing lesions, but that was the worst of it. He had had to gag her and bind her thoroughly before shoving her into the trunk, securing her in there with as many foam packing peanuts as would fit. He wanted her movement as restricted as possible, so as not to raise any suspicions.

The trunk had been locked, but Andrew had insisted on moving it himself. It had been a struggle; he was a little on the flabby side and did nothing in the way of exercise. Still, he was highly motivated and filled with nervous adrenaline, so he found the strength. He had risked getting bitten when he had gagged her and when he had removed it again once they had arrived. This was after he had dragged her out, spilling the packing peanuts across his clean new floor. He didn't worry about cleaning up. Nobody would be coming into that room other than him. During his party, the upper floor would be off limits, and his office would remain locked.

When the auspicious day arrived, Andrew watched like a hawk for the arrival of one particular invitee. Vernon Caldwell, a renowned reviewer, had been attacking Andrew's success from day one. Vernon had been an avid fan of Sharralyn Lewis, lauding her praises at every opportunity. His article after her disappearance had come across as some sort of obsessive eulogy and as soon as Andrew's "work" began to draw positive attention, Caldwell immediately began to question it. He referred to Andrew as a copycat and suggested he lacked even the slightest shred of originality. He had even called Andrew a hack on one occasion, and had gone as far as to hint that the new "it" writer had stumbled across an unpublished cache of Ms. Lewis's work, and in her absence, was parading her stories out as his own.

If only Caldwell knew how right he was, but Andrew wasn't about to let the man find out. He was going to keep a close eye on Caldwell, and if the man looked like he was trying to snoop, Andrew intended on finding some way to distract him.

The problem was, attendance at Andrew's party far exceeded his expectations, and tracking Caldwell's movements proved more difficult than he had planned. For one moment, Andrew had had the surly critic in his sights, and then he had been pulled aside to deal with an issue presented by the caterer. By the time Andrew could return to his observation, Caldwell was nowhere to be seen. Andrew resorted to asking around, casually, if others had noticed what had become of the reviewer, but he was met only by shrugs and claims of ignorance. One person did think that she had actually seen him leave the party and Andrew decided, uncomfortably, that he would have to accept this belief as fact.

When the last of the guests had gone, and Andrew had sent the caterers away, he poured himself a glass of celebratory wine and headed for his bedroom. On impulse, he decided to check in on the Sherralyn zombie, to make sure that she had not been overly disturbed by the party. He would have just stuck his head in and given her a quick peek, but something shook him enough that he had to go right in. The door, which he had made sure was locked and secure before any of the guests had arrived, was no longer locked. The fear that immediately sprang to mind was Caldwell.

The first thing Andrew did was make sure that his zombie was still where he had left her. He could see her in the computer chair in the dim light of the desk lamp, which told him that if Caldwell had entered the room, he at least hadn't released what was left of Sherralyn. What Andrew did note, however, even from behind

her in the shadowy room, was that his zombie looked dishevelled –
more so than usual. That made Andrew's stomach turn. Just how
much had Caldwell seen?

If Andrew had known that Caldwell had decided to carry his
snooping to the upper level and had jimmied the lock open, if
Andrew was aware that the nosy critic had not been satisfied with
merely glancing in the room, but had never come out again, Andrew
likely wouldn't have entered the office. If from behind her, Andrew
could have seen the splattering of blood ringing the Sharralyn
zombie's mouth and coating the front of her chest, he definitely
wouldn't have approached her.

But Andrew didn't have that knowledge, so he crept into the
room, making a point of keeping out of reach of the one loose
flailing hand. He had no knowledge that Caldwell, upon seeing what
he believed to be Sherralyn Lewis being held Misery-style by a cruel
captor forcing her to write on his behalf, had rushed over to her to
release her, and had fallen victim to her hunger for flesh. As the
partiers had reveled on the level below without him there, Vernon
Caldwell had been succumbing to the zombie curse a few feet away
from his writing idol, the undead woman who had spread it to him.

By the time Andrew realized exactly what had happened, it
was too late. When he eased the chair around and saw the mess that
the attack on Caldwell had left behind on the Sherralyn zombie, he
choked back a terrified scream. It wasn't quite loud enough to block
out the sound of the Caldwell zombie surging towards him, roaring
for blood. The undead creature was slow, but not slow enough that
Andrew, paralyzed by fear, could avoid him. The zombie was on the
rising literary star and sinking his teeth into Andrew's jugular before
the writer was able to react.

As Andrew lay dying and being devoured by the Caldwell
zombie, he considered it ironic. He had always wondered if the
critics would eat him alive...

*Chantal Boudreau is an accountant by day and an
author/illustrator during evenings and weekends who lives by the
ocean in beautiful Nova Scotia, Canada with her husband and two
children. In addition to being a CMA-MBA, she has a BA with a
major in English from Dalhousie University. An affiliate member of
the Horror Writers Association, she writes and illustrates horror,
dark fantasy and fantasy and has had several of her stories*

published in a variety of horror anthologies, online journals and magazines. She has also published ten novels to date. Find out more at: http://chantellyb.wordpress.com.

www.ingramcontent.com/pod-product-compliance
Lightning Source LLC
Chambersburg PA
CBHW072103170626
46813CB00004B/1437